FRIENDS AND SECRETS

Recent Titles by Grace Thompson from Severn House

The Badgers Brook Series

THE HOUSE BY THE BROOK
A GIRL CALLED HOPE
A NEW BEGINNING
THE HEART OF THE HOME

The Pendragon Island Series

CORNER OF A SMALL TOWN
THE WESTON WOMAN
UNLOCKING THE PAST
MAISIE'S WAY
A SHOP IN THE HIGH STREET
SOPHIE STREET

The Holidays at Home Series

WAIT TILL SUMMER
SWINGBOATS ON THE SAND
WAITING FOR YESTERDAY
DAY TRIPPERS
UNWISE PROMISES
STREET PARTIES

DAISY'S ARK
MISSING THE MOMENT
THE SANDWICH GIRL
AN ARMY OF SMILES
AROUND ANOTHER CORNER

FRIENDS AND SECRETS

Grace Thompson

This first world edition published in Great Britain 2006 by
SEVERN HOUSE PUBLISHERS LTD of
9–15 High Street, Sutton, Surrey SM1 1DF.
This first world edition published in the USA 2006 by
SEVERN HOUSE PUBLISHERS INC of
595 Madison Avenue, New York, N.Y. 10022.

British Library Cataloguing in Publication Data

Thompson,   Grace
    Friends and secrets
    1.   Female friendship - Fiction
    I.   Title
    823.9' 14 [F]

    ISBN-13: 978-0-7278-6436-9
    ISBN-10: 0-7278-6436-X

All Severn House titles are printed on acid-free paper.

Typeset by Palimpsest Book Production Ltd.,
Polmont, Stirlingshire, Scotland.
Printed and bound in Great Britain by
MPG Books Ltd., Bodmin, Cornwall.

One

'Mum, can we have a mobile?' Oliver and Rupert pleaded in unison.

Cynthia smiled at her twin sons and teasingly enquired whether they wanted toy ducks on it or model cars.

'Mum! You know what we mean,' Oliver protested, trying not to smile. 'All the boys in school have mobile phones, so why can't we?'

'It could be helpful if we were lost or something,' added Cynthia's youngest, Marcus, who was ten, five years younger than the twins. An unplanned bonus.

'Don't tell me you want one as well!'

'It would be great, no one in my class has one,' the solemn Marcus replied.

'Sorry, but you all have phone cards so you can get in touch with someone if necessary and they will have to do.' Cynthia turned and smiled at her husband. Christian was sitting listening to the exchange with amusement. How different their sons' lives were from his childhood, when a slice of bread dripping with treacle was considered a luxury – usually because of his father's win on the horses.

It was a warm, sweet-scented May evening and they were eating in the garden, from a well-used barbecue organized by Christian. The boys' friends, Jeremy and Justin, who were fourteen and thirteen, had joined them with their mother Joanne Morgan. Joanne's husband was not there. He was often away from home, as was Christian, which was partly why Cynthia and Joanne had become friends, finding solace in each other's occasional 'grass widowhood'.

Cynthia and Christian's lovely home commanded the best position on cliffs overlooking the sea not far from Abertrochi. They enjoyed fresh sea-breezes in a garden protected by a spindleberry hedge. They now saw another friend walking

1

along the cliff path with her two dogs and they waved. The smiles left their faces as Meriel disappeared.

'Poor Meriel,' Joanne said in her rather childlike voice. 'So sad, walking the dogs and probably dreading bumping into her ex with his new woman.'

'D'you think Evan's happy with that Sophie Hopkins?' Cynthia frowned. 'They seem an unlikely couple to me.'

'She's certainly different from Meriel, she's much more social. She's always dressed up and ready for fun, while poor Meriel seems to want nothing more than the beach and the company of her dogs,' Joanne said, her voice bearing a strong hint of disapproval. 'My John would soon grow tired of that.'

Later, when their guests had gone and their sons were in bed, Cynthia brought up the subject of the mobile phones.

'Do you think they need them?' she asked, and Christian shook his head. 'We agree that they don't get everything they ask for, even though we can afford to indulge them and this is one instance when we have to refuse. They have phone cards, that's enough surely?'

'I think I'll ask Millie to sew a small pocket inside their blazers and leave a few coins in it as an extra precaution,' Cynthia said. 'I'd hate them to be stuck somewhere with no means of getting in touch.'

They went up the wide, curving staircase, arm in arm, affection and love wrapping them in warmth and contentment. They had been together since they were fourteen. Even when Christian went away to buy land or deal with the progress of various building sites, they spoke on the telephone constantly. There was never a time when one didn't know the whereabouts of the other.

The boys each had their own room, filled with the paraphernalia of their many hobbies and interests. Football and motor-racing posters, pop groups and Star Wars memorabilia, filled the rooms belonging to the twins, but in Marcus's room there were more serious displays. Photographs of animals and foreign countries, warnings about the dangers of global warming and endangered species were the ten year old's apparent interests, although he really needed simply to be different from his older brothers, to display a character of his own.

As soon as the lights were out and the house became quiet,

Rupert and Oliver tapped on Marcus's door. Already fully dressed in outdoor clothes and anorak, bathers on under his clothes, he tiptoed along the passage and followed them silently down the stairs and through the dark kitchen. His heart was racing, the night hours always unnerved him, but he was determined to do whatever his brothers were planning. This time it was a midnight picnic on the rocks above the sea.

Gathering thick coats and towels, they silently left the house. Slipping through the garden like shadows, they were joined at the spindleberry hedge by Joanne's boys, Jeremy and Justin. They made their way down the path to where jutting rocks gave them a view in both directions of the wide sweep of the tranquil bay, dark now but with a few small lights from boats visible. As they watched, their eyes became accustomed to the poor light and they could make out the lighthouse on its promontory; four blinks, count six, four blinks, count six. The large bulk of a tanker far out became visible as they watched, waiting for the tide to allow it to dock.

As they shared out the food they had brought and munched contentedly, Christian crept through the garden following in their wake. He watched for a while, smiling at the innocent fun of the secret feast before creeping back to the house, certain he hadn't been seen. He and Cynthia would lie awake, listening, until the boys returned an hour later.

'Has he gone?' Rupert asked nonchalantly.

'He's gone,' Oliver replied. 'Who's for a swim?'

'I think it's too cold,' Marcus said at once.

Small for his age and inclined to be nervous, he was aware that his brothers were trying to help him become less afraid, but sometimes it was difficult not to run away from the things they suggested. He was usually persuaded though, on the promise that as soon as he could safely reach the pedals and see through the windscreen, they would teach him to drive their mother's car, something the twins were both able to do, and a skill about which their parents knew nothing.

Marcus didn't like the dark water far below them, with the strip of sand separating it from the foot of the rocks.

'Don't worry, Marcus, we won't swim, we'll stay with you.' Rupert whispered. Marcus still hesitated, envious of the others confidently stripping off their clothes.

'Come on, Marc,' Oliver coaxed. 'You're almost swimming,

just a little more practice is all you need. Think of the surprise when you tell Mum and Dad, eh?'

Stripping to his bathers but keeping his anorak wrapped around him to protect him from the cold night air, Marcus followed his brothers down the rocky path to the beach. Each taking a hand, they ran with him down the wet sand until they reached the sea then they all three fell laughing into the foam.

It was freezing. They all felt that sudden loss of breath but none would admit to it. They jumped about in the white surf, gradually accepting the painful temperature until warmed in the turbulence, then, no more than knee-deep, Oliver and Rupert helped the small, thin boy to float then pull himself along in a sort of frantic doggy paddle, praising him for his success at moving through the water. Jeremy and Justin swam out fast and circled back to the bay, calling to persuade the twins to join them.

Seeing that Marcus was beginning to shiver, Oliver and Rupert then left him to climb back up to the top and dress himself while they swam strongly with Joanne's boys, circling, racing, diving and swimming underwater, fooling about before running back up the sand and climbing up to join him.

They dressed with a speed encouraged by the cold night air and departed in different directions for home and a warm bed. 'Bathing costumes in the airing room remember,' Oliver hissed, as they opened the back door and crept back to their rooms.

Between the kitchen and the double garage was a small room filled with slatted shelves and clothes-lines and warmed by a heater, where their housekeeper Millie aired the washing. They carelessly threw bathers and towels over the lines and hurried up to bed.

Hearing the doors open and close, content that the boys were home and happily unaware of their swim, Cynthia and Christian cuddled up to each other and slept contentedly.

A few days later, Cynthia went shopping in Swansea. Christian and his partner Ken Morris, had set out for a town near Brecon, where they hoped to buy a piece of land on which to build a row of town houses. She was looking for a dress to wear at a charity luncheon, at which she was the speaker. She and Christian did all they could to help children's charities. In no hurry, she trawled the shops, not knowing quite what she was looking for, but attracted that day by the peacock green/blue that suited her so well.

She was walking through the shopping centre when she heard a laugh that chilled her with agonizing memories. Startled and filled with a primeval desire to run, the sound took her back through the years and she was a child again. She heard her father's laughter as she cried when told she couldn't go on holiday with the rest of her class, and as he drowned her kitten, and when he had found her secret diary and read it aloud to his friends. Such a cruel sound, no trace of kindness, only malicious amusement at her suffering. Her mother had always joined in with her father's mirth, her almost toothless mouth wide, her head thrown back, afraid, no doubt, of annoying him with her disapproval.

With her mind bludgeoned by shock, her legs continued to move of their own volition; tip tap tip tap, past clothes shops she couldn't see, past Debenhams, Early Learning, more clothes, heading for the bus station. Her destination was forgotten. She was engulfed in fear of what she would see if she dared to turn around. Those voices, those hated voices and the laughter, following her, taunting her, warning her that she couldn't escape her past, that one day they would find her again and today might be the one.

Retrieving some control, she turned into Thorntons and pretended to look at the chocolates on display. Then, as the voices drew closer, she dared to glance up. She saw her mother and father, with a young man she barely recognized as her younger brother Kevin.

Shaking, she stood near the counter and tried to follow their progress. It wasn't hard, they were always very noisy and the years hadn't changed that. If she could see what bus service they used, she would know if they were still living in Cardiff. Surely they hadn't moved closer, where the possibility of meeting them would fill her days with misery and her nights with terror?

Staying well back, thankful of the crowds, she saw to her relief that they had stopped to wait at the coach station for the Cardiff bus. They must have been visiting for the day. 'Please let this be a once-only visit,' she pleaded with she knew not who. She watched until the coach left. Then, almost crying with relief, she stood in a corner and phoned Christian.

Fortunately Christian had not gone far, and arrived quite soon. They found a corner seat in a quiet cafe and he held her hands and allowed her to talk.

'I felt as though I'd been stripped of my fashionable hairstyle and make-up, and my quality clothes and was standing in front of everyone in ragged hand-me-downs, waiting for the beatings to start.' She ignored the tears that fell and Christian wiped them away. 'I visualized myself and my sisters hiding under the stinking bed, listening to my parents in one of their drunken rages, and pleading with an uncaring God to rescue me.'

She fell silent and Christian added, 'While across the road, I was suffering a similar situation. But we did get away, love. We fought our way out of that squalor, didn't we? You and me, together.'

'Yes, darling, we did. And our three boys have never heard our voices raised in anger, or felt the shock and pain and humiliation of a beating.'

'Remember how Ken's mother bathed our wounds and soothed our tears, and eventually helped us to get away?' Christian said softly.

'Where is Ken?' she asked.

'Waiting in the car. I told him what you'd seen.'

'We're lucky we have Ken who knows the truth about our sordid beginnings. No need to prattle on to him about my wonderful but imaginary "Aunt Marigold", who brought me up when my loving parents died in a car crash.' She managed a smile and encouraging her, Christian said, 'Or my darling imaginary Gran, who lived in a beautiful house and adored me!'

'Dear Aunt Marigold!' Cynthia giggled.

'Darling Grandmamma!' Christian laughed.

'Were we wrong to deny our background and invent a happier one?'

'No. We'll never forget it, but why inflict it on Oliver, Rupert and young Marcus? There was nothing there they'd benefit from knowing.'

'We've been very lucky, darling,' she whispered.

'I love you, Mrs Sewell,' he whispered back.

Ignoring the glances of others, they kissed.

* * *

Ken Morris was sitting in the camper van that he and Christian used when they had to go out of town for a few days. Neither liked hotels and the camper van was comfortable for a few nights. He was reading the racing page of a newspaper. They had been on their way to examine a possible building plot when Cynthia had phoned. Also on their itinerary that day was an inspection of a barn, offered for conversion into a private home, but when Cynthia had phoned in distress, Ken, who had been driving, didn't wait to be told but had turned the van around and headed back to Swansea. Where Christian was concerned, Cynthia and his three sons always came first. While Christian hurried to Cynthia, Ken had phoned their appointments to apologize and rearrange.

Getting out of the van and locking it, Ken went to find a betting shop and wrote out a bet for an accumulator on four horses. He hadn't had a very good month and he hoped that being bold might improve his luck and pay off his debt to the bookmaker. As another display of confidence, he paid the tax in advance, so if he did win, he wouldn't pay out on his winnings.

Going back to the van, Ken turned on the radio. He was used to being alone, but sometimes, like today when Christian hurried back to comfort his wife, he felt the emptiness of his life like a pain. He gambled only to fill the hours with artificial excitement, to give some punctuation to the empty days, not because he couldn't live without the highs that only a good win could give him. He told himself that several times each day, until he nearly believed it.

Cynthia and Christian walked back to a car park from where Christian would phone Ken to pick him up.

'I still feel guilty about not visiting Ken's mother,' Cynthia said as they waited. 'We owe her so much.'

'Ken is adamant that she won't see us. Her mind was turned when she became ill and she seems to think we are the enemy. I don't understand it, but we have to do as Ken advises and stay away.'

'I wish he'd at least tell us which nursing home she's in. We can't even send a gift, or phone to enquire. It's very odd that she went so completely against us after the way she cared for us when we were young.'

'Ken's a private person. He doesn't ever invite me to the room he rents. I plead, I tease, but he won't shift. He says he's saving to build a house but he never takes up the offer of a site on which to build it. Every time we have a planning session to discuss the schedule for the next few months, I offer to fit the house into the plans, even make it a priority – he's a partner in the firm after all – but he always says he isn't ready.'

'As you say, darling, Ken Morris is a very private person. But he must be loaded. I can't imagine why he doesn't get himself a comfortable home, can you?'

Forgetting the dress she planned to buy, Cynthia went back to Abertrochi but didn't go back to the house. She went instead to Churchill's Garden, the cafe in the small shopping precinct of the same name, where she frequently met her friends. She walked in, still trembling a little, trying to shake off the shock of seeing her parents and finding them little changed from when she had run away from home with Christian. Joanne Morgan was sitting at their usual table sipping coffee and Cynthia wondered grimly how the snobbish Joanne would react if she knew the truth about Cynthia's background.

'Christian has gone to look at a barn conversion and a few sites, so I'm bereft,' she said, putting her handbag on the chair beside Joanne. 'Join me for lunch? My treat? I need comforting.'

'Love to,' Joanne breathed in her childlike voice. 'John is away all the week, some cafe he is setting up near Newport. Such a bore having a husband who's always away, isn't it?'

'Not so bad now the boys are growing up though?'

'Jeremy and Justin are getting worse. They don't do a thing to help me. Ask them to wash a dish or help in the garden and, well, you'd think I'd asked them to fly to the moon. Some mornings they can barely stay awake to eat their breakfast. I sometimes wonder if they are ill,' Joanne complained.

Remembering the occasional midnight picnics enjoyed by the five boys, Cynthia smiled but said nothing. Boys needed to be daring, and sitting on the cliff path eating food was a safe way of rebelling against Joanne's rather strict rules. If Joanne knew she would almost certainly spoil their fun.

They went to The Fisherman's Basket for lunch, and Cynthia

found it difficult to concentrate on what was being said. She was still distressed at how close she had come to being confronted by her family with the danger that they might destroy the life she and Christian had built.

Joanne went on moaning about her boys. 'When I was their age Mummy insisted on my never sitting with nothing to do,' she said.

Cynthia spouted the usual lies about her own privileged childhood and the wonderful but imaginary 'Aunt Marigold', who indulged her every whim. They were finishing their coffee when Christian came in.

'I thought I'd find you here, darling,' he said to Cynthia as he kissed her. 'Ken has gone on alone to deal with the barn and we've cancelled the other meeting until tomorrow.'

'Why?' she asked, smiling her pleasure at his surprise appearance.

'I don't know. I just thought we could meet the boys and go to the cinema and supper afterwards. We haven't taken them out for a while.'

'We'll have to let Millie know we won't be in for dinner.'

'Already done,' he smiled.

Watching them, aware of the love flowing between them, Joanne felt a stab of jealousy at the way everything else ceased to exist when Cynthia's eyes met Christian's.

'My John will be home at the weekend to spoil me and the boys,' she was forced to say. 'We *are* lucky aren't we, Cynthia, to have such caring husbands?' She thanked Cynthia for the lunch and said her goodbyes but wondered if her words had been heard.

'Nothing to frighten Marcus, mind,' Cynthia was saying as they left the restaurant after her automatic goodbyes had been said. 'You know how nervous he is and a horror film would keep him awake.' Joanne waited until they were out of sight before going into the bargain priced grocery shop, coming out with cut price sausages and corned beef. 'It's for the dog,' she whispered to the cashier. She returned to her car aware of rising irritation. What Cynthia had paid for their lunch would have bought food for herself and the boys for the whole week. How tired she was of being short of money. If only John realized how difficult it was to manage on the meagre amount he gave her each month. Ploughing it back into the business month after month was sensible, John had made her understand the need for that, but surely they didn't have to live on special offers and out of date food?

The following day, Christian met Ken for breakfast. They ate in a cafe; toast for Christian and the full breakfast for Ken. When they were walking back to the camper van, Christian asked, 'Is your Mam all right? Cynthia and I were wondering if there had been any change. We'd love to do something to help.'

'She's about the same,' Ken said sadly.

'Cynthia and I were talking about her and we really would like to do something. Couldn't we send fruit? Or perhaps we could have the phone number so we could at least ring the Home and ask about her progress. Is it in Abertrochi?'

'No, it's miles away, the best places often are. Best you don't see her. I'll tell you when she's well enough to see you, right?'

'Cynthia almost bumping into her family like that, it made us think even more about how much we owe her. She helped us so much when we were children. We owe her and feel we're neglecting her.'

'If you went she wouldn't know you and she's often aggressive with strangers. I wouldn't want to risk upsetting you or Cynthia. She's lost in a world of her own. Well looked after, locked in of course, for her own safety, but safe and fed and warm. She doesn't remember me, and it's kinder that she doesn't. Memories would be painful. Believe me, there's nothing you can to do help, honestly, Christian.'

'It seems so uncaring to know she's mentally ill and we don't even go to see her.'

They bought the barn and set the planning application in progress, turned down the other site for reasons of access and went home. Christian stepped into his beautiful home, called to Cynthia and the boys, and thought of Ken going home to a lonely room. Millie, rosy from cooking, ageing prettily and full of energy, came out of the kitchen where she was cooking dinner, and he thought of Ken's mother seriously ill with a sad mind-destroying illness, and wondered at the unfairness of life.

* * *

Ken parked the camper in the front garden of the rather run down semi and stepped through the door to savour the smells of dinner cooking. 'Hello Mam,' he called, 'Is that steak and onions you're cooking for your favourite son?'

Mrs Morris, dressed in a summery dress, her hair neatly fixed in a flattering bun, her face made-up and wearing a smile, said, 'Hello, son. Yes, I've got your favourite meal. I'll serve while you get bathed and changed. It's my bridge night and I don't want to be late.'

Two

The morning was pleasantly warm and Meriel opened the windows to enjoy the fresh air and decided that today she would sit outside and eat her breakfast, but first the dogs needed their walk. She locked her back door and looked up at the sky. It was a beautiful morning with the clouds tinted in that wonderful beige/pink which was reflected on the sea. It would be a good walk along the cliff path and with the tide out, she could take the dogs on to the beach – something they both loved.

She wondered whether Evan, her ex-husband, would be jogging on the cliff path – she really didn't want to meet him. Why had he bought a house so close to their previous home? Why couldn't he have taken Sophie Hopkins to live somewhere far away? Turning left, she walked away from where the large houses – including those of Cynthia and Joanne – stretched down from the narrow road to the cliff edge. Evan rarely came further than the point where she began the walk. She hurried until her house was out of sight, the dogs scampering enthusiastically ahead of her. When she felt safe she slowed down and enjoyed the morning. The mornings were still the worst.

Strolling along wet sand smoothed by the outgoing tide and taking in the smell of freshly washed rocks and seaweed, she calmed down, and tried to think of what she wanted to do with the rest of her life. It wasn't easy. She had given up university and started a small business selling artists' supplies. She had sold that to help Evan get started.

He had spent some time in the army and when he came out had planned to build a business importing cane and teak furniture. Having made a few contacts he needed more capital and she had sold up and given him the proceeds.

For the first year he had needed her help and she had spent as many hours in the business as he but, as the business grew and staff were employed, she gradually stayed at home. No babies came and she had settled comfortably into a routine of house and garden and meeting friends that seemed set to continue for ever. Then he had left her to live with Sophie Hopkins. Now she didn't know where to start building a life for herself.

Meriel passed groups of trees that were distorted, bending landward, forced into a submissive shape by the powerful onshore gales that ravaged the area. She looked ahead, eastwards to where the sun was back-lighting the clouds with a glorious red edging. Sighing, she reminded herself how fortunate she was to be living here in this beautiful part of South Wales and able to enjoy it. Even being alone after fifteen years and Evan with his new love, Sophie Hopkins, living near enough to taunt her, couldn't spoil everything.

Glancing at her watch, a present from Evan on their tenth anniversary, she realized it was time to turn back. Clambering down the rocky cliff face, where soil and rocks showed a well-worn path, she whistled to the dogs and made her way down to the sand. Walking back along the beach she waved at others who regularly used the path and climbed up easily a little way past Channel View, her home – for a while longer.

Cynthia, unlike Meriel, who dressed casually for the weather and her dogs, didn't appear until her make-up was complete and her hair washed and dried and her dress was immaculate. It was a habit she had begun on her honeymoon and not once had she deviated from her self-inflicted regime. Even when the twins, and later Marcus, were born, she refused to allow her husband near her until she was, what she called, presentable.

Millie presided over breakfast, the boys being called by her when she arrived at seven thirty to begin her day's work. When Cynthia appeared, her breakfast of toast and orange juice and coffee was waiting for her. Apart from critically straightening a knife, asking for a marmalade dish to be wiped or commenting on the brownness of the toast there was nothing for her to do.

She thumbed through the post, putting those for Christian – who was away on business with Ken – on one pile, 'rubbish' on another and her own on her side plate. Between bites and sips of orange juice she read one or two letters. Mostly appeals for her help with fund-raising. Millie had put a pen near her place and she scribbled a few dates on the back of an envelope ready to transfer into her diary. Almost as an afterthought she looked up and asked the boys what their plans were for the day.

'School,' the fifteen-year-old twins groaned, echoed by their younger brother.

'And afterwards?' Cynthia queried.

'Football.'

'What are you doing, Marcus?' she asked her youngest.

'I'm playing football with Rupert and Oliver.'

'Oh, no you're not!' Rupert and Oliver were horrified. 'Mum, he can't!'

'Oh, don't start quarrelling so early in the day,' Cynthia groaned. 'Your father should be home around four so why don't you come straight home to greet him? You haven't seen him for a week.'

'We've made arrangements,' Rupert said, and Oliver nodded agreement, his mouth filled with toast and egg.

'Please yourselves.' With a shrug, Cynthia washed her sons' arrangements from her mind, already planning which of the morning post's appeals she would respond to, what she needed to buy, what she planned to tell Meriel and Joanne and Vivienne when they met in Churchill's Garden later that morning.

Churchill's Garden, in the main shopping street of Abertrochi, was a popular venue for ladies – and a few men – to meet for coffee and to catch up on the latest news of friends. It was a large premises which included several other shops besides the cafe. To the right of the central doorway was a hairdressers, partitioned off with elegantly draped net. Behind that was a counter selling toiletries and perfumes. On the left of the doorway was a gift shop. Behind that, a small area specializing in dried flower arrangements. Beyond was the cafe.

The cafe extended out into a small paved area where a tree offered shade, and two sculptures added a touch of class. One was a mermaid with water gently flowing around its tail. The other was a half-open oyster-shell from which flowers and foliage tumbled. The furniture was metal; mock Victorian tables, chairs and a couple of benches.

14

Meriel was the first to arrive and, as the day was mild, she had chosen a table out in the courtyard garden, where she sat looking through a glossy antiques and decorating magazine while she waited.

Joanne arrived, dropped her shopping on to one of the chairs Meriel had saved, then went to the counter for the coffee and a cake which was her regular Tuesday treat. She was frowning, and Meriel knew this was likely to mean trouble with her sons. The session would be a long diatribe about the difficulties of bringing up children with a father who spent so much time away. At least until Cynthia and Vivienne arrived. Cynthia's husband was away from home a great deal and Cynthia didn't find it a problem, and Vivienne was a single mother, so Joanne would have little sympathy there. She hoped they wouldn't be too long. Joanne could be wearing. She was so intense about everything.

'D'you know, I don't think my boys have enough home-work,' Joanne began.

'I bet they don't agree,' Meriel laughed. 'I can remember how resentful I was when the weather was fine and I had to stay indoors and work.'

'But you've always been one for the great outdoors, haven't you, dear. I want my boys to succeed academically and the only way is to work and work.'

'I did pass a few exams, and I ran my own business,' Meriel said dryly.

'But you didn't go to university, did you? I know my boys are clever enough if only they'd buckle down and work.'

'I know, I failed miserably,' Meriel sighed, hiding her irri-tation under sarcasm. 'I married and sold my business to finance that of my husband.'

'And then he did *that* to you. Such a shame everything fell apart for you.'

Meriel was relieved to see Cynthia bustling in, loaded with carrier bags and pushing people out of her way as she made her way towards them. Her ex-husband, Evan, was a subject she wanted to avoid.

'Meriel, Joanne, dears, why are we sitting outside, the wind will be so irritating. I'll get us a place near the window, shall I?' There were no empty tables but with her loud voice and confident air, she persuaded one woman sitting alone to share with two others then spread her shopping territorially over four chairs. 'Come on,' she called, beckoning to where Meriel and Joanne were still sitting. Ignoring the fact that they both had coffee, she ordered four, plus some scones, presuming that Vivienne would join them soon.

Reluctantly, both preferring the garden to the crowded room, Meriel and Joanne joined her and Joanne went back to her tale of the neglect shown by the teachers in not setting more homework. Fortunately, Vivienne arrived as Cynthia brought the coffees, with her small son Tobias.

'Morning everyone, say good morning, Toby,' Vivienne called as she moved everyone along to get the pushchair in between herself and Meriel. 'I couldn't get anyone to look after him for an hour, but he won't be a nuisance,' she said cheerfully, filling the three year old's hands with an apple and a chocolate bar.

Vivienne was tall and dark and this morning was cheerfully dressed in bright red with an orange scarf draped around her shoulders. She had a dream-catcher on her head, part ornament and part hat, and the three-year-old Tobias also wore one across his jumper.

'What's that on your head?' Cynthia asked trying to be polite.

'Dream-catcher. They stop bad dreams and allow only happy thoughts to be sifted through, aren't they lovely? Toby loves them. We have one over the bed and over his cot and several in the living-room in case we doze off unexpectedly,' she laughed. Cynthia and the others smiled with her. Eccentric but always happy, it was impossible to disapprove of Vivienne. After exchanging news of their respective weekends, Vivienne leaned across the table and whispered, 'She's here again,' and jerked her head towards the corner near the open door to the garden. 'The Tragedy Queen.'

A young woman sat at a table for one, almost hidden in the shadow between the door and a large display of tea towels, oven gloves and aprons. She was thin and wore long, dull coloured clothes in drab browns and greens and grey. Her black hair was carelessly pulled back   a bunch held in place with a braid of the same material as her dress. She was often there but rarely smiled and she ignored any overtures the friends made for her to join them.

'I wonder who she is?' Meriel whispered. 'She seems so sad.'

16

'No one knows her, but she must be local,' Joanne said. 'She's in here so often.'

'Well, we've given her the opportunity to join us but she clearly prefers her own company.' Cynthia brushed crumbs from the table as if dismissing the woman with the same movement.

As the conversation became more general, and Joanne had been firmly quashed in her attempts to discuss the imagined problems with her twelve- and fourteen-year-old sons, Meriel studied the lonely young woman. Her dark eyes had a bruised look about them that suggested illness or at least a lack of sleep, her nose was long and thin and painfully red. She was someone who cried a lot, she decided, recognizing the signs from her own past.

'About that woman,' she whispered to the others as they began to gather their things to leave, 'We could ask Helen Symons. Working in the newsagents, she gets to know everyone.'

They agreed it would be a good idea. They knew Helen well and she sometimes joined them for coffee. When she could.

Joanne was impatient as her sons took their time getting ready for school.

'Why is it that although I put everything ready for you, you can't find your clothes?' she demanded as Justin one-handedly lifted cushions and moved books looking for a pair of socks. 'Your bedroom's a tip. It's no wonder you can't find anything. This evening you'll come straight home from school and tidy it, d'you hear? And for heaven's sake, Justin, use both hands!'

'Can I have the twelve pounds for the school trip, Mummy?' Jeremy asked as he threw the socks he had hidden towards his brother.

'Twelve pounds?'

Jeremy drooped his shoulders and gave a long dramatic sigh. 'Here we go. Why do you have to make such a fuss about everything, Mummy? You know we have a trip next month, so why do you pretend it's such a shock? It's only twelve pounds for heaven's sake. It isn't a second mortgage,' he added in a mutter that made his younger brother smile.

'I'll give it to you tomorrow morning.' Joanne said sharply. 'And if you talk to me like that again you won't have it at all. Understand?'

His, 'Sorry Mummy,' brought another grin to the boys' faces.

Having seen the boys off to school, she drove on towards the park. Her poodle Fifi needed a walk but one look at the mud and she drove back to the house. In high-heeled shoes and a smart black coat, she walked the little dog around the estate of large houses and back into the kitchen.

She then changed into a track-suit and went up to clean Justin's room. It was pointless expecting him to do it and if John saw it she would be ashamed. There was no carpet, just a few rugs which never stayed in the right place. She sighed. John had promised carpets two years ago. Life would be a lot easier if only he would spend a little money on the home. Not having a cleaner was bad enough, but using a mop and having to polish floors was archaic.

After a shower and a few minutes sitting reading the morning paper she set off to meet the others in Churchill's Garden. She hoped Meriel would be there. Today was a sad anniversary for her, it was a year to the day since her husband had left her, and she wanted the chance to let her know she remembered. Poor Meriel. She'd be glad to know she had such loyal friends.

Meriel thought her house seemed particularly empty this anniversary morning. The ticking of the clock was very loud in the silence: it marked the passing days she spent alone, mocking her. She picked the newspaper up from the doormat and tossed it on to the table. She ought to cancel it because she rarely read it and it was a hurtful reminder that Evan was no longer there to enjoy it. She wondered whether he still read *The Daily Telegraph*, or whether his new love had persuaded him to read something different.

It wouldn't have been just herself Evan had left behind. He would have moved on in a hundred different ways. He probably watched different television programmes, saw different films. Lovemaking would have changed too, she reminded herself with a jolt of longing.

On the verge of tears she put down plates of food for Nipper and Patch and hurried upstairs to the bedroom to change. Trying to shake off the melancholy was impossible. The bed, with its large expanse of sheets and pillows and a solitary indentation, taunted her. She sat on the edge and gradually slipped down until she was resting on the pillow and allowed her tears to seep into its softness.

Below, Nipper barked to remind her he liked a drop of milk after his meal, and she ran into the bathroom and angrily washed her face, forcing herself to lift her thoughts from her unwanted and, she thought, her undeserved predicament, and face the day. This was no way to behave. Evan had gone and she was alone. Punishing herself about him in this maudlin way had to stop.

After giving the dogs their milk and replenishing the drinking bowl, she changed out of her walking shoes and, with a deep sigh, prepared her smile for greeting Cynthia and Joanne and hopefully, Vivienne too. Please let them be unaware of the importance of today, she whispered, as she got into the car and set off for Churchill's Garden.

As the late May morning was now calm and bright, Meriel found Joanne, Vivienne and Helen in the cafe garden. Joanne was smartly dressed in a beautiful two piece suit with blue leather shoes and matching handbag while Vivienne wore a short black skirt and a bright red top. Her white jacket was thrown across a chair, reserving it for her, she presumed. Helen, the oldest of the group at forty-two, was slightly over-weight so she always wore long tops over loose trousers in cheerful blues and greens. Her badly permed hair was untidy and held back with an unbecoming braid. 'Bandbox and jumble sale,' she frequently joked when she sat beside Joanne. The three women had their heads together as though sharing a spicy piece of gossip, confirmed by the way they hurriedly stopped talking when Meriel approached them.

'Where's Cynthia?' she asked after greetings had been exchanged. 'She's usually here on Tuesdays.'

'Trouble with her boys,' Joanne whispered, disapproval tightening her lips. 'At the last parents and teachers meeting I was told they had been absent from school on two occasions.'

'Mitching, we called it,' Vivienne said, with a lack of concern. 'They all do it sometime, don't they? I know I did. I remember mitching more than twice, don't you, Joanne?'

'I do not! I wouldn't have dreamed of disobeying my mother!'

Meriel and Vivienne exchanged glances of amusement and Meriel said, 'No, of course you wouldn't, Joanne. But I did. Like Vivienne, I sometimes felt stifled by school and stayed out in the fields until it was time to go home.'

'Once I discovered an injured fox cub and I didn't know what to do,' Vivienne said. 'I could hardly tell Mam and Dad that I'd found it in the classroom, could I?'

'What did you do?' Meriel asked.

'I went to a neighbour and owned up to mitching. She took it to the vet and paid for its treatment. I was in a terrible mess, my clothes were muddy and streaked with blood so I had to own up to Mam in the end. But she didn't mind. Said she was proud of me for caring enough for a wounded animal to admit my bad behaviour.'

'Proud of you?' Joanne frowned in disbelief. 'My mother would have given me a good hard slap for staying away from school!'

Cynthia appeared just then, slipping out from behind the net separating cafe and hairdressing salon, smelling of shampoo and looking bandbox smart.

'Wait till you hear this,' Joanne said. 'Go on Vivienne, tell her your mother's reaction when you stayed away from school.'

'Mitched,' Vivienne explained.

'It's hardly a crime,' Cynthia said. 'As I told the head-teacher, I think it showed a sense of confidence and adventure. When I ran away from a House Craft lesson to go to a gymkhana, dear Aunt Marigold roared with laughter and said she didn't blame me for preferring horses to housework.'

Leaving Joanne and Cynthia to exclaim over the amazing remarkable tolerance of the oft-quoted and saintly Aunt Marigold, and Vivienne's mother, Meriel went to the counter to collect coffee. Thank goodness the conversation had centred around Vivienne. It was unlikely now that they would remember the date she had repeated so frequently over the past year, declaring it to be the worst day of her life.

But she wasn't to escape. In a lull, the dreaded moment came and she took a deep trembling breath as Cynthia lowered her voice to denote sympathy and asked, 'How are you today of all days, Meriel dear?'

Fighting down the pain and the dread of tears, Meriel smiled brightly as she said, 'Today, I might have found myself a job.'

'You have? Well, isn't that marvellous?' Joanne turned around to include the others in her approval, her voice soft and caring. 'You're so brave, Meriel. Isn't she brave?'

Meriel rather unkindly thought that Joanne sometimes sounded like a purring cat.

'Nothing boring I hope,' Vivienne remarked.

'Gardening, for a teacher over in Holly Oak Lane. Two men sharing but neither likes the work so I offered to do a morning a week and keep it under control for them.'

'What?' Joanne was amazed for the second time that morning. 'Just think what it will do to your hands!'

Quickly, Vivienne said, 'Don't you think that's a stupid name? Holly Oak? There's no sign of either.'

'It used to be Holy Oak I believe and the name somehow changed,' Meriel informed them with determined brightness.

'But gardening! I wouldn't have the stamina. Not after I'd done my own house and garden properly. I'm up at six thirty, winter and summer as it is. I like to have everything perfect for when John comes home as you know and—'

'I thought you had a "Woman Who Does?"' Cynthia said.

'I do,' Joanne lied quickly, 'But they never give it that final finish, do they?'

'Any chance of one of you Toby-minding on Saturday? It's weeks since I went clubbing and—' Vivienne tried but failed again to change the subject.

'Gardening is a skill given to few,' Cynthia said, with an approving glance at Meriel. 'My gardening lady is amazing and I admire her enormously for what she does. People don't consider it a career for the lowly any more, Joanne, not with so many facinating programmes on the television. I did a bit myself in my student days, but I wasn't very good at it.'

'So did I,' Vivienne said. 'I was sacked after a day! I nurtured the ground elder and pulled up the aubretia which I thought looked a mess. Anyway, whatever Meriel does, it's better than moping about wondering what Evan's getting up to with that new woman of his – rot his socks.'

21

'I kill off anything I'm given for indoors or out,' Helen said with a rueful sigh. 'My Reggie doesn't even trust me with the grass – thank goodness!'

'That young woman isn't here today,' Joanne whispered, after a brief lull.

They glanced towards the isolated table just inside the door, now occupied by an elderly gentleman. As they watched, the man stood up, gathered the paper he had been reading and went out. A moment later, the young woman they called the Tragedy Queen sat down and placed a coffee on the table and took out a magazine.

'I wonder who she is,' Joanne whispered. 'Poor thing, she looks as though life has hurt her terribly.'

'Her name is Cath Lewis and she lives in the end one of the three chalets,' Helen informed them. 'The one tucked right up against the rock face. Dark it is and damp for sure. Poor dab. I suppose she can't afford anything better.'

'What does she do?' Cynthia asked, attempting to keep her loud voice confidential, and failing.

'She cleans for the two men Meriel's going to garden for,' she added with a wink, 'so we'll be able to find out more, won't we? It's over to you, Meriel.'

Meriel frowned. 'D'you think that's sufficient for me to go and talk to her, ask her about the men and whether they're easy to work for?'

'She must have to gather wood for her fire, there's only a shower and an outside lav and she'll have to boil water for a tin bath if she wants one. That's according to old Megan Philips who lived there until she went into a home.' Helen mused, half to herself. 'Poor dab her. What a life, eh?'

'Now we know her name, we might give her one more chance to join us,' Cynthia said. 'It's always interesting finding someone new and learning all about them.'

'Gossip!' Helen sniffed.

'Who's talking!' Joanne laughed. 'We don't call you "fount of all knowledge" for nothing, dear.'

'Well, working in a newsagents I can't help learning about people, can I?'

'What if she's a bore? We could be stuck with her for weeks.'

'We can change our time, or buy coffee at The Artist's Palette for a while.'

No one was prepared to ask. Meriel didn't think she could, and besides, she and Cath Lewis might meet naturally if they both worked for the same two young men. As she went out, she heard Joanne say in a stage whisper, obviously intending her to hear, 'Poor Meriel, it's so sad. I do feel sorry for her, even though she brought it on herself.'

'We did our best to make her see the dangers,' Cynthia agreed.

'Poor dab,' Helen whispered sadly. 'And doing nothing to deserve it.'

Meriel winced and hurried from the shop. Those were the remarks her so-called friends had been making ever since Evan had left her. Remarks made just loud enough for her to hear and, presumably, to wallow gratefully in their sympathy and concern.

The two women who watched her go were both dressed in stylish clothes and both oozed confidence. They were also complacent that a marriage breakup wouldn't happen to them.

'I wonder how long it will be before Meriel gets a real job?' Joanne mused as Helen stood up to leave. 'Her ex has been extremely generous. She can't fault him there. He isn't in a rush to sell the house, he's allowing her to stay there while she sorts her life out and there aren't many who would do that.'

'Perhaps he's just not burning his bridges? If it doesn't work out for him with this Sophie Hopkins woman, he might want to go back?'

'Would she let him d'you think?'

Cynthia opened her compact to check her face once more, adjusted an eyebrow with a delicate touch of her little finger. 'Who knows, my dear?'

'I think she might,' Joanne said thoughtfully. 'Meriel is the type to take the simplest route.'

Cynthia gathered her shopping and began to rise. 'Lunch at The Fisherman's Basket?'

'Lovely,' Joanne smiled then the smile turned to a frown. 'Oh dear, I'm forgetting, Cynthia. I can't. My cleaning lady is there and I do like to make sure she's done all I asked.'

'I thought her day was Monday?'

'Oh, just a few extra things needed doing, you know how it is.'

Cynthia shrugged. 'Another time then? I just happen to be free.'

'Sorry.' How could she explain to Cynthia of all people that she couldn't afford to eat at The Fisherman's Basket? Cynthia, Meriel, Helen, Vivienne and several others met for lunch two or three times a week and it was increasingly difficult for Joanne to find excuses not to join them to spend a few hours and a lot of money. She watched them go with a surge of envy in the pit of her stomach. Why was life so unfair?

Evan hadn't been ungenerous to Meriel when they parted. His guilt revealed itself in many ways. He had agreed that she could stay in the house for up to a year before putting it on the market and he knew she was half-heartedly looking for a flat that wasn't too expensive. He quickly learned of everything she did and she had been working for Tom Harris and his brother in Holly Oak Lane for only two weeks before he found out. The knowledge worried him.

Although he was living with Sophie Hopkins and was happy, he still had strong feelings of responsibility for Meriel's welfare – a notion that irritated Sophie more than a little.

'She isn't your wife any longer, Evan,' she complained when he told her, with some dismay, about Meriel's choice of job. 'She can decide for herself what she wants to do with the rest of her life, she doesn't need to ask your permission.'

'But it's embarrassing, darling. I earn a good salary and what will people think when they see my wife – I mean my ex-wife – working for other people?'

'Most people do that, work for other people, don't they? There's no shame in that.'

'She's clever and intelligent and, she always hated working in the garden,' he finished lamely.

'Did she really hate gardening? Or was she pushed out of something she enjoyed because you thought it was your job to do the heavier outside work? You are an old-fashioned dear, you know. Weak little woman and big strong man. It's really old hat.'

In fact Evan needn't have worried unduly about Meriel's new career. The month of June was one of the wettest on record and she found that most of her appointments had to be cancelled. The money was left out for her at the Harris's but she didn't take it. She left a note each Monday letting them know she had actually arrived, but didn't attempt to deal with the tasks she had been set. Apart from the initial interview she didn't see the brothers. Neither did she see Cath Lewis, their Tragedy Queen.

At Churchill's Garden one Wednesday towards the end of June, she went in, to see Vivienne sitting alone.

'Only me today,' Vivienne smiled. 'Joanne has gone to the school insisting her boys are falling behind would you believe. Cynthia has gone shopping.'

Meriel nodded towards the tall thin young woman in her usual solitary state. She looked far from happy. 'Now might be a good time to invite her over,' she suggested.

To their surprise and pleasure, Cath Lewis picked up her cup, tucked her newspaper into her bag and joined them.

'We don't want to intrude,' Meriel said, 'But as we all meet here several times a week, it seemed churlish not to invite you to join us.'

'We're talking about jobs,' Vivienne began. 'Meriel has a gardening job but the weather has put paid to that. She's divorced you see and is wondering about the best way to restart her life.'

'It isn't easy when you've been out of the working fraternity for fifteen years,' Meriel added. 'I thought gardening might be an idea, get me used to being out of the house at certain times. A routine of sorts.'

'You must have some skills?' Cath said in her low, melodious voice. 'Everyone has, and it's amazing the varied ways in which people earn money these days.'

Meriel frowned and shook her head. 'I ran my own business for a while, but before that I worked in offices. My shorthand and typing skills are no longer needed and I haven't the first idea about computers.'

'What about a hobby which you can develop into a business?' Cath queried. 'The happiest people are those earning their living with an interest that began as a hobby.'

That made Meriel start guiltily. There was something. Something she had told no one about, not even Evan. But she denied it, shaking her head and lowering her eyes to hide the lie.

'What do you do?' she asked, and at once wished she hadn't.

25

A cloud came over Cath's face as though she were wondering how to answer without giving a truthful reply. 'Sorry, I didn't mean to pry. It was just another idea to throw into the pot.'

'I don't mind you asking, really I don't.' Cath reached out a long, slender hand and touched Meriel's arm. 'I was wondering about the best way to answer. I clean for two men on Holly Oak Lane, and I do a bit of buying and selling. Anything I can make a few pounds on.'

'You own a shop?'

'Nothing so grand,' she replied solemnly. 'I buy all sorts of things at charity shops and car boot sales, repair them, then I take a table at a sale and sell them on.'

'Is there much money in that?' Vivienne asked.

'I don't need much.' The long thin hands played with the coffee cup. The dark eyes, rimmed with purple so they looked bruised, were filled with melancholy. Both women looked away, afraid their stare would be an intrusion.

She was such a quiet, sad and lonely creature that Meriel and Vivienne were bursting with curiosity, but they talked about themselves and avoided further questions, afraid too much probing would send the girl away. She was obviously a very private person and whatever was making her so unhappy was not their business.

Vivienne talked about the previous Saturday night, when an ex-boyfriend had Toby-sat and she had gone to a nightclub with friends. Cath smiled as Vivienne exaggerated the stories she told to make them laugh, but made little comment. Then her eyes went misty and she appeared to sink back into her own thoughts; thoughts that were far from happy.

They had discovered enough for a first conversation. They left her there ten minutes later and when they looked back from the doorway they saw she had taken out her newspaper and was staring at its pages. Meriel thought she was not reading it, but using it as a screen.

Meriel spent some time in the shops, choosing food and buying a few items in the chemist. When she reached home she was hungry and her mind was filled with thoughts about what she would have for lunch, and how she would spend the rest of her day. But the first thing she noticed when she stepped inside was a note pinned to the cork board. It was from Evan, telling her he had called to take Nipper and Patch for a walk.

She and Evan had always used the cork board to let each other know where they would be. Now, seeing his note pinned there and realizing he had been inside as though it was still his home, she tore it down angrily. How dare he? She couldn't walk into his new home so why should he treat hers in this cavalier manner?

Changing into her walking shoes, forgetting everything she had planned to do, she set off to retrieve her dogs, seething, anger adding to the speed of her footsteps.

Evan and Sophie's garden was reached from the road on the landward side of the houses but knowing Evan had walked into her house although he had agreed not to do so without invitation, made her reckless. Leaving the cliff path and climbing over the low wall, she pushed her way through the hedge and stormed up to their back door and knocked loudly.

There was no reply. 'Both of them walking my dogs!' she said aloud. 'How dare they?' Retreating the way she had come, she went back to the path and headed for home, her anger unsatisfied.

She had been in for about fifteen minutes and was sipping a cup of tea, not because she wanted it but for something to do, when she heard the car.

'Don't come in here unless you're invited,' she said by way of greeting. 'We agreed.'

'Sorry,' he said. 'But Nipper recognized my voice and I thought the old chap would have been disappointed.'

'He had an hour's walk this morning, he'd have survived!'

She took the leads from him and called the dogs but they seemed unwilling to come to her. She stood at the door glaring at Evan, as he stood beside his car door smiling. Then she saw that Sophie was in the car and she was talking to the dogs. Meriel called sharply for Nipper to come; it was a tone he rarely ignored but this time he did. Then she saw Sophie lean down and give something to the dogs. Their tails wagged enthusiastically. It was obviously one of their favourite treats.

So that was why they didn't come to her! What was Sophie trying to do, make it clear that she could take the dogs too, if she wished? She ran to the car, picked up both dogs and took them inside. She slammed the door unnecessarily hard and listened as the car reversed out of the drive. What else would the woman take from her? What else was there left?

27

Three

When the sound of the car had faded, Meriel looked out of the window, glaring at the roadway, sending anger and dismay in equal proportions chasing the couple who had ruined her life. She scolded Nipper and Patch for their part in the scene and looked around wondering what she could do to ease her unhappiness. If only Evan and Sophie had moved right away, she thought for the thousandth time, instead of moving into a house she passed almost daily. She might have stood a better chance of rebuilding her life without him if Sophie hadn't been so near that she could look at her and smile like a sleek and satisfied cat.

She smiled then herself. Sophie was hardly like a sleek cat with her generous folds and her long thick hair that fell in untamed curls down to the small of her back. Sophie dressed in a blatantly sexual way, revealing just a little more than was acceptable. Blowsy is the word my mother would have used she thought, with another smile.

Sophie's interests did not lie within the home and she boasted about her inability to cook a decent meal. She liked dressing up and going to clubs and discos. Both things for which Evan had previously shown no interest. Perhaps, a hopeful voice within her whispered, perhaps he will soon grow tired of the hectic life Sophie demanded?

She stood up and snapped herself out of the foolish daydreaming. What was she doing thinking foolish and self-indulgent thoughts about Evan? She had to wipe him clean out of her life. Going into the bedroom where they had once slept together but which was now relegated to being the spare room, she looked at the chest of drawers that still held some of his clothes. Packing them up and taking them to a charity shop would be a start. Once she began, the job took hold and when the drawers were emptied, she started on the wardrobe where two of his suits still hung. She dumped them unceremoniously on to the pile.

The loft was next. Books he wanted to keep but for which Sophie wouldn't find the space, filled a small tin trunk and these she now efficiently packed into smaller boxes. She found a cricket bat that hadn't been used for years in an old sports bag together with white leather boots scuffed and grass-stained, and a few cricket balls and score cards. Sophie wasn't the type to watch cricket. She paused a while, remembering the fun of supporting Evan's team when he played for one of the local pubs. Everything went down to the hall, ready for delivery to the charity shop.

She remembered a pair of velvet curtains long abandoned and which she knew she would never use again. These were also packed and added to the collection. She felt the grumblings of hunger and remembered she hadn't had lunch, but she didn't stop to eat, she needed to get these things out of the house. It was almost two thirty, there was sure to be someone there to receive her offerings.

To her surprise it was Joanne who was in charge of the charity shop. She had forgotten Joanne's boasting about the generous way she gave up her time to help those less fortunate than herself. Having had the reason for the clear out explained to her, Joanne laughed and promised to try and sell the items as quickly as possible.

'We don't want Evan coming in and buying them back, do we?'

Meriel stayed for a while, watching as Joanne attended to the few customers who called. Most were idle browsers looking in the hope of a bargain or perhaps an unrecognized treasure.

'Not much chance of one of those these days,' Joanne told her. 'People are too well informed, what with the television programmes and magazine articles.'

'But it still happens sometimes. In fact,' Meriel said, as she picked up a small white plate with black sketches of household items on it, 'I would like this Home-maker plate.'

Joanne pulled a face as she took it for wrapping. 'I can't understand the fascination with old things,' she frowned. 'I can't bear the thought of using something that's been used by dozens of people. Give me brand spanking new every time.'

'I like the thought of it being used and loved and enjoyed by others.'

'But you don't have anything second-hand in your house?' Joanne queried.

'Evan's choice.'

'Such excellent taste,' Joanne breathed.

'But, Evan's choice,' Meriel repeated although with little hope of Joanne understanding.

'Lucky old you!'

Meriel bought a small trowel and fork set, paying double what was asked. 'I think Toby might like these next time I Toby-sit,' she explained.

'I don't know why you look after him just so Vivienne can go out and enjoy herself.'

'I don't mind. I could only look after him during the day when Evan was around, but now I'm on my own I sometimes have him in the evenings. Even to stay the night when Vivienne goes to a club.'

'Or on the pull! Isn't that what they call it these days?' Joanne gave a ladylike sniff of disapproval but Meriel didn't reply.

Seeing a pressed glass jug with an appealing shape, Meriel bought that too. How could she explain to people like Joanne the pleasure of a beautifully shaped jug? Or her fascination with articles that had led former lives? It was a contact with history, a glimpse of how people had once lived. She loved to run her fingers over a piece of furniture that had been lovingly polished by many hands over several generations, or handle a kitchen utensil worn by years of use.

Thanking Joanne she went across the road to the newsagents. Helen was browsing through the greetings cards and so she stopped to share a few words.

'Buying a card for my daughter Henrietta I am,' Helen smiled. 'It's her birthday and she and the boys will be coming to tea on Sunday. Fifteen she'll be mind. Hard to believe, eh? So I don't suppose she'll be wanting to see her Mam on her birthday much longer.'

'Do you see them often?' Meriel asked, aware that, since her divorce, Helen's sons William and George and her daughter Henrietta lived with their father and his new wife.

'They come more in the summer. Like the beaches they do and they spend a lot of time up with Cynthia and Christian's

30

boys. Henri doesn't seem to mind being the only girl, in fact, she's more like a boy herself,' she laughed.

They chatted for a while then Helen lowered her voice and whispered, 'There's a few rumours flying about, I hear it all, working here, mind. It seems that Joanne is no longer as well off as she pretends. So I've heard anyway. Never invites us to coffee no more. And she's got rid of her cleaner and her gardener, even though she denies it. And, this is the clincher, she doesn't shop in Sainsburys no more. She goes to the cut price store and for a snob like her that shows things must be serious don't you think? She wouldn't have been seen dead in one of them bargain shops up till a few months ago. D'you think her John's business is in trouble?'

Meriel was careful not to respond more than was necessary for politeness. It couldn't be true. John was opening new premises every few months and Evan had remarked more than once on the success of his enterprises. Small cafes offering fast food for a reasonable price, the All Day Breakfast had caught on and was showing no sign of fading. No, Helen must be wrong.

She went home and, letting the dogs out into the garden, she climbed up into the loft and began unwrapping some of her stored treasures. She remembered her start of guilt when Cath had asked whether she had a hobby or interest. These valued pieces had been kept a secret from Evan all through their marriage. For years she had been buying and storing pieces picked up in second-hand shops and car boot sales and wherever she saw something that appealed. Mostly china and glass, but hidden in the back of the garage she had a few small pieces of furniture. If Evan had noticed he would have thought it was junk, to be carted off to the tip one day. Her interest spanned from fifties memorabilia, to much earlier items. One day, when she left this house which she had shared with Evan, she hoped to find a place where she could indulge her interest and furnish it to suit her personality. Everything her own choice.

The prospect of living alone in a strange new house was frightening, but perhaps it was something she had to come to terms with. A second marriage was not a prospect that excited her. She couldn't risk being hurt again like Evan had hurt her.

She fingered a Susie Cooper teapot that had been her mother's, valuable now, but something she would never sell.

Perhaps she should put it on show, somewhere prominent where she could enjoy it every day? She began thinking of places where she could add shelves and corners where she could display her favourite things, but then she sadly rewrapped it and put it back in its box. One day, but not yet. She had to dig up her roots here, not make the place more attactive, more her own, more difficult to leave.

Her friends Cynthia and Joanne had a rivalry about owning the latest gadget and the newest designs. Although, she pondered, remembering Helen's latest 'news', she now wasn't sure about how well Joanne actually kept up with Cynthia. We none of us tell the truth, she mused silently. I certainly don't tell all of it when we meet and chat as if we were true friends. We all boast a little, perhaps Joanne boasts more than the rest of us? Perhaps the need to pretend a little is the reason we meet? The thought was a sad one. No, she told herself, we meet because we are friends.

She made a sandwich, then walked the dogs, making sure she didn't go in the direction where she might see Evan or Sophie. She didn't want to see them for a very long time.

After Meriel had left the charity shop, Joanne began to look through the offerings her friend had left. Apart from the curtains, which she put on display, everything in the boxes had belonged to Evan. She closed the lids and looked up expectantly as a customer entered the small, overfilled shop. She was pleased to see that it was Cath, the sad young woman they saw in Churchill's Garden.

'Hello! Mrs Lewis, isn't it? Cath? What a lovely surprise. Are you just browsing like most of my callers or can I tempt you to look for something specific?'

Cath only nodded in response to Joanne's greeting, making no comment on the use of her name. She asked the price of the curtains Meriel had brought in, which Joanne had hung on a rail.

'For you, five pounds.' Seeing Cath begin to retreat, she said hastily, 'Two pounds fifty?' Cath hesitated, touching the soft fabric with her long thin fingers and Joanne said, 'Go on, two pounds and they're yours.'

Smiling her thanks, Cath took out some silver coins. 'I need this material to cover a chair I've been given,' Cath explained,

'And perhaps make a few cushions. I don't have much furniture but what I do have, well, I like it to look warm and comfortable.'

'You sew then?'

'Fortunately yes.' She thanked Joanne again, bundled the curtains under her arm and left.

Ken Morris felt like an honorary uncle to the Sewell boys. Now and then he took them to Swansea for a MacDonalds and the cinema. One day in June he met the boys from school in his old van and they set off for town. Abertrochi didn't have a cinema but Swansea did and they were excited at the prospect of a film and before that a meal at a restaurant of their choice.

Ken wasn't surprised when they chose MacDonalds and he parked in a multistory not far away. When they had eaten, there was still an hour before the film began so they were in no hurry as they walked through a small laneway on their way back to the car park. When the three men suddenly came out of the shadows and stood in front of them, Marcus yelled in fright and Oliver and Rupert moved swiftly to stand protectively beside him.

'Let the boys go,' Ken yelled as one of the men grabbed him and pinned his hands behind his back, with an arm across his throat.

'Go back to the car! Scat!' the man standing in front of Ken hissed at the boys. But they couldn't move, being frightened and disorientated by the suddenness of the men's appearance and their threatening behaviour. One of the men sauntered menacingly towards them and they shrank together for comfort.

'Go, boys. Go back to the van and wait for me,' Ken said, his voice distorted by the arm around his neck.

'No police, mind!' the one holding Ken threatened. 'No clever tricks or you'll all be sorry, right?' Oliver and Rupert grabbed Marcus and hurried away.

When they reached the car they stood glancing around, avoiding each other's eyes and the fear they knew was there. Oliver and Rupert comforted Marcus soundlessly by holding his trembling shoulders tightly. Tears bulged and fell silently down his face. His foot tapped an involuntary rhythm on the cold concrete.

Ken arrived at last, walking slowly and awkwardly, but waving cheerfully and they ran towards him. He held them at arm's length, explaining that he'd fallen earlier in the day and was a bit tender.

Oliver and Rupert shared a knowing glance. They had watched enough police programmes on TV to guess what had happened. During the film, Ken got up and went to the toilets and when he came back Oliver was aware of the sour smell of vomit.

They were all subdued when they drove home even though Ken tried to cheer them up by talking about the film they had seen. Once outside their house, Ken made them promise not to say anything about what had happened. 'Just a bit of a misunderstanding, see? Those guys thought I owed them money but they'd got the wrong man!'

To Millie's surprise the boys went straight to bed without the usual arguments. She wondered whether they had eaten too much. Ken was inclined to indulge them when he took them out.

Cynthia's birthday was fast approaching and having faced the awful truth that she would soon be forty, she decided to celebrate boldly rather than pretend it wasn't happening. That way she'd feel better about it and enjoy it instead of feel the dragging dismay at the loss of her youth.

'It's the '0's,' she explained to Joanne and Meriel when she rushed in to join them for coffee one morning, 'It's the ending of a decade that makes it so serious, isn't it?'

'I don't agree,' Joanne said brightly. 'Twenty was marvellous, you're still wanting to grow up and be considered a person of note, to have your opinions sought after and valued. Thirty makes you think you're over the hill and any ambitions you might still have must be abandoned. But at forty, you're wise enough to know it's never too late to begin something new and succeed. Oh, no, Cynthia, the big "four oh" is a wonderful age. The children are less worry and everything is less urgent somehow. I can't wait,' she added as a reminder that she hadn't reached that wonderful milestone herself.

'You won't have to wait long, dear,' Cynthia said dryly as she checked her lipstick in her mirror, 'A year soon passes.'

'How will you celebrate?' Meriel asked.

'A party of course. Is there another way?'

'Plenty I'd have thought.'

'Well, I think my darling Christian has something planned. He asked me to check that the passports are in order last week and he hasn't mentioned a holiday, so – a surprise is likely, don't you think?'

The actual day of Cynthia's birthday was Friday, July the tenth but Christian decided to arrange the surprise for the following week. Coming out of the hairdressers and into the cafe one morning, an excited Cynthia waved for Cath to join them.

'Come on, I've got something to tell you all!' Pushing the coffee Meriel had bought for her to one side, she waved a sheaf of papers and announced. 'We're going to Paris on the seventeenth! A whole weekend together, with no children, no interruption for business emergencies or family problems. Christian has promised not to go near a telephone from Friday until Tuesday!'

'What about the children?' Joanne asked.

'They'll be all right with Millie. She and Christian have arranged it all, aren't I lucky? We're staying at the George Fifth of course. Oh, I'm so excited.' She went to the counter to remind the staff to bring out the birthday cake for all she had previously ordered and the friends sat and enjoyed a morning party, listening to Cynthia's plans for her romantic weekend.

'I'm buying everything new – underwear, night clothes, a new outfit for travelling in.'

Cath was quiet as usual, although she did make a few comments on Paris, which she described as her favourite city and suggested a few places Cynthia and Christian might visit.

'You know Paris well, do you?' Joanne asked.

'I've been a few times yes.'

They waited for her to explain but Cath added nothing more.

When they were leaving, Vivienne walked with Meriel down the road towards the sea.

'Toby and I are thinking about going away for a few days this month,' Vivienne said. 'Are you planning anything this summer?'

'I hadn't thought about going away. I feel tied to the house, afraid of leaving it in case Evan and Sophie go in to snoop. And the dogs. I wouldn't want those two to look after them. Silly I know, but it's how I feel. I won't feel able to go away until I've decided what I'm going to do with the rest of my life.'

'Make a decision about the rest of your life! What a terrifying thought!' Vivienne laughed. 'I never plan more than a month or two. It's too boring to know so much of what lies ahead. Impulse is much more fun. Why don't you come with us? Toby's funny, fascinating, exhausting at times on holiday but not difficult. After all, you know him well enough – which reminds me, can you look after him tonight? I was hoping to go out with two girls I met a couple of weeks ago.'

'Yes, to minding Toby, but I'm not sure about going away. There's the house—'

'Lock it.'

'And the dogs—'

'Ask your ex to mind them. Might as well make use of him.' Then, seeing that the suggestion was not well received she added, 'Or, why not bring them?'

'We couldn't manage two dogs and Toby. Could we?' She couldn't admit that she wouldn't leave the dogs with Sophie because she was afraid she would steal their affection like she had stolen her husband, coaxing them away from being her own dogs.

'The house will still be there when you get back. Dusty perhaps, but unharmed.'

'I don't know,' she said doubtfully.

'Kennels. A friend. A house-sitter. If you want to come I can obliterate all your objections.'

'Where were you thinking of going?'

'That's better! I thought we could just set off for West Wales and see where the car takes us. Pembrokeshire is particularly lovely in summer. It shouldn't be that difficult to find bed and breakfast. What d'you think? If there's some other area you'd prefer, I'm not averse to a change of plan, in fact, I *love* changes of plan.'

'If you're sure you want me along, I think I'd like to come. Thanks.' Meriel went home feeling more cheerful than she had for a long time, a year in fact. Although she did have a slight apprehension as to how many evenings she would sit alone, Toby-sitting, while Vivienne went out!

'John and I will be going to Spain,' Joanne told them when holidays were being discussed again a few days later. 'Not a very exciting choice, but the boys love it. Sea, sand and swimming pool. That's all they want. Plus plenty of good restaurants to satisfy their giant-sized appetites.' She sighed theatrically. 'Soon it will be sea, sand and sex, I suppose, then the troubles start. But at the moment that's all in the future and Spain is a restful break for John, and easy for me, not having to choose meals, and shop and cook.'

'Where are you staying,' Cynthia asked.

'Oh, Menorca,' Joanne replied, saying the first name that came into her head. She couldn't admit that John had told her they couldn't afford a holiday this year. Later on, she could explain they'd had to cancel owing to pressure of work or something.

'North or south?' Cynthia wanted to know.

Joanne frowned as though trying to remember. 'West – I think.'

'Cuitadella?'

'Mmm, that might have been it. I'm a bit vague actually. John sees to the bookings. I leave everything to him.'

'Pretty little town, there's a river running through and the island's so small you're never far from a beach.'

Anxious to change the conversation, Joanne invited Cath over and began to ask her about her recent purchases from the shop.

'I covered my chair and made two quilted cushion covers,' Cath told them. 'The velvet looks lovely. So rich.'

'You'll have to invite us up to see them,' Joanne suggested, knowing she would never set foot in the place no matter how many times she was invited. It was bound to be a tip.

'Perhaps I will.' Cath gave one of her rare smiles.

'Lovely,' Joanne breathed.

'I'm beginning to sort out what I need to keep and what I won't use and I have a couple of shelves you might like,' Meriel said. 'And a couple of kitchen chairs I no longer want.' She wrote down her address. 'Call if you'd like to see them.'

Cath thanked her and promised to do so the following day.

* * *

Cath arrived at three. She stepped out of an old Saab wearing a long flowing dress made of assorted patchwork and dyed a uniform green, with a crotcheted shawl low on her shoulders to take away the slight chill of the ever-present breeze coming in from the sea. Walking slowly, her head held high, her hair undulating gently around her, a velvet shoulder-bag swinging against her hip, Meriel could imagine her looking quite at home in a scene centuries back in history.

She would have fitted perfectly in a film of a Thomas Hardy story, or one about a Celtic queen, Meriel mused, as she watched the woman approach. As she drew near, she realized with sudden surprise, that Cath was very beautiful.

After a coffee, Meriel showed her visitor into the garage where, stacked along one wall, there were tea chests and boxes all neatly labelled, in which Meriel kept her treasures.

Cath was pleased with the shelves she was offered.

'I have some baskets abandoned by a florist that I'll fill with dried flowers and grasses,' she explained, a faraway look in her dark eyes. 'I'll display them on these shelves fastened to the wall. My tiny kitchen will be a brighter place in which to work. Thank you very much.'

'It sounds lovely,' Meriel smiled. 'I wish I'd thought of it myself.'

'If you've changed your mind and want to keep them, I'll help you fill them?' Cath said at once.

'No, no. I'm gradually taking my home apart, not building it up,' she said lightly. 'I have to move soon. When I've decided where I want to live.'

'That must be exciting.'

'That's a better response! I usually get, "poor you". And I have to admit that's usually how I feel. I thought I'd stay here, with Evan, for the rest of my life.'

'Better to pull up roots at least once. You know who you are after living in a house for a while, then you can move on and choose what you really want.'

'I thought I had what I wanted.'

'Two years from now you will know it was not.'

'You sound so sure.'

'Two years,' Cath repeated softly. 'Then you'll know I'm right.'

One of the tea chests was still open, only partly packed,

and Cath spotted a wooden fire engine. It had been well used but was still strong and ready for more rough handling. She picked it up and fondled it with her long elegant hands, a frown clouding her lovely eyes.

'You don't have children?' Meriel asked softly, about to explain her own lack of a family and, to her alarm, she saw the dark eyes flood with silent tears. Unable to decide what to say, wishing the words could be revoked, she stood and watched as Cath coped with the sudden rush of emotion before replying briefly,

'No.'

'I wonder whether things would have worked out differently if Evan and I had had children,' Meriel said as she gathered up the shelves and put them beside Cath's car. She had turned away from her and was talking to give the woman a chance to recover, aware she should have chosen a different subject but unable to think of one. 'We wanted them, but it just didn't happen. I'm afraid it's too late now.'

'There you go again, Meriel. Think positive, isn't that the slogan for today? You're young enough to remarry and have children, so why shouldn't it happen?'

'Perhaps I can't?'

'Perhaps *he* couldn't.'

Meriel laughed aloud then. 'Keep trying, Cath. You'll teach me positive thinking in the end.'

'Would you like to see where I live?'

'Really? Well, yes. I'd love to,' Meriel said in surprise. 'Thank you.'

Packing the shelves into Cath's car, and an old, unwanted watering-can Cath had admired, plus two slightly damaged urns, they set off. Meriel was quite excited. She had an idea Cath's home would be unconventional, but would certainly be a calm, peaceful and attractive place. She also thought it was a place to which few were invited.

It was high on a hill, backed by trees growing out of the rocky higher ground behind it and leaning over its roof as if for extra protection. From the front there was a view over the town and the distant sea. There were three houses similar to Cath's but hers was the furthest in, tucked into a corner cut from steeply rising rocks, close to the narrow path which led to the back entrance of the houses.

The impression Meriel had on entering was more or less what she had envisaged: drapes of material, tassels and ropes, wind-chimes, gold embroidery and polished brass and copper. Carpets and rugs were piled on the floor one on top of another in casual disarray yet looking elegant and tasteful. Cushions offered comfort and relaxation. Amid all the draperies, the windows were unadorned to allow the view to be enjoyed to the full.

There were several soft toys around and they looked well used. Meriel didn't comment on them. The subject of children was, for whatever reason, one to be avoided.

She wasn't shown any of the other rooms, so Meriel presumed that the rest had yet to be furnished. The kitchen was filled with jars of pulses and dried herbs and several kinds of rice and pasta. Draped around the walls were garlands of hop vines.

It was not a home in which she would have enjoyed living, there was an all-pervading air of sadness, but it was the perfect setting for the tall, slim, mysterious and beautiful woman who was pointing out to her with obvious pleasure, where the flower shelves would be fixed.

'Tom Harris, one of the brothers I work for, is very kind. He'll come and fix them for me,' she explained.

'I work for him too,' Meriel explained. 'Although I haven't seen Tom since the day he hired me, and Roy not at all.'

'They lead a very full social life, belonging to various organizations and with a variety of interests which they share.'

'They seem remarkably close, for brothers.'

'They have so many interests in common I suppose.'

'And gardening is not one of them,' Meriel laughed.

Meriel felt it a privilege to have been invited and knew her visit wasn't one she would share with Cynthia, Joanne or Helen. Not even Vivienne would be given the opportunity to discuss Cath so intimately. They wouldn't understand and might ridicule Cath's style.

When she was back in her own place, she sat and stared into space for a long time, wondering what had brought Cath to live in Abertrochi and what had happened to the children for whom she grieved.

Four

Meriel's ex-husband, Evan Parry, drove back from Newport, feeling utterly exhausted. He had broken down on the motorway and had spent hours getting the car fixed. This had made him late for his appointment with a prospective buyer for the last of a recent consignment of conservatory suites. The cane was not the best quality and the cushions were looking a bit jaded and he had offered a low price to get them cleared. The buyer was not soothed by his explanations and apologies and the result was a wasted day.

This morning's two appointments had been cancelled to enable him to go, which meant a very full day tomorrow and to add to that, Sophie had expected him home an hour ago. Belatedly, he thought he should call to let her know that he was on his way. He'd never had to bother when he was with Meriel. She had accepted his odd hours and irregular meal-times without a murmur. That was because she was dull, he reminded himself. She never wanted to do anything in the evenings except walk the dogs or watch television or read, so it had never made much difference to her if he had been held up. Yet, he wished he was going home to the peace she created.

Inexplicably he felt he needed to see Meriel, needed her to soothe away the tensions of his day, and he found himself outside his previous home. He sat in the car for a while, allowing the agonies of the day to settle, and fall from him. He was stiff when he finally stepped out of the car and walked to the door. He knocked and there was the sound of excited barking. He smiled and opened the letterbox. 'All right, you two, I'll see you in a moment.' When nothing further happened he said, in the foolish way of dog owners, 'Where's your mum, eh? Go and tell her I'm here.' Disappointment was powerful as he accepted that Meriel was not there. She wasn't the type to hide and not answer the door. He wondered with slight

41

irritation where she could be. She rarely went out in the evening.

Returning to the car he dialled Sophie's number. When the phone was picked up he heard the sound of music played very loudly and in his imagination saw her dancing around their untidy kitchen. He smiled in spite of his tiredness. Peace was not why he had chosen to live with Sophie.

'Darling, I'm running late, but I should be with you in an hour.'

'I can't wait,' she said, sending kisses down the phone. 'Shall we go out this evening? There's a good band at The Farmers.'

'Well, I do have a lot of paperwork. I should stay in and get on with it.'

'But you won't,' she said. 'It's no good trying to sound serious, I can almost see the smile on your face which shows me you're teasing. I'll be freshly bathed and perfumed and waiting for you, darling.'

Smiling, Evan drove towards home, only a few minutes away, reminding himself of his good fortune. Sophie is wonderful, he told himself. Young, beautiful, sexy, and altogether wonderful, and she has chosen me! He glanced at the package on the seat beside him. He'd bought a new shirt. It was unlikely there would be a clean one hanging ready in his wardrobe. Young, beautiful and sexy maybe, but Sophie wasn't that kind of wife, he thought ruefully. Perhaps he should suggest getting someone in to deal with the ironing as well as the cleaning.

As he opened the door, he stopped to take a deep breath, aware of mild irritation. If only she didn't have the CD on quite so loud. She was dancing around the kitchen, as he had guessed, her face flushed, her long hair a glorious cloud around her lovely face. Her eyes were wide apart and a summer-sky blue, more intense now with the heat of her exertions adding colour to her face. She lowered the sound and ran to him, sweet-smelling, warm and soft and so desirable.

'You tease! You were just around the corner and not an hour away.'

He laughed, enjoying her delight.

'Can we eat out?' she pleaded. 'I was going to defrost some chicken and do a stir-fry, but I haven't started preparing anything and I'm starving.' Seeing the hesitation on his face she added, 'Your fault, you phoned and told me I had plenty of time.'

'Give me an hour first, and—'

'That long? Are you tired of me already?'

'I'll never tire of you. I love you.' he said. 'Come here and let me show you.'

Meriel opened her door later that evening to see Cynthia standing there, with her youngest son, Marcus.

'I've come to beg a favour,' Cynthia said as she bustled in. 'I can't stay a moment as I'm on my way to a committee meeting. The fourth this week would you believe. The end of school year coincides with the end of season for so many other organizations I don't know how I can fit them in. Anyway, I won't keep you.'

'Coffee?' Meriel suggested when she had a chance to speak. 'And orange juice for you, Marcus?'

'It's about this weekend in Paris that darling Christian has arranged. I've been let down by Millie. She wants to go away to some cousins in Hampshire. Could you possibly stay with the boys? I would be ever so grateful to you if you would.'

'We wouldn't be any trouble, Meriel,' Marcus smiled. But as his mother looked away from him, he gave a broad wink.

'Of course I'll stay with the boys, but will it be all right if I bring the dogs?'

'We hoped you would,' Marcus said, patting the two inquisitive dogs who had come to greet the visitors.

'Don't do any housework, nothing at all. Millie will catch up when she gets back, and I'll leave money for you to eat out whenever you wish. It's only a few days.'

'Why don't I come over tomorrow so you can show me where everything is?' Meriel suggested.

When Meriel walked into the imposing house near the cliffs, a team of decorators were clearing up having refurb-ished the hall, landings and staircases. A new chair, upholstered in yellow velvet, stood beside what Cynthia called the post table at one side of the hall, which had a tooled-leather top, bearing stamps, pens and four brass trays, in which the separate piles of post had been sorted and placed.

'Christian's business, my committee work, family letters and bills,' Cynthia explained. She pointed to the waste-basket underneath, 'And of course, the bin for rubbish.'

Briskly she opened doors and explained where everything

was kept. At the back of the garage was a room adjoining the airing room, which, she explained hurriedly, as though with embarrassment, was full of junk. 'I've discarded a lot of old ornaments and rugs, even some furniture now I've redecorated the hall,' she said. 'Some of it was abandoned years ago, stuff from when Christian and I first married when we had no idea of what we wanted. If there's anything you think you can use, please help yourself. Just don't tell anyone you got it from me,' she said with a self-deprecating laugh. 'That would be too embarrassing, so tasteless. If you don't fancy anything,' she went on airily unaware of the implied insult, 'I'll give it to Joanne for her charity shop. People will buy anything, won't they?'

Meriel stared at the carelessly stacked items and asked, 'Surely you don't mean *all* of these things? Some of this china and glass is lovely.'

'You can't mean it, Meriel?'

'Oh, I do.'

'Then take it. Bring the car tomorrow and we'll fill the boot.'

'But, that looks like a chandelier,' Meriel said, pointing at a collection of glass and brass in a corner, dumped half in and half out of a large flat box. 'You can't mean to discard that?'

'It's so old, dear. It belonged to my grandmother in the large house in Llandrindod Wells. I wanted something new. I chose one in hand-wrought iron. Much more attractive.'

'But if it belonged to your grandmother, doesn't it have any sentimental value?'

'It was in the house before my grandmother's time. Mummy liked such things but not I.'

'But, it must be valuable.'

'Must it?'

'If it's that old – I would love it but I could never afford to pay anything near its value.'

'All right, if it makes you feel happier and you really want it, give me something for one of my charities. Oh, and there's another one somewhere, a matching pair.'

'If you're sure—' Meriel at once wrote out a cheque which made Cynthia raise her eyebrows. 'Meriel, you must be mad, but thank you!'

They went upstairs to glance into the five bedrooms and

44

the bathrooms, with Cynthia pointing out the various store cupboards and their contents.

'Now, this is our bedroom. Mine and Christian's and – I don't want you to take this the wrong way, but I've hidden all my jewellery. It isn't that I don't trust you, please believe me. It's because, knowing we're away, someone might force a way in and look for it. It is rather valuable. Picking up a box with everything in it makes it too easy, doesn't it? You do understand, don't you?'

'Of course. But won't you be wearing some of it?' She glanced at Cynthia's fingers unusually lacking ornamentation.

'I most certainly won't, Meriel dear. Bare fingers will more likely tempt darling Christian to buy more! Neither will I be taking sufficient clothes, for the same reason!'

As Meriel prepared to leave, having had the mysteries of the microwave and dishwasher explained, Cynthia said, 'There is one thing. Marcus is a bit nervous lately, he's had some bad dreams. I think it's from the time Ken last took them to the cinema. Will you make sure you don't take them to see anything frightening. He's such a sensitive boy, so easily upset.'

'I don't like horror films myself,' Meriel admitted.

'It doesn't need to be horror to frighten him, dear, just something awful happening to an animal and he's uneasy for days.'

'I'll make sure he doesn't see anything to upset him,' Meriel promised.

Driving home, thinking about the wealth that could allow Cynthia to discard so many beautiful things without a thought, Meriel turned around and went up to see Cath Lewis in her house high above the town. She might like to be involved in the transporting and assessing of the contents of Cynthia and Christian's 'junk room'.

They made three trips, both cars filled with the discarded items from Cynthia's house which were stored in Meriel's garage. Much of it was cheap china and glass including vases and drinking glasses of every type.

There were incomplete dinner services and teasets. 'These teasets are rather nice. It appears that when one or two items were broken Cynthia threw away the rest. And some of this glass is lovely. No complete sets, but they are nice enough to sell individually,' Cath said, handling a tall champagne flute with obvious pleasure. 'These coloured cups and saucers might

45

go well too if we show them individually. What d'you think, fifties or sixties?' The cups and saucers were white china and each was a different colour around the base of the cup and the centre of the saucer. Once a set of six, there were just three left plus a couple of odd saucers.

They carefully sorted the collection and packed them away in boxes marked with a code they devised to show contents and approximate age. The chandeliers had been packed into two large containers and they left these until the last. Opening the box, pushing aside the protective sheets and paper, they looked at their prize items. The light in the garage was not good but the glittering marvel they expected didn't materialize.

'They aren't glass, they're plastic,' Cath gasped. 'I thought you said they were from her grandmother's large house?'

'Perhaps they were, but they weren't bought before her grandmother's marriage, that's for sure.'

'Perhaps her grandmother replaced them?'

'Perhaps Cynthia is making it up!'

'No, why should she?' Cath frowned. She found that hard to believe.

'Well I have often wondered why she never talks about her parents or any brothers or sisters. And this grandmother and the house in Llandrindod, when did you hear about any of that before?'

'Family quarrels do happen,' Cath excused. 'Plenty of people have left all or part of their family as they grow and move away. Move not just geographically, but in attitude and interests.'

'You're probably right. But that doesn't explain these.'

'Perhaps "Grannie" sold them and bought these because the originals needed repair that was too costly?' Cath suggested.

'We'll be able to sell them, but not for the amount I had in mind,' Meriel said ruefully. 'Lesson number one. Look closely at something before you buy and don't believe everything you're told by the seller!'

They arranged for extra locks to be fitted on the garage door and took as much of the more valuable stock up into Meriel's spare room, the one she had once shared with Evan, as they could manage.

'I think I should start selling some of the less valuble items at a table top sale,' Meriel said, looking at the odds and ends she had collected over the past few years. 'Will you help?'

'Love to.' Animation warmed Cath's face. 'I'll share the cost of the first one and we can each sell our own stuff, if you agree.'

With the contents of the garage made as safe as possible, Meriel made plans to go to look after Cynthia's family. 'I'll call every day to make sure it hasn't been stolen!' she said to Cath.

'It would be a bit late if you found that it had!' Cath said dryly.

Cynthia's holiday in Paris and London with Christian was an expensive spending spree. She came back with suitcases filled with new clothes and happily discarded half the contents of her wardrobe into Joanne's charity shop. These were sorted by Joanne, who selected several garments to sell at the nearly new shop in town. It wouldn't be a lot of money, but the few pounds she gathered seemed a reasonable way to pay for the extra expenses that John chose to ignore.

Meriel and Vivienne's holiday later in July was cheap, relaxing and enjoyable. They travelled in a leisurely way around Pembrokeshire, enjoying the warmth of the welcome they received, enchanted by the views unfolding with every mile and the fascination of the history of the area. Toby was easily entertained, enjoying visits to farms and theme parks and was contented for hours on the many clean sandy beaches they found.

Vivienne, as Meriel expected, disappeared often to look at shops or to find ways of amusing herself in the evenings. Night-life was sparse in some places they stayed, but she usually found a public house where music was played or on one occasion a village barn dance in progress during which she quickly made friends. Meriel and Toby went with her on this occasion, but Meriel took the little boy home when he began to tire. Vivienne had been promised company to walk her back to their B and B and followed them later. Much later.

Meriel had taken books to read and occasionally she wandered around the second-hand and antique shops, buying a few items to add to her growing collection of fifties memorabilia, trying to explain their fascination to a bemused Vivienne.

Discussing their vacations in Churchill's Garden on their return, it was clear they all wanted different things from life. For

Cynthia the full wallet and comfortable hotels where she was waited on and made to feel important, were essential. For Meriel and Vivienne it was the simpler pleasures dependent only on the weather, in which they had been fortunate.

Helen had her three children staying with her for a week. William who was twelve, George thirteen and Henrietta who was now fifteen. Helen managed to squeeze them into the flat she and Reggie called home and they spent a happy week exploring and bathing, and eating all the things their father didn't allow.

'My holiday in Spain has been cancelled,' Joanne told them, displaying great sorrow. 'John can't even manage a weekend between now and when the boys go back to school. I don't mind for myself, but it's so disappointing for the boys.'

'Why don't *you* take them?' Cynthia asked. 'I took mine away a few times when Christian was building the business.'

'I can't. I like to be here when John gets home for a few days. He needs looking after, his life is so stressful.' She glanced at Meriel before adding sweetly, 'We don't want him given the opportunity or the excuse to stray, do we?'

'If I was so worried about Reggie, or my first husband, Gareth, I wouldn't have married them in the first place!' Helen said loudly. 'And if you're wondering about my first marriage, it was a mutual parting. He didn't leave because I hadn't stirred his tea!' She touched Meriel's arm understandingly and glared at Joanne.

Embarrassed by the following silence, Meriel stood to collect more coffee. Joanne touched her shoulder and gently pushed her down. 'I'll get it, Meriel, I'm sorry if you misunderstood what I said.'

'That's the trouble,' muttered Helen. 'She *did* understand!'

Cath watched, listened and said nothing.

Later on, as they were about to leave, Cynthia sympathized with Joanne. 'Such a pity your holiday had to be cancelled.'

'Oh, I don't know. I wasn't that keen, and the boys find plenty to do in the garden and on the beach. Why do we need to go away when we've everything they need right here?'

'Why indeed,' Vivienne agreed.

'My holiday is having my three children to stay,' Helen said. 'I don't see them often enough to miss a moment of their visit. And they love the beaches around here.'

Cath got up without a word and hurried from the cafe.

Meriel thought once again, it was the talk of children that upset her. One day she would ask.

Cath Lewis didn't appear at the popular cafe so often in the following weeks, and Helen Symons – fount of all knowledge – told them that besides working for Tom and Ray Harris, she was also working for two men living on Gregory Way. 'They work in some nightclub or other,' she explained, 'So they don't rise very early. The bedrooms get done on the mornings following their nights off.'

Cynthia and her family had now gone to New York for ten days, Helen was doing extra shifts in the shop to help over the holiday period, Meriel was decorating the house preparatory to offering it for sale, so the table was never full.

One morning Helen called in and was telling Vivienne and Meriel in urgent whispers about the breakup of the marriage of a mutual friend, when Cath came in and said to Meriel,

'Can I have a word?' Refusing the invitation to join them, she said, 'There's a table top sale on Saturday. Would you like to come? We might pick up a few things cheaply.'

'And get pointers ready for when we take a table ourselves.'

As Vivienne continued to listen avidly to the lurid details of Helen's latest newsletter, Meriel agreed to meet Cath at eight o'clock on Saturday morning and drive to the village where the sale was to be held.

It was the start of a new routine for them. With summer sliding quietly into autumn, on most weekends there was a sale somewhere and they didn't need to travel more than twenty miles to attend one. They had to leave before seven a.m. to get the best of the car boot sale bargains and sometimes they went for a coffee before going home.

Meriel had found the summer months easy so far as the gardening was concerned. Both men were away for most of the six weeks that the schools were closed, touring France, Tom had told her on a rare occasion when they met in July. The beds were planted and it was too early to think about spring bulbs. There was little to do apart from weeding and cutting the grass. She went often to get out the hosepipe, though, especially for the many planters she had filled.

For Meriel, dealing with the garden for the absentee employers and decorating the house was a way of helping to take her mind off Evan and Sophie. She began to realize that on some days, hours would pass without thoughts of them entering her mind and causing a revival of her distress. Mail sometimes came for him and she readdressed it and posted it on. Phone calls came from people involved in his business activities and these she dealt with sharply and unhelpfully, as though they were automatically on his side, as much to blame as Evan himself for his abandonment of her.

During one of her gardening mornings she met Tom. She had hoped to see him at some time before the school holidays ended, but the house always appeared to be closed up. Then, during the first week of the autumn term, he was waiting for her at the door. He was tall, fair and rugged-looking, in corduroys and a thick aran sweater, like a hero from a 'forties film, she thought with a smile. He held out a hand and greeted her warmly.

'I had to stay and thank you for all you've done,' he said, waving an arm encompassing the neat borders and the well-tended grass. To Meriel it sounded like the beginning of a 'goodbye' speech and she frowned. 'Don't worry,' he laughed, having guessed her thoughts. 'I don't want to lose you. I just wondered what to do when the weather gets worse. Will you come when you can? We'll pay you of course.' As she began to protest, he said quickly. 'We'd prefer to retain you rather than get to springtime and have to look for someone else, someone who might be far less skilful than you.'

They discussed what was needed and finally agreed that she would be paid a half fee on the days she didn't come, although, she decided silently that even if she had to change her day to accommodate the unreliable weather, she would do enough to earn the money he gave her.

'Do you do much of this kind of thing?' he asked as he handed her the money he owed her.

'No, in fact I haven't done this sort of thing before.'

'You surprise me! But you must be keen on growing things. A hobby maybe?'

'Not even that. I'm hoping, one day, to learn enough about antiques to start a business of my own,' she explained.

'I don't know anything about running a business, but my brother Ray tried and failed. He made the mistake of renting an expensive premises in the main road. Better I think, to find a cheaper place and make your customers find you.'

'Thank you, that's worth remembering,' she smiled.

In late September Cynthia decided to organize a large charity dinner in aid of the NSPCC and, having persuaded most of her circle of friends to attend, she insisted that Joanne put aside her usual excuses and join them.

In case her husband wouldn't help with the money, she began using the usual excuses.

'I can't leave the boys, Cynthia, dear,' she said baby-voiced. 'John is away. I'd love to come but I simply can't leave Jeremy and Justin on their own.' A look passed between Joanne and Cynthia, an awareness of their differing views on childcare.

'She could at least offer to contribute if she can't come,' Cynthia complained to Millie later. Rupert who had overheard the conversation, offered to help.

'Why don't we go down and stay with Jeremy and Justin, Mummy? Oliver and I are over fifteen.'

'What a good idea, darling. I'll telephone at once. She won't get out of this one!'

'Do I go with them?' Marcus asked hopefully.

'I don't see why not. If you'd like to.'

'I'm still not sure,' Joanne was saying as she dressed carefully, watching the clock, seeing the minutes pass before Helen and her husband Reggie were calling to pick her up. 'There's still time for me to cancel.'

'Don't Mummy, you deserve a night out,' fourteen-year-old Jeremy said.

'Can we go to bed *really* late?' asked twelve-year-old Justin, before being hushed by a glare from his brother.

Oliver, Rupert and Marcus arrived at that moment and they unpacked a game of monopoly and several books. They conversed politely, until the toot of a horn announced the arrival of Helen and Reggie.

'Just be good, don't make a mess and don't cause any trouble.' Joanne left the house after a last warning about tidiness and good behaviour as the five boys were settling down to read one of the story-books they had brought. She heard Oliver saying, 'Come on, we'll read it aloud, a page each, right?' as the door closed behind her.

As soon as the sound of the car faded, they threw the books and the monopoly in the air and turned on the television. They looked expectantly at Oliver who had promised them a special treat. Slowly he pulled from his coat pocket a video.

Laughs and catcalls filled the air, nudges and looks were shared, but after the first illicit excitement the scenes began to pall and they lost interest. They looked around for something to do to celebrate their freedom from adults.

The autumn evening was humid and, ignoring Joanne's instruction, they trooped out into the dying light. Calling for Joanne's poodle, Fifi, which they didn't like to admit knowing and whom they called Stupid, they set off down the garden and on to the cliffs.

The night was calm, the air heavy making them feel sticky and uncomfortable. The leaves on the trees were still. The only sound was the distant shushing of the sea. The moon was full and already high in the sky, yet looking so close they could imagine being able to touch it.

'Let's go and look at the sea,' Rupert said, holding his arms out in the hope of a cooling breeze. 'It'll be colder there.'

'I don't think we should,' Jeremy said. 'We promised Mum and—'

'You come out when she's here, so what's the difference?'

'I don't know. It's creepy somehow, walking away and leaving the house empty at night.'

'Don't be a wimp!' said Marcus, brave in the company of his brothers. Pulling the door closed, he walked towards the cliff path and the others followed, the twins laughing affectionately at their young brother's bossiness.

The tide was hardly moving, slipping quietly in with hardly a sound, no frilly white underskirt to reveal the extent of its journeyings. The sky was pink and yellow and orange, with fingers of dark clouds signalling the day's ending.

It was no one's suggestion, nothing was said as, in unison, they stripped off their trousers and tops and clambered down the sloping rocks, ran across the strip of wet sand and plunged headlong, with shrieks of genuine shock, into the sea.

Rupert and Oliver, Cynthia's twins, left Jeremy and Justin to get on with enjoying their unexpected and strictly forbidden freedom, and concentrated on Marcus's swimming lessons before leaving him kicking about near the edge and going for a swim themselves.

When they eventually looked up, they realized that the night had fallen and the tide was approaching the rocks.

Above them, ghostly white in the failing light, was Fifi alias Stupid, barking and growling, playing with something they couldn't see.

'Come on,' Oliver shouted. 'Time to go.'

Shivering now they were out in the night air, they clambered back up and began arguing about whose trousers belonged to whom, laughing like conspirators. Joanne's boys were almost delirious with delight at their adventure. Until Justin failed to find his shirt and socks.

Laughter ceased and they all began to search for the missing clothing. The shirt wasn't found and only one sock was discovered before they admitted defeat and walked back to the house. The one sock they had found was full of holes.

'So that was what Stupid was playing with,' groaned Justin. 'What shall I do?'

'Throw it in the bin and swear you know nothing,' Marcus advised. The laughter that followed eased Justin's anxiety and they made some hot chocolate and ate the biscuits Joanne had left for them. Then they used a loaf of bread making toast and drank more hot chocolate before declaring themselves thoroughly warmed.

When Joanne came rushing in at eleven thirty, anxious to reassure herself that everything was all right, she found the five boys, dressed in pyjamas and dressing gowns, feigning sleep, sprawled across the chairs and sofa and the floor. Coming in behind her with much sentimental 'aw'ing', Helen and Reggie helped her get the boys to their allotted beds. When she was alone, Joanne plumped cushions and straightened the furniture minutely to get it correctly aligned and looked around in satisfaction. They must have behaved remarkably well.

The books Cynthia's boys had brought were neatly stacked and the kitchen had been left without a trace of their having eaten supper. Perhaps she might do this again? If only money wasn't so short, she sighed.

The next morning after breakfast, all five boys diligently helped her to search for the missing shirt and socks and declared themselves utterly puzzled by their disappearance.

Five

K en Morris called into an empty house and collected his mail. He put the assorted envelopes down on the passenger seat of his van and drove to a lay-by to examine them. One with an American stamp he opened first. His daughters both lived there and he was smiling with anticipation as he broke the seal. As well as the hastily scrawled note, typical of Sue, there were photographs of her family. A husband he had yet to meet and two grandsons he knew only from the regular supply of snaps. He looked at them several times, read the note twice and put them down. The letter from his Turf Accountant was next. He smiled as he opened that one too, expecting the amount he owed to have fallen. But it had increased.

Worse, the account was closed until he paid the whole amount off. As he had been told, they didn't like him using their money to try and recoup his losses. The figure owed was frightening, and the tone of the men, when they had met him coming from the cinema with Christian's three boys, had been clear: pay up or be used as a warning to others. He had paid something off his account after the three men had warned him, by borrowing more from moneylenders and now his debts were escalating alarmingly. He had a nasty letter from the moneylenders too.

He looked again at the snaps of Sue and her family. When would he ever be able to go out there and meet them all? With both daughters married and settled permanently in the States he had to find the money to visit them. He couldn't stop gambling. How else was he going to find the money to pay off his ever mounting debts and arrange to visit them? As he drove home, he changed direction a few times. Perhaps he was becoming paranoid, but if someone followed him and learned that he was living with his elderly mother – the thought was too terrifying to hold on to. He had to do something, but what? To begin with, he would ask one of the labourers to go in and place a bet for him, borrowing money from the petty cash. He could put that back at the end of the month. He had to win some time.

The night of their escape, as Jeremy and Justin called it, was the first of many that month. Being reassured by the orderly state of the house and the apparent good behaviour of the five boys, Joanne began to accept more invitations, explaining to John that, as long as the boys were properly looked after, she felt confident to leave them for a few hours. John was surprised but pleased.

'Just tell me where you'll be, so I can get in touch with you if necessary,' he said.

'Really John, we ought to have mobiles so we can keep in touch more easily. It's ridiculous, everyone else has one these days. Everyone but me.'

'There's no need to add to our outgoings. You have a phone in the house, that's enough.' He had a mobile, but dealt with the account via his office. He didn't want Joanne to know about it. She fussed so much she would be bothering him too frequently during his working day, and at most inconvenient times.

Travelling a lot, dealing with his widespread cafes and houses, he needed to be free of her while he was involved with work, as he explained to Cynthia's husband, Christian, one day when they met at one of his lorry parks about fifteen miles from Abertrochi.

'I talk to Cynthia a lot during the day,' Christian said. 'She always knows where I am and what time I'll get home. We both have such busy lives we need to be in constant touch or we'd lose our way as a couple.'

'Lucky you,' John said. 'I hate to admit it, but Joanne irritates something terrible.'

'I am lucky,' Christian said. 'Cynthia keeps the home going so smoothly I never have to worry about a thing, and the boys have always been happy and easily managed. She touches everything so lightly it seems effortless. And, d'you know, John, I don't remember ever having a cross word.'

When they parted, Christian to return to the camper van

where he and Ken were about to travel north, and John to return to Abertrochi, John went to a phone box and told Joanne that he'd been held up and wouldn't be home that evening as promised. He drove away from the lorry park with a lighter heart.

Cynthia's boys became regular visitors to Joanne's house, pleading with Cynthia and explaining that Jeremy and Justin had so little fun that they welcomed them going over with video games and tapes they rarely saw. Apart from these 'official' times, they were often there without her knowing. They would arrive at the gate and whistle for Jeremy and Justin to join them on the cliff path, after the boys – and sometimes Joanne too – had gone to bed.

With the dark autumn evenings, she was pleased when they went to bed early and settled down, convinced that it was her firmness and management that had made them so amenable. She frequently boasted of their good behaviour to Cynthia and Meriel, explaining that it was the result of her strict regime. Cynthia didn't disabuse her of her theory. She only glanced at Meriel when Joanne went on, 'Children need firmness, a framework from which they can find themselves.'

'If my guesses are correct,' Cynthia whispered to Meriel with a chuckle, 'They find themselves by running along the cliff path and into my airing room for midnight feasts and freedom!'

With Joanne blissfully unaware, Jeremy and Justin would creep down and through the door within moments of her light being extinguished, having been fully dressed and waiting for the signal. Their outings were fewer now the weather was colder. But it was with the same excitement that they always ran down the drive and on to the cliff path. Sometimes they would let themselves into the warmth of the airing room with its clean smell of wood and soap, where they just sat and talked, the Sewell three making the Morgan two envious, with their tales of their easy-going mother and the easily outwitted and kindly housekeeper, Millie.

After a week of violent storms which dislodged a large section of the cliffs making it too dangerous and unpleasant for them to venture near, Rupert who, although identical in age to Oliver, was self-appointed leader, announced that, with the sea and midnight picnics no longer an attraction, he would teach them all to drive.

Joanne continued to enjoy her free evenings. Money was still a serious problem but many of the 'evenings out' entailed nothing more than a visit to friends for a drink and a chat. She often called on Meriel and sat with a glass of wine until the ten o'clock news began before walking home, confident that the five boys were still at their homework as they had been when she had left them. She rarely took the car, it hardly seemed worth it for a ten minute walk, and Meriel always drove her home if it was raining, or cold, or when they had sat talking too late.

Cynthia called one evening when she and Meriel were watching a television programme and managed to persuade them both to buy a ticket for a wine-tasting evening in aid of one of her fund-raising schemes. She at once forestalled Joanne's protests by saying, 'Oliver and Rupert will stay with Jeremy and Justin. They all have homework and settle down to it so well together there's no reason for you to say no, dear.'

Joanne began to panic when she got home. The tickets were expensive. And there was always a raffle. How was she going to find the money? She had something to wear, but the cost of the ticket was impossible. Taking some of the items given for charity was risky, the person who gave them might mention them and ask how much they raised. But, desperate to avoid the others knowing of her poor circumstances, she took a vase of her own which she had never liked, plus a small brooch, wondering if she could sell them for enough to pay for the ticket. Then, when she was doing her shift in the charity shop, someone brought in a beautiful set of silver backed brushes and hand mirror. She took them all to a shop in town and received the cost of the ticket with some to spare. Generously – and to soothe her troubled conscience, she gave the remainder of the money to Cynthia's fund and glowed in her praise.

It was when Joanne was at Cynthia's wine-tasting event that Rupert made his announcement, that tonight was the time to begin driving. The night was dark enough, and the parents would be out until quite late. Eleven o'clock at least. It was the work of a moment to reach up to the hook where Joanne kept her car keys.

Keeping to the quiet roads of the housing estate, Oliver

drove carefully around, explaining his moves to Jeremy. By the time they returned the car to its place, Jeremy had driven around several times, reversed into a parking place, managed a three point, or rather a nine point, turn and felt able to drive across the world.

Justin and Marcus, who were too small to be competent, were promised that they too would be able to control a car, long before their seventeenth birthday, when their fathers might be expected to pay for lessons.

'I'll never be tall enough,' Marcus moaned. 'I'll be this height until I die!'

'Look at your trousers,' Oliver said. 'They're showing too much sock. Of course you've grown.'

Delighted, Marcus informed his mother that he'd outgrown his trousers and needed new ones if he wasn't to look a fool in front of his friends!

For Meriel and Cath, the autumn was one of a gradually developing friendship. Their mutual interest in antiques began it, but they soon felt able to talk about almost everything with ease, knowing they would be understood, even when their opinions differed, although Meriel still avoided the subject of children.

They continued to attend antique fairs, car boot sales and table top sales whenever they saw one advertised, although they had yet to rent a table themselves and try out their skills at selling. Their knowledge of prices was slowly improving, and they bought and sold a variety of objects, sometimes losing a little and sometimes gaining.

Meriel refused to bring out her 'fifties memorabilia though. In fact she was adding to it as she and Cath searched for choice items amid the dross.

'I'm keeping it all, until I know exactly what I've got and what it's worth,' she told Cath, who quite understood.

It was December when they finally tried out a sale of their own. They rented a table at a small venue in a church hall intending to display a variety of less valuable china. Cath brought some cushion covers she had made and small items like appliqué pictures depicting Christmas scenes, and calendars with pictures of the four seasons. When the sale ended at midday, they were both satisfied with the response.

The following week in Churchill's Garden, Cath joined them and as it was Helen's day off, all six of them plus Toby sat down to coffee. Vivienne was talking happily about a man she had met who loved Toby. Helen spoke of her dismay that her three wouldn't be spending Christmas with her and Reggie.

'I'm going to make sure the New Year is a good one,' she said. 'Henri is fifteen now and she'll soon want to spend these occasions with her friends. I have to do what I can for as long as I can.'

Cynthia jokingly told her, 'My Rupert is quite smitten with your Henrietta, whose name he refuses to shorten.'

Cynthia told them of the guests she expected. People living alone and without family. 'Are you having any visitors?' she asked Joanne. 'You have a sister, haven't you?'

'Only my sister Samantha, and we have lost touch.' Quickly she added, 'My John will be away right up to Christmas Eve, and he always takes the dog for a long walk on Christmas morning while I prepare lunch.'

'Dinner,' Cath whispered. 'We always called it dinner.'

Meriel watched Cath anxiously as the talk of families continued but she seemed calm and unaffected.

Then Helen surprised them by saying, 'Joanne, what was your son doing driving your car the other night?'

'My Jeremy? Surely you were mistaken, Helen,' she said with a laugh. 'It must have been me. I'm not very tall and with my hair back in a chignon, well, that must be the explanation, there isn't another. Jeremy can't drive and at fourteen, he's hardly likely to be learning, is he? No, I'm the only one to drive my darling little Fiat.'

But privately, although she didn't think it possible, she was always prepared to believe the worst of her sons, even without any reason to do so. So for the next few days she checked the mileage on her car. Once there was a discrepancy of ten miles; she convinced herself she had misread the dial. John's car was beside her own and for no reason apart from looking to see whether the two numbers were easy to confuse, she looked at his mileage too.

That evening, when the boys were finishing their homework, Joanne cleared up after the evening meal, she repaired her make-up and changed into a long evening gown that John had bought her years before. The whisky bottle and a glass were set out on a tray beside John's chair so he could help himself to the one drink he allowed himself when he was home for the evening.

She arranged the lighting just as he liked it and settled down to a pleasant evening, during which she intended to bring up the subject of extra money for Christmas.

'Darling,' she began, when the boys had gone to their rooms. 'Christmas is nearly here. We have to decide what we're going to buy for the boys, and I need to know what entertaining we can do. Shopping is becoming an urgent priority.'

Within ten minutes of her broaching the subject of finance, John stood up and said he was going to the pub.

'Shall I come with you?' she asked. 'Cynthia's boys would agree to come for an hour or two. They never seem to mind, and the five of them get on so well. Oliver and Rupert, the twins, are very sensible, and young Marcus is a darling child.'

'I'd love you to, but it's a boring meeting to discuss some repairs needed on one of the houses. Why don't we arrange something for later in the week instead? Invite Cynthia and Christian and go out for a meal?'

'Are you sure we can afford it?' she asked.

'Not really,' he grinned, giving her a hug. 'But let's do it anyway. It isn't often we give ourselves a treat.'

It was past eleven before he returned. He explained that he 'got chatting' and forgot the time.

'You didn't drink too much, did you?'

'I stuck to low alcohol beer, you know I don't take chances, Joanne,' he said irritably. 'My business depends on my being able to drive, doesn't it?'

'Was it a successful meeting?'

'Well, I got the price for the repairs to the Tenby place whittled down a bit, so, yes, I suppose it was.' He smiled then, a smile reminiscent of the early years of their marriage, when that smile was capable of weakening any protest she made about the risks he took financially.

In those early days they were rarely apart. Much of his work was local and his commitments were few. Joanne had worked for five years, besides running the home and helping out in the business whenever John needed it. It was when the boys were born she had become less involved, and even then there had always seemed to be enough money for a comfortable life.

Since then, John had expanded more and more, widening his ownership of cafes to include houses, and his absences from home had become a part of every week. Their marriage had drifted down to fewer hours together and less and less money to spend.

'If only you didn't have to work so hard, John darling,' she sighed.

'Come and show me how you've missed me,' he said and with an arm around her, he led her up to their room.

The next morning she went to get his overnight case from his car, in order to do his washing, while he and the boys were eating breakfast. For no reason at all she looked at the mileage and saw with surprise that it had increased by forty-seven miles.

'Which pub did you go to last night?' She asked the question casually, but her heart was racing as though her life depended on the answer.

'The Boathouse,' he told her, naming one about twelve miles away, and she sighed with relief. If he had called for the man he was meeting and had taken him home again, the mileage was easily accounted for. Then he spoilt it.

'I saw Cynthia and Christian Sewell while I was waiting for my builder friend,' he said. 'I didn't have a conversation, but I did suggest that meal we discussed. It's on for Friday, all right? Pleasant couple, aren't they?'

Not forty-seven miles then, if he didn't call for his friend. The words were like daggers. Where could he have been? And she could have sworn that when he first came in that evening he'd had no intention of going anywhere. The thought had come on him suddenly, as though he had needed to get away from her. Having to meet a builder had been an invention. So where had he gone?

'I said, they're a pleasant couple and—'

'John, Helen said my car has been seen with a young boy driving it. Helen thinks it was Jeremy.'

'Nonsense. She must have made a mistake. She's a bit woolly at the best of times. Nice enough though.'

'But you have to question the boys. She was very certain.'

'Why should I act like a Victorian father because she thought she saw your car? There are others, just like it! Really Joanne, do you think either Jeremy or Justin could drive without lessons? Forget it for heaven's sake! The woman was mistaken.'

His irritability made her hold back from further argument. She would have to talk to them herself. Worried about having to confront the boys but still more concerned with the mileage on John's car, she was quiet as she watched the three of them leave after breakfast; the boys running with school bags flying, and John more slowly, carrying his freshly packed overnight bag, waving, blowing kisses and promising to be back in a few days, when they would have that promised evening out.

When she drove to meet her friends in Churchill's Garden later that morning she was still puzzling over the extra miles John had travelled. The story about Jeremy driving was forgotten. It was John's car not her own that worried her.

'What did John say about your Jeremy taking up driving then?' was Helen's greeting.

'It couldn't possibly have been Jeremy. I'm not the only person in Abertrochi to prefer a small car you know.' Her voice came out sharper than intended and she quickly added, 'He's too young, Helen. How could he have learned?'

'I haven't taught Rupert or Oliver,' Cynthia laughed, 'But I know they both drive the car around the drive and through the lanes to the old stables, where they practise turning and reversing.'

'You don't mind?' Joanne frowned.

'I've warned them not to go on to public roads. They'd hate to have their licence taken from them before they're old enough to have one.' She shrugged, as she touched up her lipstick after finishing her first cup of coffee. 'They know what's involved so I can leave it up to them.'

Continually surprised by her friend's strange attitude to bringing up children, Joanne said nothing more, but went to order her coffee and cake. A large sticky one today, she decided. She felt the need for some spoiling. Imagine leaving important decisions like that to fifteen-year-old boys! Cynthia was heading for trouble. That was as clear to see as the cherries on her iced bun.

She and Cynthia discussed the proposed meal out and decided that, although it was not the most exciting place, The Fisherman's Basket was a suitable venue. 'It doesn't entail a long drive,' Cynthia explained, 'And we can all drink if we want to. We can easily get a taxi or even walk if we feel like it.'

'That would be a change,' Joanne said mildly. 'It's usually me having to stay on tonic water so I can drive.' She was disappointed. She and John went out so rarely together that she had hoped for a more exciting place.

'Perhaps you could go on somewhere to dance afterwards?' Vivienne suggested. 'If Meriel would have Toby I'd come with you.'

'Why don't you?' Cynthia said enthusiastically. The idea of an evening spent with Joanne and John was daunting; all that serious conversation. Vivienne looked hopefully at Meriel who agreed to look after the little boy and no one noticed the look of dismay on Joanne's face.

Joanne sat with a stiff smile on her lips which didn't reach her eyes as Cynthia and Vivienne discussed the various places where they could dance. She wanted to cancel the whole thing. John didn't dance and neither did she. What a prospect, sitting in a crowded room being blasted with music and unable to talk.

'Cynthia suggested The Fisherman's Basket,' she told John when he telephoned that evening from his office.

'No, I've already booked for four at Fuschia Palace,' he said. 'I called in on the way from the pub the other evening.'

Joanne smiled and dialled Cynthia's number.

Instead of reverting to the original plan of a meal then back to her house for coffee, it was once more taken out of her hands. The telephone lines buzzed for the next hour and then Cynthia rang her back.

'John has changed the booking to five and suggested that as you don't drink much anyway, you'd be willing to drive us, then we can go straight on to the club afterwards.'

'Lovely,' Joanne breathed, before slamming down the phone. She bought a bottle of wine and rang Meriel, arranging to see her the next evening. 'As I can't drink on Friday I might as well indulge tomorrow,' she explained.

She was having her brown hair tinted and cut and set the next morning, and planned to see who was in Churchill's Garden. Tidying up before leaving for her appointment, she found a letter from the boys' school. It was folded small and was tucked in between the shorts and football boots in Jeremy's sports bag. It was addressed to parents, asking them for their permission to arrange a trip to France during the following spring. Jeremy and Justin were just leaving and she called them back.

'Jeremy, why didn't you show me this?'

'I don't really want to go,' he replied, staring down at the floor.

'I don't think that's true. You've often told me how much you're looking forward to the time when your class will be going.'

'He said you can't afford it,' Justin piped up, and suffered a fierce dig from his older brother.

Upset that he should try to hide it out of consideration for her, she turned away and pretended to reread the letter while she recovered.

'I'm sure you'll be able to go,' she promised, while wondering how she could possibly find the money. Surely John would find a way of affording this? How could they make their son face being left behind while every other child in the class went to France? 'I'll talk to Daddy this evening and we'll tell the school that you're going. All right?'

'There'll be spending money, and clothes,' Jeremy warned.

Guessing his fear was having less than the others, she reassured him further.

'There'll be an upper and lower limit on what you can take and you'll have the same as the rest, Jeremy. You won't have a penny less than you're allowed, I promise.' She hugged him and said, 'It was so kind of you to think I might worry about this, but it's all right, this is what Daddy has been saving for, so you can take advantage of these opportunities. You're going and you'll enjoy every moment.'

'Jeremy is going skiing with the school,' she announced to Meriel and Cynthia when she emerged, neatly coiffeured, from behind the net curtains separating the hairdressing salon from the rest of the shop premises. 'There's such a lot to organize. New clothes of course, and currency, you know what it's like, but I don't mind. Jeremy's such a good boy, never given me a moment's worry. He deserves a treat.'

She was talking bravely but so far she hadn't been able to reach John. He hadn't telephoned and, as usual, the office phone was unmanned. If he told her they couldn't find the money she

64

didn't know what she would do. If only she were trained and able to work at something glamorous. John was so snobbish, and wouldn't be willing for her to find just any old job.

Pulling her thoughts away from her money worries she joined in the general admiration of the diamond ring Christian was going to buy Cynthia for Christmas, as well as listening to Cynthia's memories of their trip to Paris and London. Cynthia could afford to send her boys without a moment's thought. Meriel's ex-husband could afford to give her enough money to enable her to live comfortably without seriously looking for work. Vivienne was supported by an ex-boyfriend so she could look after Toby without the pressures of work. John worked all the hours he could and they were still struggling. It wasn't fair.

She was the last to leave the cafe that morning and when she stepped out into the cold gusty day and her hair was in danger of losing its style, she realized she had left her scarf behind. It had a habit of slipping off her shoulders. Going back to their table, still uncleared by the waitress, she saw something on the floor, half hidden by her scarf. A purse. Cynthia's purse. It was a split second to pick it up and put it in her handbag.

No one could possibly have seen. The coffee clientele were gone and the lunch crowd had not yet arrived. She hurried back to the car and drove home feeling as though a thousand eyes were upon her and knew what she had just done: stolen from a friend.

Deliberately she made herself a sandwich and a cup of tea before she looked at it again. There was still time to return it. Her eyes strayed to the telephone. Telling Cynthia she had picked it up would be so easy. Her hand reached out but before she touched it it began to ring and she jumped back as though from an electric shock. Her heart was beating in her throat, almost choking her as she answered.

'Hello Cynthia,' she said casually.

'Joanne, you didn't see what I did with my purse, did you?'

'Your purse? No, you paid at the counter so I wouldn't have, would I?' She gave a stiff little laugh, 'Don't tell me you've mislaid it?'

'Oh, I haven't really looked yet. It's just that it wasn't in my bag when I got home. Don't worry, it'll turn up.'

'Have you phoned Churchill's Garden?'

'Yes, no one has handed it in. I'll look in the car again, it's probably there.'

'I hope you find it,' Joanne said. Her hand was trembling as she replaced the receiver.

Ignoring the sandwich and the cooling tea, she opened the wallet part of the purse. Fifty pounds in tens. Enough for the deposit on Jeremy's skiing holiday. The purse held another nine pounds in silver and she slid it into her hand and stared at it for a long time before putting it into her handbag.

The talk next day was about children. Cynthia explained in a rare moment of revelation that she had been an only child. Untrue but an essential part of the story she had invented about her childhood. 'Because of that I wanted more than the generally accepted two children, so they would have brothers and sisters and eventually inlaws and nieces and nephews. An extended family, some of whom would hopefully become friends. Unfortunately, we didn't have another after our darling Marcus.'

'I don't have anyone,' Meriel said, 'And I can understand why you try to make sure there's someone for your boys, even if they don't become as close as you hope. Aunts and uncles are all I have, and a few cousins. The aunts were great when I was small but I became less and less important to them as I grew up and they became more involved with their own burgeoning families. I haven't seen some of them for years, even though they aren't that far away.'

'I've got three brothers and two sisters,' Helen told them. 'I hate and love the lot of them! But it was wonderful growing up with a large family. I wish I could have had more but the marriage breakup spoilt any chance of matching my mother's achievements.'

They turned to Joanne questioningly.

'As you all know, I have a sister but we don't see each other,' she said crisply.

'Aren't you going to tell us why?' Helen demanded.

'No.' Joanne replied, then she laughed. 'All right, we quarrelled over my John. My sister met him first you see, but it was me he fell in love with and Samantha accused me of stealing him. There, doesn't that sound silly? As if I could have stolen him. I can assure you he came willingly. We both knew straight away that we were meant for each other.'

'Don't you speak to her at all?'

'Never! I don't even know where she lives or what she does.'

'You might have nephews and nieces. You're depriving your boys of cousins!'

'They don't know I have a sister and I hope they never will.'

'Joanne is so rigid about everything,' Helen sighed when Joanne went to the ladies. 'I'm surprised she's agreed to send Jeremy on this skiing holiday. She's so hard on her boys. There's a strict regime in that house that's almost an obsession. Mealtimes are the same every day even if the boys want to go out somewhere with friends. Bedtimes, a time to bath and she has a timetable for homework that would terrify my lot!'

'She even checks with the school to make sure they aren't cheating on the work they're given,' Meriel added.

'I like to be organized,' Cynthia said, 'I couldn't fit in all I do if I didn't work within a system, but everything in Joanne's house happens like clockwork. It's soulless somehow. Between you and me, I sometimes wonder how John puts up with it.'

'Oh, there are all kinds of marriages,' Meriel offered. 'And perhaps John likes the security of a formal and controlled home life.'

'Hardly, when he isn't there half the week!'

The discussion was inevitably turned to Christmas. Cynthia and her family were going away but she promised a celebration during the week before. 'I've promised the boys a party too, so I hope your two will come,' she smiled at Joanne. Turning to Helen she said, 'I don't suppose there's any chance that your three will be home? It would be lovely if they could come too.'

'I've got a few things planned,' Vivienne said. 'But as usual, it depends whether I can arrange the necessary Toby-sitting.' She pulled out a diary. 'Any offers? My neighbour is free for one night and someone I met at Keep Fit has promised to do Christmas Eve.'

Joanne looked disapproving. 'Toby is only three and that seems a bit young for him to be left with so many different people,' she said in the babyish tone she used, as though afraid to offend.

'One morning,' Vivienne cheerfully told them, 'I left him with the postman while I went to the shop for milk.' Joanne tightened her lips but said nothing more. Meriel was thankful that Cath was not there.

Dates and times were discussed until it was arranged that the party would take place on the fourteenth.

Joanne decided to drop in on Meriel that evening to thank her for the nice evening they'd had the night before. She left her boys alone, as she didn't intend to be long, saying she'd be an hour or two. But she found Meriel's ex-husband there.

'Oh, I'm sorry Meriel, I didn't know you had a visitor, hello Evan, how are you?'

'Hardly a visitor,' he smiled stretching over to kiss her cheek. 'I used to live here, remember.'

'Used to,' Meriel reprimanded quietly. 'You no longer call this home – remember.'

'Really, I wish he'd stay away!' Meriel said when Evan had gone. 'That's the third time this week he's called on some pretext or another. I didn't tell you but I came back from shopping yesterday and he was cutting the lawn. December, and he's cutting the lawn!'

'It is a good idea to tidy up before the winter makes it impossible,' Joanne excused. 'I like things to be neat.'

'But it isn't his lawn! At least, it won't be once the house is sold and until then this is my home and I invite who I want to see.'

Joanne was surprised to see Meriel so irate. It was rare for her to lose her temper.

'You still miss him, do you?' she said softly.

'I've accepted that he's now married to someone else, so why doesn't he?'

At Joanne's house the five boys were getting into her car. Jeremy was driving, with Oliver beside him and Rupert sat in the back with Justin and Marcus. They drove around the expensive houses near their homes and along the lanes into the outskirts of Abertrochi. With a bravado they didn't really feel, aware that they were supposed to be home and in bed, Jeremy and Justin got out and bought chips and they drove to a large car park overlooking the sea and ate them. Justin was still too small to reach the pedals but he sat beside Rupert on the way back and watched as Rupert explained the sequence of starting and driving off, with the gear changes and the correct signals.

Concentrating on instructing Justin might be why Rupert failed to notice Joanne on her way home.

Joanne had realized that Meriel was upset by her ex-husband's visit and had left earlier than intended. She was also feeling a bit guilty at having left her boys on their own for the first time. When the car passed her she only glanced at it. It was Jeremy in the back seat who recognized her. Putting his foot down, Rupert drove back to Joanne's house faster than he had driven before. He parked in the exact spot where they had found the car and, glowing with the excitement of near discovery, pushed Jeremy and Justin into their house.

'As long as she doesn't touch the bonnet and realize it's warm we'll be all right,' he said gleefully, as the three of them hurried away through the darkness, giggling like conspirators.

When Joanne entered, she found her boys in bed and deeply asleep. A touch of a cover might have revealed that they were fully dressed, but she only opened the doors and glanced at the two shapes before going downstairs again.

The boys were eating breakfast the following morning and Joanne was washing dishes when John arrived with a suitcase and an assortment of parcels.

'John, darling! I didn't expect you until this evening.'

'An appointment was cancelled, and an assistant who had given notice decided not to leave after all, so I had the morning free and drove back through the night. Breakfast then bed, I think,' he said after greeting the two boys and handing them each some chocolate.

When the boys had left for school, John pointed to the parcels. 'There are a few presents for the boys,' he said as he finished the meal she had made for him. 'What do we do about their main presents, any ideas?'

'Well, with the skiing trip in February we can't give them anything too expensive, can we?'

'What skiing trip?' he demanded.

'Didn't I tell you?' she asked innocently. 'Surely I did.'

'No you didn't. You know damned well this is the first I've heard of it. They can't go.'

69

'It's only Jeremy, Justin isn't old enough and it's too late, I've already told him he can. And, I've managed to find the money for the deposit.'

'Cancel it. We can't afford it and he isn't going.'

'But John, we can't do that. He'd be so upset. D'you know he hid the paper, he wasn't going to tell me – us, worried that we couldn't afford it.'

'He was right, we can't.'

'But we have to. This time we have to.' She rarely stood up to his arguments about money, but this time, having stolen from a friend to pay the deposit, she had to persuade him to pay the rest of the money. To do such a thing was bad enough, but to have done such a wicked thing for nothing, would be impossible to live with. She would have to stop going to Churchill's Garden, avoid all her friends. She wouldn't be able to visit Meriel again. No cinema trips, no social life at all. John couldn't do it to her, she wouldn't let him win. Not this time.

She stood up and stared at him, her eyes steady as she held his gaze. 'John, however you get the money, whatever you have to do to get it, Jeremy is going on that school trip. Do you understand?' She was shaking when she walked into the kitchen, and as she heard him run up the stairs to their room she began to cry.

Then she rang Cynthia and asked her to cancel the dinner for that evening, she was feeling ill and thought it might be flu.

In Churchill's Garden a few days later, Cath was sitting at her usual small table. Her eyes never left her newspaper but Joanne knew she was aware of their arrival. Rather half-heartedly she invited her to join them but Cath smiled, thanked her and declined. Irritated, Joanne pushed past her and went to their usual table in the corner from where they could look out at the bleak winter garden beyond the glass doors. She didn't want company herself today but had made herself come. Anything to get out of the house and away from the worry about the money she needed and which, so far, John had refused to give her.

Meriel and Cynthia came in together, Cynthia having been to look at clothes for the holiday period and a few last minute gifts, and Meriel to keep her company. Cath turned and smiled at Meriel and giving in to her persuasion, agreed to share their table. Coffees were brought and a dish of scones stood in the centre of the table.

'No work this morning?' Meriel asked Cath.

'I didn't like the two men in Gregory Way.' She shuddered. 'There were women there some mornings, the last time they were very young girls. I couldn't cope with that so I left. So, there's only Tom and Ray twice a week.'

'They are all right are they? Pay you well and not much trouble?' Vivienne asked. There was an expression on her face that Meriel couldn't read.

'Do you know them?' Meriel asked.

'I used to know Tom but I haven't met his brother,' she said and quickly changed the subject before Meriel could ask why she hadn't mentioned it before.

'I'll let you know if I hear of anyone needing a bit of cleaning done,' Helen promised Cath. 'We pick up all sorts of information in the shop, so I'll keep an ear wagging.'

'Don't you always?' Vivienne teased.

Christmas again became the main discussion, each of them talking over their plans.

'The boys are growing up and only want clothes,' Joanne said.

'Mine too,' Cynthia agreed, 'Except darling Marcus. He wants a book on insects and a new bicycle.'

'My boys still want toys,' Helen said. 'William is twelve and George is ten. But Henri wants clothes, the skimpier the better.'

Only Cath was quiet.

'Are you planning to go away?' Vivienne asked her.

Cath shook her head. 'No, I've nothing planned at all.'

Vivienne looked at Joanne and began to ask, 'You couldn't look after Toby for me this evening, could you – I was hoping to—' she stopped seeing from Joanne's expression that the answer would be a refusal. 'No, I can see it isn't convenient.'

Meriel explained that she had a prior engagement and Vivienne turned to a startled Cath. 'Could you look after Toby for me?' she asked.

Cath jumped up and glared at Vivienne in horror. 'How can you ask me? You don't know me! You can't tell whether or not I'm a suitable person to care for your child. How can you be so careless of his safety!'

'Cath?' Meriel frowned. 'I think I know you well enough to know you'd be an ideal person to look after Toby.'

'You don't know me at all!' she shouted, glaring angrily at Vivienne. 'You invite me to sit and chat and pass an idle hour and think because you know my name and I take my turn at buying the coffee, that I'm decent and reliable and a suitable person to trust your beautiful and precious child to?' She banged her half empty cup on the table and ran out into the street, shouting, 'You don't deserve to have a child!'

Meriel ran after her but when she reached the street there was no sign of her among the shoppers milling around the pavement. Forgetting her own intended purchases, she hurried home.

Getting into her car she drove up to the small chalet where Cath had made her home, but although she waited for almost an hour, her friend didn't appear. Leaving a note asking her to call, she drove home.

Six

Vivienne was shaken by Cath's outburst. She knew she was careless about Toby, but, she told herself, nothing dreadful had happened to him, most people were genuine.

'There's no point in worrying about what fills the newspapers,' she defended herself to Cynthia. 'The chance of someone harming Toby is so slight it isn't worth thinking about. People are decent and if they don't want to look after him they say so. Those who do are kind people who love children. It stands to reason.'

Cynthia said nothing for a while then said slowly, 'I suppose, by some standards I've been neglectful of Rupert, Oliver and Marcus. I leave them with Millie quite a lot, and although it's part of her job to keep an eye on them, I wouldn't leave them with her unless I completely trusted her. We can't allow a few dangerous people to run our lives.'

'Exactly,' Vivienne agreed.

'I've never been an over-anxious mother. I work really hard for several charities, especially for those involved with children's welfare. I simply couldn't do all the work I do if I'd been a mother hen and one chick type of mother, could I?'

'My reasons aren't so noble,' Vivienne sighed. 'I just like to go out. I like the cinema, I enjoy the atmosphere in a decent pub and I love dancing to good modern music. I expected to give up those things when I married but now, with no marriage and no serious relationship, I couldn't stand being home night after night on my own. I think I'm a better mother to Toby for escaping like I do.'

'You're probably right,' Cynthia agreed.

'I'll have Toby for you,' Helen offered. 'Reggie won't mind, he likes children and he'll enjoy amusing him.'

Vivienne looked thoughtful and Cynthia also had a slight frown on her carefully made-up face.

'Perhaps I shouldn't—'

'Your house or ours?' Helen insisted.

When Helen had gone, Cynthia and Vivienne sat quietly for a long time. Eventually, Cynthia asked, 'This marriage of yours, what happened?'

'It's difficult to explain. There was Toby you see and—' Vivienne waited for Cynthia to come to her own conclusion.

'You didn't really love each other, and Toby was the reason you married?'

'Something like that. Now!' Vivienne said. 'I have to pick the boy wonder up from nursery in half an hour, but first, some shopping. Will you come with me and help me choose a dress for tonight?'

Cynthia understood that the subject was closed.

Cath hadn't gone home when she had run out of Churchill's Garden. She had driven out of town without a clear idea of where she was going. She was simply getting away from her stupid outburst. What business was it of hers how Vivienne chose to look after Toby? What made her set herself up as an expert on raising children? Angrily, she rubbed away insistent tears.

Driving around the lanes, her first thoughts were that she couldn't go back to Churchill's Garden. No more trips to antique fairs with Meriel, no more pleasant mornings searching through car boot sales and looking through the fascinating assortment offered on table top stalls. Slowly, she had been beginning to accept the casual meetings with Cynthia, Joanne, Vivienne and Helen too, slowly beginning to make a life in Abertrochi. Now, with that stupid outburst, she had lost it.

Returning to the town by a different route she saw the huge sign advertising a toy store and again without fully clarifying her thoughts, she parked and went inside. She began to feel tears threaten again as she walked along the aisles and studied what was on offer. There was a familiar tightening of her throat and a stinging behind her eyes. She almost ran out, but stopped herself. This was the opportunity to make a proper apology and get back what she had almost thrown away.

Struggling to the car a few minutes later, she put the large box into the boot and drove towards the road where Vivienne lived. She had insisted on the assistant opening the box and making sure the toy was complete. She had always hated to see a child unpack a long awaited parcel then have to wait longer for someone to put the thing together.

There was no reply when she knocked at Vivienne's door. The quiet road was bereft of passers-by. Neat curtains hid neat little rooms and in the neat front gardens there wasn't a sign of a living, breathing human being. She was not the only person to live in isolation. Even in a group of houses like this, a person could be lonely, she mused sadly, remembering her mother's stories about the friendliness of neighbours and going out together on enormous picnics to the beach. It was an uncaring world today where people only did a kindness for the glory and praise.

She knocked again and when there was nothing but the echo of the sound, she was tempted to go away and forget it. But no. She had run away too often in the past and it was time to stand still.

She sat in the car for an hour, then saw Vivienne's car turn into the road. Getting out she waited at the end of the drive while Vivienne drove in and parked. Lifting up the box she heaved it out of the boot and walked towards the little boy.

'Toby? I have a present for you. Not Christmas, it's too early for that, and not your birthday, it's just for being a lovely little boy.'

Any uneasiness she felt having to face Vivienne after her inexplicable behaviour was quickly dispelled as the excited little boy opened the flaps of the box and stared in undisguised delight at the sit-on tractor. Vivienne's thanks were brushed aside as Cath explained,

'I was in a depressed mood this morning, I didn't mean any of it and in any case, I don't have the right to criticize you. Toby is a happy, well-adjusted child and you should be very proud of him – and of yourself.'

Vivienne was embarrassed both by Cath's apology and by the size of her gift. She thanked her, admired the tractor then suggested inanely, 'Cup of tea?'

'No thanks, I have to get back. I need to see Meriel and try to explain my dreadful behaviour to her too.'

As she drove past the estate close to the cliffs and parked outside Meriel's door, Cath felt light-hearted. Somehow the morning's hysterical outpourings and the following apology had lifted a burden from her. She smiled when Meriel opened the door and said, 'I can't really explain how or why, but I needed that. Will you forgive me?'

'It's forgotten,' Meriel hugged her and invited her inside. The only comment she made was an assurance that they need never refer to it again, 'But,' she added, taking Cath's shawl and offering her a seat, 'If ever you want to talk, in confidence, I'm here. Will you remember that?'

Sinking into armchairs facing each other across the hearth, they began making plans for the sales they would attend during the following week. With the approach of Christmas there was a spate of such events and they were determined to attend as many as possible, sometimes separating so they didn't miss anything when two were taking place at the same time.

On the weekend following Cath's outburst, Vivienne had been invited to a party. Meriel had agreed to look after Toby and keep him overnight. The small third bedroom was full of boxes which Meriel had half-heartedly begun to pack ready for the move she would one day have to face. Normally she had the little boy in her room in a small foldaway bed, but something made her want to make an effort. Maybe the approach of Christmas.

She decorated the plain walls with a few bright posters. After dragging a small armchair up the stairs, she called at the charity shop where Joanne worked and bought a few toys, which she washed and then used to fill the armchair and a small pine box. Looking around she smiled with pleasure. Everything was in readiness for her small visitor. Toby would be sure to feel welcome.

Vivienne had arranged to bring Toby at six and long before the appointed time Meriel sat and waited, excited at the prospect of Toby's surprise, but they didn't arrive. Meriel telephoned and, at eight o'clock, she drove up to Vivienne's house and knocked. There was no reply and, puzzled, she drove back home.

She tried phoning several times that evening and again the following day but failed to contact her friend. Cynthia and Joanne knew nothing of her plans and even Helen, who bore the nickname, 'fount of all knowledge' couldn't shed light on the mystery.

It was midday on Monday before an apologetic Vivienne arrived and gave a very incomplete excuse.

'Sorry, sorry, sorry,' she said as she burst into the kitchen. 'My weekend was changed at the last minute and I had to go away. I know I should have phoned but, well, didn't get the chance.'

Toby climbed unaided out of the car, where Vivienne had left him in her haste to explain. Meriel said, 'Go and look in the back bedroom, Toby, it's all ready for when you come and stay with me.'

His little fat legs took him step by step up the stairs and he disappeared into the room.

'Well, Vivienne? What's the real story? Are you in trouble?'

'No trouble. Something came up that I couldn't refuse and there wasn't a phone and—' She gabbled on, talking but without saying much and Meriel sighed and interrupted, saying,

'All right, I don't want to know if you don't want to tell me. But next time something irresistible comes up, will you please let me know?'

'I promise. And, before you ask, Toby was with me. I didn't dump him on someone I hardly know. You can tell Cath if she asks.'

They didn't stay. Toby climbed into his car seat carrying a gaudy green teddy and with small cars filling his pockets, content with his brief visit and unaware of the friction between his mother and one of his 'aunties'.

Angry with Vivienne for messing up her weekend and not even giving her a satisfactory explanation as to why, Meriel decided to go and do some work in the Harris brothers' garden. She thought some strenuous work would help rid her of her irritation. As usual, she knocked as soon as she arrived but, as usual, the house was empty.

She went to the shed and gathered the tools she would need for clearing out an overgrown pond she had discovered. She began pulling at tough old grasses, irises and other pond plants, having first loosened their roots with a fork. She worked steadily, discarding her gloves in frustration so that she could finger her way through the overgrown tangle, gradually clearing the round edges of the cement pool and exploring its depth. Deep enough for fish, she decided when she had reached the bottom. She would leave a note for Tom and ask him if he would like to restore it and fill it with water.

Her back was beginning to ache so she used the key Tom had given her – it was too cold to use the shed in winter – to let herself into the kitchen. Washing her hands and allowing the hot water to run over them to ease the stinging of a dozen cuts and grazes, she stared out at the garden. Since she had started coming, it was beginning to open up. The lawn was still patchy but the mosses and the determined plantains and dandelions had almost given up. Flower-beds were clear and ready for spring planting. Soon the pond would be revealed. This evening she would study the gardening year book she had bought and later, discuss with Tom what they should buy for the borders and beds. They had already planted a hundred bulbs. She would be sorry to leave it behind when she moved away and found herself a proper, full-time occupation, she thought sadly.

Reaching for the kettle, she was surprised to notice a small glove on the work surface. She smiled. The brothers obviously had family, a sister perhaps and they had been entertaining a young relative. It reminded her to make sure she covered the pond before she went. A fall down there would frighten a child if not actually harm him.

The door to the rest of the house was usually locked, but, probably because they had not been expecting her, today it was ajar. Curiously she peeped around the door and saw that the floor was spread with children's videos and, in a corner, was a large tractor, just like the one Cath had described as having given to Toby.

Meriel was not overly inquisitive, but something made her explore further. The opportunity, and seeing the toys, made her intensely curious about the two people for whom she worked.

A second room was neatly and rather sparsely furnished with a three-piece suite and a nest of tables, a music centre and a television. Telling herself she would make the excuse of needing the toilet should either of the brothers suddenly appear, she walked slowly up the stairs. She walked with her back to the wall, moving from step to step sideways, a need to protect her back unrecognized, instinctive, her breathing shallow, her heart racing. She really shouldn't be doing this, she scolded herself silently.

The first room was a small one containing little furniture,

only a single bed, the covers neatly in place and with a few toys scattered about. The smallest room was used for lumber, the third unfurnished. It was only the large front room that looked as though it was used. A double bed, with lots of men's clothes thrown casually about, the two pillows indented from sleepers' heads. The bathroom was untidy, razors, men's after-shave balanced on the edge of the bath, shirts and underwear thrown carelessly towards a clothes basket. Aware of the implications, Meriel ran down the stairs, closed the door and shut herself in the kitchen.

Why had she invaded their privacy? She would have given a great deal not to have known what the use of that bed told her. Tom and Ray were not brothers, that much was certain. Again she went to tackle the stubborn roots around the pond, again needing hard physical work to blank out her feelings. Not anger this time, but embarrassment. Her feelings were ambiguous. She wasn't anti gay men or women, she just hadn't knowingly met any before. Would Tom guess she knew next time they met? Could she face him again?

Time passed without her being aware of it and it wasn't until it was too dark to see the fork she was wielding, that she stopped and cleaned up and went home. She hadn't left a note. She didn't think she could go there again, she would be afraid her expression would give away the fact that she had sneaked into their house without permission and learned their secret.

Heaving her wellingtons into the boot of the car with the mud-covered coat, she got in and drove off. When she pulled up outside her house she felt too stiff to move and sat there for a moment, still thinking about the secret she had discovered. She had no one with whom to discuss it. That, she decided sadly, was one of the worst aspects of being on her own. She was very tired and for a weak moment imagined Evan coming out and hugging her.

She would walk through her door and step into a cold, empty house, tired and confused, with no one there to hold her and comfort her and help her to understand how she felt. No man had held her, touched her, even with an arm around her shoulders, since Evan left her for Sophie Hopkins. She wanted to be held now, she wanted it badly.

In a melancholy mood she stiffly eased herself out of the

driving seat and gathered her filthy clothes out of the boot. As she stood there, smelling of rotted vegetation and stagnant pond, a mud-spattered coat over her arm, her hair limply hanging around her far from clean face like an abandoned floor mop, her wellingtons in her hand, a voice called, 'What the hell have you been doing! Get into the house before anyone sees you!'

Evan stood at the door staring at her before running towards her in great agitation and bustling her around the house and in through the back door which, she noticed with irritation, he opened with a key. 'Why are you working like a navvy? Is it just to humiliate me? If it is then you're doing a fine job.'

'I like what I do. The garden is a fascinating hobby and I've no intention of giving it up,' she shouted back. They were leaning towards each other like fighting bantams.

'I insist that you stop!'

'You can't insist on anything! And if this is the way you behave, I pity Sophie. I realize I've had a narrow escape! And, give me that key!' she demanded. 'You promised not to come here unless invited and you'll wait a long time for that to happen!'

She was tired and longed to flop into a sudsy bath and was prepared to argue furiously, knowing it was the quickest way to get rid of him. Evan always walked away from confrontation. 'Go away, Evan! You don't belong here any more!' Her voice sounded ugly and harsh. She felt ugly, her anger making her so, and she hated him for making her like this. She took a deep breath ready to shout over his next criticism but, to her alarm, his shoulders dropped and he said quietly:

'I was worried. I called this morning and again at lunchtime. Patch and Nipper were desperate to go out. It isn't like you to neglect them. I remembered I still had the back door key and I took them out. I've been waiting for you.' He took out a key-ring and, slipping off the one for the back door, he placed it on the kitchen table.

In a calmer tone she said, 'I got involved in what I was doing and forgot the time. I really do enjoy taming that garden, I do it for me, nothing to do with you or your hang-ups. I'll make it up to the dogs tomorrow.'

It was almost dark, the only light was from the porch light. The key was glinting slightly as it sat on the table between then, a reminder of their separation. Neither of them moved and Meriel felt an aching longing for Evan to take her in his arms. To end the tense moment, she deliberately and slowly picked up the key.

'Would you like me to run you a bath before I go?'

She shook her head. She didn't want him to see the look in her eyes; he would guess how much she still loved him. Turning away, she said, 'Goodbye Evan,' and placed the key in a dish on the dresser. As he left, unnoticed, he reached out and retrieved it.

Christian and Ken were negotiating for a plot of land on which they planned to build three houses and two shops. When they left the site they called at a smaller site where two semis were nearing completion.

'It's almost Christmas,' Ken said. 'Let's send in the estimates and then let it go until after the holidays. You and I could both do with some time off. The men here will work for a couple more days then they'll want to be off.'

'Will you be seeing your Mam?' Christian asked.

'Oh yes. I'll visit her although she's so far gone she doesn't seem to know me,' he said sadly. 'It's a hell of a thing, especially after the life she had. Now, when I could afford to give her some comforts, it's too late.'

'Are you sure we can't go and see her? Perhaps, if we talked about the old days, and of her kindness to Cynthia and me, it might bring her memory back, for a while at least.'

'No, I've spoken to the doctors and they don't advise it. Sorry, Christian, I know how much you want to help.'

When Christian had gone, Ken called one of the labourers over.

'Will you go to the betting office and put this on for me?' he asked, taking a note and some money from his wallet. 'You don't have to say who it's for, tell them it's yours if you like but, try and run off with my winnings and you're dead,' he said with a grin.

The young boy smiled and went off to do as he was asked. He had tried a few bets in the past but with little success and, seeing the large amount with which he had been trusted, he was tempted. It couldn't win. The odds were too high for it to be more than an outsider. He decided to pocket the money. Why should the bookies get all the luck?

81

When the results were broadcast later that day, Ken sighed with relief. He'd actually won! Perhaps his luck was changing at last. It wasn't much, but if he paid off some of his spiralling debts it should keep a few of his debtors happy, at least until after Christmas, he thought.

Perhaps he would treat his old mum to a video and a take-away tonight. It was lucky that Christian wouldn't be able to see them. The way his mum laughed at the innuendoes and tucked into a curry there was no doubt that she was strong and healthy!

Joanne resentfully prepared a meal for John and some of his friends and colleagues. As a small retaliation she invited Cynthia and Christian to join them.

'Sorry Meriel,' she breathed, sweetly apologetic, 'I can't include you without a partner. It throws out the seating arrangements.'

John had given generously for her to prepare good food but she had planned the meal with great care and had managed to spend far less than he thought. Pasta as a base for both starter and main course was filling and cheap. An exotic-looking dessert containing cream and chocolate hadn't cost much and she was flattered by the praise she received from guests and John.

She used the money she saved to pay for Cynthia's lunch at The Fisherman's Basket. It gave her a good feeling. Besides, Cynthia would reciprocate at the first opportunity. A guilty thought about the money owing for Jeremy's skiing trip she pushed aside. New Year, that was the time to worry about that.

Cynthia's Christmas party was simply arranged. Millie did some of the food preparations, set out the extended table, brought in extra chairs, and the rest was left to caterers. A clothes rail was brought in from the garage for coats and Millie left to spend a few days with her sister.

Joanne's two arrived first and they joined Rupert, Oliver and Marcus in preparations for some party games. Helen's three children were staying with her and Reggie for the weekend, so they came too, accompanied by Reggie, who promised to collect them at ten thirty.

'Eleven,' they pleaded and Reggie relented. Eleven o'clock

was what Helen told him anyway but, knowing the awkwardness of teenagers, he offered less to get what he wanted.

Henri, the only girl to arrive so far, was given the task of handing out paper hats to the guests as they arrived. But only as long as it took Cynthia and Christian to get ready and go out. Once their car had left the drive, the paper hats were thrown aside, games discarded, the music changed and bottles of wine revealed. The lights were turned low, doors opened and closed with increasing regularity and the volume of excited chatter rose as more and more guests arrived; approximately double the number Cynthia had expected.

Many of the guests were not known to Joanne's boys. Jeremy and Justin went to a different school from Oliver, Rupert and Marcus. Some of the girls looked much older than the hosts and Justin stared in jaw-dropping amazement as girls he had only seen wearing uniform, took off coats and revealed minuscule dresses.

Cynthia and Christian went for a meal and on the next table saw Vivienne.

'Vivienne! What a surprise, would you like to share our table?' Cynthia asked.

'Thanks but no, I'm waiting for someone.'

The restaurant was decorated for the season, with a great deal of sparkle, and boughs of holly and mistletoe, some real most not. Cynthia looked around while Christian, always a slowcoach at choosing his meal, made up his mind. A tall, rather effeminate but elegant man entered, dressed in an evening suit that fitted just a little too well and, walking with a swagger, looked around the room in a way that suggested he was used to being admired. He joined Vivienne but, from the way he greeted her, the effeminate impression was wrong.

Slightly embarrassed by her thoughts, Cynthia took out her compact to check her make-up. She moved her chair slightly to enable her to look in a different direction and saw someone else she knew.

'It's Meriel's ex, with his new wife, or woman. I don't think they're actually married,' she whispered to Christian. 'According to Helen, she wants to but he won't agree.'

'Blimey, we might as well have gone to the local pub for all the privacy we're getting,' he muttered as Evan left his table and came over.

'How is business?' Christian asked. 'Keeping you busy?'

'I have to keep busy with the rate Sophie spends,' Evan said jokingly, but the smile was forced and didn't reach his eyes.

'Seen your Meriel lately? I hear she's doing gardening. At this time of year too.'

'She doesn't have to,' Evan defended at once. 'I give her a generous allowance and she only has to ask if she needs more.'

'Sorry, I wasn't criticizing you, old man. She's your ex, after all, and no longer your responsibility. I just think she's admirable, doing something like that. She was filthy when I saw her coming home one day last week, cleaning out an old pond she told me. I could get her a job with my gang of labourers any time!'

Evan looked tense and tight-lipped as he made some brief comment about it being her choice, and women having minds of their own, before returning to his table and Sophie. A few minutes later, when Cynthia and Christian looked, the table was empy, Evan and Sophie had gone.

'What's she trying to do to me?' Evan demanded of a sulky Sophie. 'She doesn't have to work, and if she wants a job I've no objection. But why choose something like that? Is it to humiliate me d'you think? She says not, but I don't believe her.'

Sophie made some uncommunicative grunt and quickened her pace as they headed for the car, leaving Evan behind as he went on complaining. She got into the car and, when he joined her, still discussing the gardening and the alternative work Meriel could find, she got out and ran for the bus stop as a bus loomed into view.

'Where are you going?' he shouted, hurriedly trying to lock the car and follow.

'Going for something to eat, where I don't have to listen to you whining on and on about your ex!'

The bus slowed for her to jump on and Evan had almost reached it when the door closed and it drove off. 'Damn!' he shouted after it.

He thought for a moment of following the bus and trying to repair the disastrous evening, but he watched it go then turned away and drove home. He wasn't in the mood to soothe her feathers.

He sat outside his house for a while. It was one of two small semis, built by Sewell to fill an unwanted corner and tucked out of sight in a small vee where the cliff curved inwards between the bigger gardens and more expensive properties belonging to the Sewells and Morgans. Small and with very little ground, they had sold because of the prestigious address.

Damp night air penetrated his feet and worked up his shins like cold water, creeping insidiously under his clothes and chilling him as he sat with the engine off. He was stiff when he stepped out and the noise from the party at the Sewells' house hit him. He began to walk back along the cliff path towards Meriel's house.

The dogs barked their welcome when he knocked then called through the letter-box. Meriel opened the door and asked, rather ungraciously, what he wanted. She was dressed for bed, smelling sweetly of soap and shampoo, wearing a fluffy pink dressing-gown, her hair still damp from the shower.

'It's this job of yours,' he said, pushing past her and going towards the gas fire, rubbing his hands to warm them. 'Any chance of a coffee, I'm freezing.'

'Before we row or afterwards,' she asked coolly.

'I don't want to quarrel, Meriel. But I do feel rather strongly about you doing heavy, labourer's work and coming home so filthy people remark on it, and look at me as though it's my fault.'

'I like what I do and I've no intention of stopping just because it offends your idea of what's right for me. I am no longer your concern, Evan.'

'But you are, you always will be. Divorce doesn't make the past disappear. We can't forget the years we were married.'

'Isn't that what we're supposed to do? Forget how I worked to get you started? How I sold my profitable business to give you the deposit you needed? That's a part of a different life, a life that's gone for ever. You chose to move on and I have to do the same. At the moment, I choose to work a couple of mornings a week rescuing a garden from years of neglect.'

'What about these antique sales? Couldn't you develop that instead?'

'How did you know about that?'

'I've known for years about your secret hoard of treasures in the loft,' he grinned. 'And you've been seen at these local table top sales and the like.'

'It's a hobby, nothing more.'

'But when you get more experienced, a shop isn't such an impossible dream. You're an astute businesswoman, running your own artists' supplies business in your early twenties and helping me establish mine.' He moved a step closer and spoke more softly. 'Don't think I don't know how much I owe you. You were an enormous help, darling.'

Trying not to show it, determined to remain aloof, the endearment was a painful shock. She was nevertheless pleased with his flattery, even though the 'darling' was an empty, rather offensive ploy. A boost to her confidence was welcome. 'Perhaps I'll try again, one day,' she replied coldly. 'But that is my decision.'

They had a coffee and when he remarked that he was 'peckish', she made him a plate of sandwiches, making him smile at her assurances that she had scrubbed her hands after dealing with the pond.

When he left an hour later his thoughts were in turmoil. Walking back westward along the cliff path, oblivious of the icy chill of the wind coming from the sea, he had the strangest feeling that he was walking in the wrong direction.

Rupert allowed the party to degenerate from reasonably orderly dancing to a sort of free-for-all where couples sat and did their own thing, kissing, finding a room for some privacy. He began to be bored, just wandering through the noisy crowd and offering more drink where required. All evening he had been watching Helen's daughter Henrietta, and gradually he realized that the way she was looking at him was no longer casual. At ten o'clock he suggested she went with him to the garage, where his parents had stored their recently bought Christmas drinks and 'Find something a bit more exciting than the cheap plonk we managed to sneak in.'

'You don't mean spirits?' Henri looked shocked.

'Of course not. But they have some better quality wine, I thought you and I might try it.'

He led her through the kitchen door and into the garage, where Cynthia's car stood. From the sounds coming from it and the movement of the chassis, it seemed occupied.

'Pity, I could have taken you for a little drive,' Rupert whispered.

'You aren't old enough to drive!'

'I'm old enough for plenty of things, Henri. Hidden talents I've got, want me to prove it? I know where we can find a car that won't be missed for half an hour.'

Hesitating only briefly, Henri followed him at a fast walk along the road to Jeremy and Justin's house.

Cynthia and Christian had promised not to return home until eleven fifteen so, after they had eaten, they went to a club. The first person they saw there was Vivienne.

'Are you following me, spying for Cath?' Vivienne laughed. She introduced the man she was with, whom they had already seen at the restaurant, as Sidney Deetam, a salesman in a men's tailors and ready-to-wear shop.

'We've been thrown out of our home for the evening,' Christian explained. 'The boys are having their first Christmas party without us being there.'

'I have four sisters and we used to have some really wild dos at our house,' Sidney said. 'I have a large family, so with all the sisters and their friends and all the cousins and their friends, we had no difficulty organizing a party. Wild we were, mind. If our parents had seen half of the things we got up to—' He emphasized his words giving them a confidential tone and Cynthia wondered whether her first impression had been correct.

Sidney was an excellent dancer though, and a good raconteur, and the hours passed happily in his company. As so often happens, they discovered mutual friends, and while Vivienne and Christian were dancing, Sidney told Cynthia that a friend of his owned one of the houses in her area.

'He's selling though, some worry with subsidence, but I think he's crazy. It's probably untrue and he'll regret selling, I'm sure of that. He'll never get such a beautiful house with such a wonderful view again.'

'Subsidence? That's nonsense! My husband's firm built them and he wouldn't own one himself if there was the slightest danger of subsidence, would he?'

'There you go then,' Sidney said cheerfully.

At ten forty-five, Joanne put on her coat and picked up her car keys to collect Jeremy and Justin. She couldn't wait any longer, their first grown-up style party had made her edgy all evening. As she opened the door she saw at once that her car was not there. Disbelief was quickly followed by the thought that she couldn't collect her boys. She phoned the B and B where John usually stayed when he was in Newport but he wasn't there. Police? But that would delay her going to get the boys. At this moment, they were her priority. She would have to walk over to collect them and deal with the loss of the car when they were home.

She couldn't find her handbag and stood unable to think clearly of what to do. She couldn't go out and leave the house unlocked. She stepped towards the phone. Why didn't John get a mobile? He should be here to deal with this, or at least be reachable. Spare keys. Not on their hook. In the drawer? She tugged the drawer open with unnecessary force and spilled the contents over the floor. She scrabbled about to find the key-ring. House keys were there, but where was the car key? She pushed the contents of the drawer around in panic. But she didn't need the car key without a car, did she? She took a few deep breaths to calm herself.

Grabbing the dog's lead, she hurried from the house. The cliff path was quicker but it was late and very dark. She took the longer route around the roads, half running, half walking, and was out of breath when she reached the Sewell's still noisy house.

There were several cars in the spacious drive, obviously parents calling to collect their children. Children unwilling to go by some of the arguments going on and the way coats were snatched from parents by sulky owners.

Cynthia tried to put the words Sidney Deetam had spoken regarding subsidence out of her mind and at five minutes to eleven she did a Cinderella act and dragged Christian away as though their taxi, ordered for five minutes time, would be transformed into a pumpkin and no longer large enough to hold them if they waited another moment. During the short journey she said nothing to Christian.

'That Sidney's a decent fellow,' Christian remarked as the taxi stopped at their gate.

'Ye-es.' Cynthia didn't sound convinced and as soon as they stepped out, the noise coming from the house made any further comment impossible.

The first person to greet them was Joanne. 'My car has been

stolen!' she said before they reached the front door. 'I don't know what to do.'

'Ring the police, surely?' Cynthia said, hurrying past with bated breath wondering about the state of the house. Millie was not available to help clear up. She had been stupid to give her time off when the party was already planned.

'Do you want this taxi to take you back?' Christian offered.

Joanne shook her head, she didn't have any money on her and didn't want the embarrassment of borrowing some from Christian or Cynthia. 'It's all right, we'll walk and I'll phone the police as soon as I get back.'

As they turned the corner to their house, to meet the icy wind coming in from the sea, Jeremy pointed. 'What d'you mean, missing, Mummy? It's there, in its usual place.' He laughed uncontrollably, bending down, hands on knees, as the giggles took his strength, guessing why it had not been there a few minutes before. 'That Rupert's a cheeky one,' he whispered to his brother between fits of laughing. 'Him and that Henri were no doubt using it for a bit of fun.'

Accepting the teasing from the two hyped-up boys Joanne went to examine the car. The bonnet was warm. Someone had used it, but who, and why? Saying nothing further to the boys, she got them to bed and tried again to contact John, and failed.

Henri and her brothers declared the party a huge success when Helen and Reggie went to pick them up. William and George had spent most of the evening in the games room with Marcus. Henri said little and Reggie thought she might be a little drunk but he didn't say anything. Like Cynthia, he thought that kids had to learn. But perhaps he'd have a quiet word with Cynthia and let her know that alcohol had been available. He doubted that she knew.

Cynthia hadn't known but she soon did, having discovered the assortment of empty bottles the next morning. For the first time she berated her sons for their foolishness.

On the following day, Joanne had a call from Cynthia. 'Look, I hope you aren't offended, dear, but there's a lot of food left from last night's bash and I wondered whether your boys could help us out. I could bring enough for their meal tonight, chicken, ham, some salads, and lots of desserts. I've offered some to Meriel too and I could bring some for you at the same time.'

Thanking her, Joanne replaced the phone and sat racked with guilt. She couldn't get the thought of stealing Cynthia's purse out of her mind. It was Cynthia's kindness in offering to bring some of the leftover food that brought upsetting memories of the half forgotten incident. Unwanted food was hardly a gift of great value, but it was a kindness from someone she had robbed.

It had hardly helped anyway; that fifty pounds' deposit on the skiing holiday would be lost as John had refused to pay the rest. But they couldn't be so short of money that Jeremy couldn't do the same as his friends. How could things be so tight, with John working practically around the clock and the businesses continuing to thrive?

She no longer dealt with the accounts for the firm, but until John had taken them from her and given the responsibility to a firm of accountants, everything was looking good. So why was he so mean with his family?

She heard a car arrive and, presuming it was Cynthia with the promised food, she quickly glanced in a mirror, touched up her lipstick and straightened her hair before going to open the door. But there was no one there, just an envelope on the mat in the hall. The postman had already been so she was curious as she picked it up. The envelope bore no message and inside she found a cheque for the amount needed for Jeremy's school trip.

Curious, she sat down and stared at it. John must have asked someone to pop it in, but why hadn't they knocked? It was rather off-hand. She tried to phone but as usual these days, he was nowhere to be found.

It was almost Christmas. What could he be doing that kept him away from home so much? She put the cheque in an envelope ready to go to the school after the holiday and within minutes was worrying about how she would find the money for the extra clothes Jeremy would need.

When Cynthia arrived bearing large platters holding enough food for a small party, she showed the envelope with the name of the teacher scrawled across it. 'I've just written the cheque for Jeremy's skiing trip,' she said casually.

Seven

After Joanne had settled the boys in bed the night after Cynthia's party, she sat for a long time puzzling over who had used her car, and why. Could it have been John? The cheque pushed through the door must mean he had been around, but if so, why hadn't he come in? No, she was being ridiculous. It couldn't have been John. He would hardly push an envelope through the door of his own home, he would have brought it in, had a meal, stayed the night. What was she thinking of? Of course it wasn't John. He had obviously sent someone to deliver it but, if that was so, she was back to the question of who had used her car, and why?

Although it was very late, she went to look at the mileage then realized she had nothing with which to compare it. From now on, she would check very thoroughly. She looked thoughtfully at the garage. If only John would take out some of the rubbish he insisted on storing there, she could put the car away and that would stop whoever it was from using it, surely?

It was past midnight but she knew sleep wouldn't come. She wandered aimlessly around the house, picking up magazines, searching for a place to put them where they would be least obtrusive, and ending up putting them back in the same place. From time to time she looked out into the blackness of the night as though expecting the faintly seen silhouette of the car to vanish once more. To catch the person who was using her car seemed an impossible task and she could hardly go to the police and tell them the car was being stolen and then returned.

Oh, why wasn't John here? She envied her friends with husbands who worked for someone else, and did a reliable nine till five every day.

Taking out her purse and cheque-book she sat for a while

working out how much she had to last until the next pay-day. Not much. A pity the opportunity to pick up someone else's purse didn't come along very often. The thought, darting so easily into her mind, frightened her. What was she becoming? John was changing her from a decent, honest person to someone who thought of stealing as a way to augment the housekeeping.

It was a long time since she had handled John's business accounts and, on a whim, she went to his desk. The top was neat and orderly, with a few of the incoming sales dockets in one pile, the outgoings for the houses during the past month in another. The desk and all the drawers were locked. From what little she could see it seemed satisfactory, with more coming in than going out, but she knew that any profit went into the fund for acquiring new premises. Four houses let room by room and five small but busy cafes. There must be enough for him to increase her housekeeping. Jeremy and Justin were growing and their appetites, and clothing needs, were growing with them. Perhaps if she told him she had resorted to stealing from a friend it would frighten him into reassessing her pitifully small allowance?

She shuddered at the thought. Confessing would make it all more real and add to her guilt. In her opinion, whoever said 'confession is good for the soul', didn't know what he was talking about.

Early the following morning, Meriel was walking past with the dogs and saw that a light was on in Joanne's house. Surprised that her friend was up at seven a.m. during the school holidays, she knocked softly and waited.

A bleary-eyed Joanne opened the door and stared in surprise. 'Meriel? Is something wrong?'

'I'm fine, I just wondered if you were. It's early to see a light as the schools are on holiday, and I thought perhaps someone was unwell?'

'I haven't slept to tell the truth, in fact I was just dozing on the couch when you knocked.'

'I'm sorry I disturbed you.' She turned to go.

'Don't worry, I have to start getting breakfast for the boys soon, although they might be late after Cynthia's party. Come in and have a coffee.'

'If you're sure.' Meriel looked at her two dogs, at present playing around outside the door with Joanne's Fifi.

'Bring the dogs, I'm past caring about the kitchen floor. The boys in and out and bringing half the cliff path in – I won't attempt to revive the colour of the carpet until school starts again.'

Meriel sat at the kitchen table and watched as Joanne filled the cafetière, guessing something was wrong, and wondering how to ask.

'Did the party go well?' she asked eventually.

'The boys enjoyed it. But, Meriel, someone used my car last evening. I went to collect them and it wasn't there. I flapped a bit, tried to ring John, who, as usual, wasn't reachable – and when we got back from Cynthia's it was back. And before you say it: no, I didn't imagine it.'

'Of course you didn't imagine it. You park it close to the window, don't you? You could hardly have been mistaken. It wasn't John? He didn't call and, as you were out, borrow it?'

'I wasn't out. It was there when I came back after walking the boys to Cynthia's and when I went to collect them at ten thirty it was gone. A few minutes later it was back.'

Meriel was alarmed to see that Joanne was tearful. 'Did you have any other visitors?'

'No. That is, yes, sort of. An envelope with the cheque for the skiing holiday was slipped through the door and I can't understand who left it. John would hardly do that and I can't think why it was delivered by hand in such a casual way.'

'Where is John? Perhaps he was unable to get home and wanted you to have it so you wouldn't worry?'

'Why should I worry? I have enough money to send my son on a school trip for heaven's sake!'

'I think the coffee's ready,' Meriel said quietly.

Coffee was being prepared in the Sewell household and, as with Joanne, their sons were still fast asleep. Cynthia had appeared from the bathroom with her make-up fully applied and her dress immaculate. Her hair was attractively styled and although short and rather mannish, looked less harsh by the addition of the earrings she habitually wore. She had been thinking about what Vivienne's friend Sidney had said about subsidence and this was the first opportunity she'd had to mention it.

'Rubbish!' Christian laughed. 'D'you think I'd be living here myself if there was danger of the house falling down? Come on, Cyn, you know me better than that. The foundations on this estate are the best. Much stronger than the depth and strength demanded by the building regulations. Believe me.'

'I do, darling. Of course I do. But I was worried, hearing a rumour like that. I thought you should know, that's all.'

'Did he give a reason for saying what he did?'

'No, but—' she hesitated before going on, 'The boys said they were covered in soil one day back in the summer, when they were swimming near the place where the rocks are low down, closer to the sea and the soil is thicker. They said earth was sliding down and making the sea like mud.'

'Reddish soil was it?' When Cynthia nodded he said, 'I knew it. They were making excuses. They've been in that cave. I told them never to go near it.'

'No, they wouldn't. I rarely insist on anything and I know they wouldn't disobey me on that. The cave is out of bounds.'

The cave they referred to was not a cave at all, just a deep cavern where, years before, an attempt had been made to build a sewage system and had long been abandoned. Cynthia knew her boys wouldn't go near it. 'The mud was definitely from the sea,' she insisted.

'I'll go and look if you like, but there's no need, darling. These houses are set well back and most of the footings are on solid rock. Don't worry.'

'I'm not worried, I know you build houses to last. And perhaps it's best if you don't look. If people see you it will only add to the rumours.' She smiled and tried to put the subject out of her mind.

'You're right love,' Christian said. 'Best we both forget it.'

As soon as Cynthia went out, Christian rang Ken Morris.

'That's funny,' Ken said. 'I've heard that rumour too.'

'Where can it be coming from? There's been no trouble with any of the houses.'

They discussed it for a while and decided to ignore the story in the hope that it would die out from lack of fuel.

'D'you think the boys will want to come to the pantomime

after Christmas with me this year? Or are they too old?' Ken asked.

'I don't think you're ever too old for panto. Yes, I'm sure they'll come but I'll ask and let you know.'

'I've already booked.'

Christian could imagine Ken's grin. 'You're a big kid, Ken Morris.'

'I only wish it was my girls I was booking for,' Ken said. 'I had a letter from them both yesterday and I always feel lonely for a while after hearing their news.'

'When are you going to make the effort and go to America and see them?'

'I don't know. I suppose I keep hoping for a miracle, and that Mam will get better and be able to go with me,' Ken sighed.

Mrs Morris was putting the finishing touches to a casserole ready for Ken's tea. She had been watching a programme about America and wondering whether Ken would take her as he promised. His excuse was that he needed a lot of money and once his house was built . . . One day. It was always one day, she thought with a sigh. One day she would go to America to see her granddaughters. One day, Cynthia and Christian would visit her.

Ken had explained about their new life and their invented past, but she would hardly shame them. She knew better than talk about the hovel in which Cynthia lived and the drunkard Christian had for a father. Perhaps next year. She sighed again. At her age, hope was a frail ol' thing.

In Churchill's Garden that week, everyone was loaded with last minute Christmas shopping. Vivienne was there with an excited Toby, who had been to visit Santa and had been given a small clown puppet.

'What was your Christian doing on the beach at crack of dawn this morning?' Vivienne asked as she settled Toby in a chair. 'Toby and I went to look for driftwood and pretty pebbles to make some decorations.'

'On the beach?' Cynthia frowned. 'Are you sure it was Christian?'

Vivienne nodded. 'Him and that partner of his, Ken isn't

it? They were crawling about on the rocks and on the beach and a right mess they were in too. Covered in red mud.'

'Oh, that. It's just some initial survey to see if they can build further out towards the cliffs.' Cynthia smiled as she lied but her heart was racing. Was there a problem with the houses? And if so, would Christian be held responsible?

'Here comes Meriel,' she said. 'Let's have a piece of gateau shall we, as it's Christmas? My treat.' She left the table and waved to Meriel, and Helen, who was close behind her, telling them she would bring coffee for them all.

She hoped the chatter would be of Christmas and the family arrangements they had each made and not the subject of subsidence. That was a rumour Christian could well do without, even if it were unfounded. It could affect the outcome of his bid for a large contract he felt certain he would win. The timing of such a story couldn't have been worse.

'What are you doing for Christmas?' she asked Joanne when she returned to the table. 'How many days will John be free?'

'Not many,' Joanne sighed. 'The cafes are open practically every day and when he can't get the staff to work he has to go in himself.'

'I thought Reggie and I would be on our own,' Helen said excitedly, 'But Henrietta wants to come and stay, at least for part of the holiday, isn't that great?'

'I don't know how you fit three extra into that small flat of yours Helen.'

'It is difficult and I know the boys don't stay as long as I want them to because of the crush, but this time it's Henrietta on her own.' She turned her small bright eyes on Cynthia. 'I suspect that your Rupert might had had something to do with her decision, mind.'

'A crush of a different sort, eh?' Cynthia laughed. 'Tell her to come any time she likes. The boys will be pleased to see her I'm sure.'

'Thanks, I'll tell her that.'

'Meriel and I will be on our own so we're sharing Christmas Day,' Vivienne told them. 'And, if Meriel can persuade her, we thought we'd invite Cath as well.'

They looked towards the table where Cath still sat when she came for coffee and to read her paper, but an elderly man sat there, blocking the aisle with some untidily strewn packages.

'No sign of Cath today. Do you think she'll come, Meriel?' Helen asked. 'Better to spend the day with you and Vivienne than to be on her own, eh?'

Meriel thought it unlikely Cath would come for Christmas Day with Toby there. She had a serious hang-up where children were involved and Meriel had never found the right opening to coax the reason from her quiet friend. 'Maybe,' she replied.

'Christian is going away tomorrow and he won't be back until Christmas Eve,' Cynthia said, repairing her lipstick after the gateau had left its evidence. 'He and Ken had finished till the New Year but Ken wants him to look at a place ripe for conversion. They'll be taking their old camper van. They both hate hotels and prefer the van when they have to stay away.'

'Don't you mind him being away so much?'

'Of course I do, he's my best friend as well as my loving husband. But I understand that it's a part of what he does. We phone each other regularly on our mobiles, and I always know where he is so I can get in touch if I have a problem, although I rarely do.'

'I refuse to have a mobile,' Joanne lied. 'Even though John has begged me to. They're such a nuisance sometimes, aren't they?'

Right on cue, Cynthia's phone began to bleep and she glared at Joanne before answering it. 'Darling? . . . All right, I'll be there . . . Yes, I'll take the boys, they love to visit the farm, don't they? . . . Bye, darling.' She replaced the phone in her bag. 'He forgot he was going to collect the turkey and I have to pick it up on Christmas Eve,' she told them glaring at Joanne. 'It's so handy sometimes.'

Cynthia was the first to leave that morning and when she was out of the shop, Helen whispered, 'I wonder if there's any truth in the rumour I've just heard about those houses being unsafe?'

'It's a worry for Cynthia and Christian of course, but as my ex, Evan, lives in one with that Sophie Hopkins woman, I wouldn't be desperately upset if they all fell into the sea,' Meriel confessed with a chuckle.

Christmas was an unhappy time for Joanne. John was home but extremely irritable. He went out in the car, stating that he needed to go for a walk, and refused to invite her or the boys to go with him. Everything she suggested he vetoed. He criticized the excellent meals Joanne served and told her not to be boring when she asked what he *would* like to eat. He bought her a dress which she thought too matronly, and in navy, a colour she never wore. She had dealt with the boys' presents from the money he had provided and had given him a watch, for which she was paying weekly from a catalogue. Before the evening of Boxing Day she was seriously considering sending it back!

The boys went to see the Sewells after Joanne had telephoned to make sure they wouldn't be intruding on the family occasion and Joanne was left, sitting on her own, flicking through the channels of the television searching for something she could enjoy.

For Meriel, Christmas was a time she had dreaded, knowing that Evan would be sharing it with his new love. But with Vivienne and Toby promising to share Christmas Day and Cath joining her for Boxing Day, she was content. On Christmas Eve she opened the door to see Evan standing there with a bunch of flowers and an extravagantly wrapped parcel.

'Evan?' she tilted her head questioningly but didn't move to allow him to enter.

'I've brought this for you and I'd like you to open it now, so I know whether or not you like it.'

'If it's a Christmas present I don't want it. We're divorced, remember?' She tried to close the door but he stepped inside and stood in the hall, offering both the flowers and the gift.

'Please, Meriel. I never want us to be less than friends. Please open it. I want you to have it.'

He put the flowers on the hall table and handed her the gift. With a show of reluctance she began to take off the carefully designed ribbons and stars, curious but trying not to show it. It was only a bar of soap, she decided, examining its shape. Just an excuse to call, nothing more. 'I haven't bought anything for you,' she said.

To her surprise the torn wrapping-paper revealed a jewellery box and, inside, a watch that was not new but probably, she thought, from the fifties; a tiny but exquisite cocktail watch decorated with marcasites. It was something she had often mentioned in the past and she was impressed at his remembering.

Joy at the sight of the beautiful object swiftly changed to anger and she thrust it back at him. 'I don't want it. Give it to that woman of yours!' She pushed him so fast, so unexpectedly she caught him off balance and he almost fell as she pushed him across the hall and out of the door. She slammed it shut then seconds later, before he'd had time to recover, she reopened it and threw the flowers after him. 'Flowers for that Hopkins woman, not me!'

Evan called twice more and she ignored his impatient ring, standing behind the corner in the hall, giggling as she imagined herself to be a bad payer, avoiding the rent man. The second time, he went around to the back and stood for a while, then picked up a garden chair that had been blown over by the wind, and replaced it in its usual corner, before finally leaving.

When the doorbell announced another visit, she opened the door fast, prepared to tell him to go away, but saw, not Evan, but Tom Harris. She laughed in relief, apologizing as he stepped back in alarm. 'Sorry. I thought it was someone else. Come in.' He carried flowers and explained, 'I found them outside, perhaps they were meant for you?'

Taking them from him, she put them, upside down, in the kitchen refuse bin.

Tom stood there obviously embarrassed and, for a fleeting moment, Meriel remembered that it was she who expected to be embarrassed when they next met. Anxious now to put him at his ease, she explained. 'My ex-husband just called and brought me flowers. I didn't want them. I'm not usually so indifferent to flowers, I assure you.'

'You thought he was back when I knocked?'

'Sorry,' she said again, with an embarrassed grin. 'Will you have some coffee?'

'I won't stay, I've just brought you this. My brother and I are so grateful for the work you did last week. He's delighted to have the pond unearthed.' He handed her an envelope, which she guessed contained money.

'There's no need,' she said hesitating to take it.

'We wondered what you think of the chances of restoring it, perhaps making it into a wildlife pond?'

'That would be wonderful. In fact,' she said, 'I've already looked up a few ideas.'

Tom placed the envelope on the hall table and followed her into the kitchen where she set about making coffee. She invited him to sit, then handed him a gardening book in which she had placed several markers. 'Frog-spawn will be unlikely to appear spontaneously, but we can apply to get some from one of the wildlife rescue organizations, I think. The rest will probably come naturally once the pond is established.'

They discussed the necessary requirements and Tom made notes. An hour passed in easy conversation which ranged from the garden, to birds and other inhabitants, to families.

'You don't have children?' Tom asked.

'No, we didn't manage that. Perhaps if we had—'

'You would be less able to make a new life for yourself,' he finished for her. 'I have a son,' he told her and she stared in surprise. 'He doesn't live with me. I thought it better he stayed with his mother.'

Meriel was unable to ask further questions with the bigger question buzzing in her head. She must have been wrong about that solitary bed. How embarrassing if she had mentioned it to anyone. Thank goodness she wasn't like Helen who would have blurted it out the moment the idea had taken root!

Evan phoned an hour after Tom had left, demanding to know who her visitor had been. Meriel replaced the receiver without saying a word. She was pleased with her self-control.

Evan was not in a good mood when he finally went home to Sophie. His irritation was increased when she appeared ready to go out.

'I don't want to go out this evening, can't we have something at home for once?'

'Pizza and salad?'

'I hate pizza. Haven't you learned that much?'

Sophie knew perfectly well that pizza was his least favourite meal, which was why she offered it as an alternative to going out.

'Eggs then?'

'Oh all right, we'll go out but only for a meal. I don't feel like dancing tonight.'

He picked up his coat and didn't hear the jeweller's box fall from his pocket.

As they went out, Sophie picked it up and opened it. She frowned. An old secondhand watch? What was he thinking of? He didn't think she'd want that for a Christmas present, surely? Evan stood at the open door, the cold night air blowing through the house, the hall light touching the top of his head and silvering his fair hair.

'Thank you, Evan, but I think you should wrap this,' she said as suspicion began to grow.

'Where did you get that? Been going through my pockets?' he said, snatching it from her.

'If it's for me, you don't know me very well, either!'

'I bought it and changed my mind. Realized I'd made a mistake. It's going back to the shop after Christmas, I bought you something else.'

Her suspicions were confirmed when she saw the tip of some wrapping-paper sticking out of his pocket. She pulled it free and said slowly, 'It was for her, wasn't it? Threw it back in your face did she? Or are you planning to take it down tomorrow morning for a sentimental reunion to talk over old Christmases?'

On the quiet air, the silence was broken by someone knocking at the door of the adjoining semi. Then the thin voices of a couple of young carol singers reached them and touched Evan with their magic. He felt himself relax, aware of the anger draining away, and it was a shock when he was pushed aside by Sophie as she ran down the short path to the road, her tap-tapping heels giving a harsh discordancy to the gentle words of the carols.

For Helen and Reggie, having Henri to stay during the last part of the Christmas holiday was wonderful. Helen told her she had booked to take her to the pantomime, which Henri thought terribly embarrassing. 'Mam, I'm fifteen! I don't go to pantomine any more!'

'Well I want to go and I can't go on my own. You'll love it, no one outgrows panto.'

'I have and so have all my friends!'

'All right, a shopping trip as well. Both or neither,' she coaxed.

Henri was not convinced but she couldn't turn down the prospect of a shopping trip.

During the interval, Henri was persuaded to buy an ice-cream and, still hoping not to bump into anyone she knew, she walked with head down, trying to avoid faces.

'Henri? Fancy you enjoying panto. Or were you forced into it by a daft adult, like us?'

'Rupert! I was trying to hide. They don't know how they shame us, do they?' Henri sighed.

'Oliver and Marcus are here. Uncle Ken took a box for us and we're missing everything that happens on the right of the stage,' Rupert added. They both laughed at the stupidity of adults.

'Soon be over,' she said with yet another sigh.

'There's a disco next Friday, d'you think you'll be able to come?'

'Love to. I'm sure I can persuade Mum to let me go.' They discussed this for a while and Henri returned to her seat with two rather soft ices and a wide smile.

Helen was pleased that, after the interval, Henri seemed more cheerful. But she made the mistake of saying so and Henri resorted once more to deep sighs and a refusal to smile.

Two men he immediately recognized were waiting for Ken when he reached home on Boxing Day. They were sitting in a car parked on the other side of the street and when he stepped out of his car they came to stand one each side of him, smiling but clearly threatening.

'We have a proposition,' one of them said. 'A way of helping you to clear your debts.'

Hope and fear showed in Ken's eyes as he waited for them to explain. Then as he listened, disappointment and then panic set in. He couldn't do as they asked. Taking the consequences seemed the easiest way out, until his mother came and stood at the door, smiling, innocent, trusting. He could take a beating and would suffer it knowing he deserved it, but how could he put his mother at risk? The spokesman whispered softly, 'I'll be generous as it's the season of goodwill and all that. I'll give you until the New Year to decide. In the meantime, take care of your mother, won't you?'

Ken was trembling when he went inside and his mother was curious to know why he hugged her that bit longer than usual.

* * *

Tom was there when Meriel went to Holly Oak Lane to do a morning's work during the holiday period between Christmas and New Year. Ray was there too and she tried not to look at them, still unsure about their relationship and afraid that her doubts would show.

The pond was completely cleared and waiting for a liner and some broken slabs, which they had decided would form the surround.

'You can leave that to Ray and me,' Tom said when he found her studying the layout of the area. 'While it's dry we thought we'd go and get the liner and perhaps put it in place this afternoon.'

'It will want some sand below the plastic to protect it, and please make sure it's level,' she warned. 'Use a spirit-level. You might not notice when it's empty but when the water goes in it will look really silly if the level isn't perfect.'

Laughing and promising to do precisely what she had told them, Tom and Ray left for the garden centre. The ground was too wet for digging and she looked around to decide on the best way to spend her morning. She had intended to deal with the pond but, as that had been taken from her, she went behind the shed and continued to clear the abandoned rubbish of years.

The wood she unearthed was rotten and crawling with beetles and she found a small toad, asleep and looking dead which she carefully re-covered. Amid a pile of pots and broken pottery, she found an old sink, which she dragged and pushed and finally placed on the path near the back door. A small herb garden? Or alpines? Or some wallflowers for their scent? She left a note with suggestions for Tom and Ray to consider.

Looking down at her clothes she was horrified at how muddy she had become. Unfortunately as she had been expecting to visit the garden centre and deal with a clean plastic pond-liner, she had dressed more tidily than usual and the clothes she was wearing were ruined.

To add to her annoyance, directed solely at herself, she took off her filthy coat only to find that the car wouldn't start. The motor whined and did nothing more. She waited and tried again but eventually she put on her muddy coat and set off to walk, after adding to the note she had left for Tom and Ray.

She went home via the lanes wherever possible, dreading

meeting someone and convinced that if she did, it would be the immaculate Cynthia in her spotlessly clean car. It wasn't Cynthia whom she bumped into at the end of the road when she was almost home and safe from embarrassment, it was Sophie Hopkins.

Sophie too was far from immaculate. Her dress was creased and stained, her hair was in desperate need of attention and her make-up was ill-applied. She looked unwashed, as though she had just got out of bed and Meriel thought it likely that she had. Boasting that 'easy-going' was an accurate description of herself, Sophie had never been one to care too much what others thought, and it was quite likely she had just popped out without preparing herself for the day, to collect some milk – a bottle of which she held in her hand. All of which made it more irritating that the woman could see her like this and criticize her.

'Been on another mudlark have we? If you're trying to get Evan's sympathy you're wasting your time. He won't fall for that old trick!'

'Trick? What a devious mind you have,' Meriel smiled. 'A sign you're lacking in confidence would you say?'

'Hardly! I'm the one he chose to live with, after years of putting up with you.'

Meriel walked past her and, when she got to the gate, realized that Sophie had followed her. 'Did you want something? Is there something else of mine you want to take?'

'Didn't you like the watch he bought for you? He offered it to me first,' she lied. 'But I don't like old-fashioned, second-hand rubbish. So he offered it to you.'

Meriel said sweetly, 'Watch? What watch? He didn't give me a watch, perhaps it was for someone else entirely?' Satisfied she had returned as good as she had received she went in. Placing the post unexamined on to the hall table, she stripped off and soaked in a deep bath scented with a generous helping of one of her more luxurious Christmas gifts.

When she looked at the post there were several for Evan. Why hadn't he arranged for the post to be redirected like everyone else? she muttered. She picked up a pen and started to readdress them but stopped. The dogs needed a walk and she had no reason not to drop them through Evan and Sophie's letter box. She was surely past the stage of trying to avoid them?

It was not yet three but darkness was hovering on the horizon, obliterating the distant coastline. Soon it would be spreading its cloak across the sea, and the blinking of two or three lights from small boats would be visible like fallen stars. A few of the houses she passed were lit but all still had their curtains open, unwilling to see the short day ended.

The curtains in Sophie and Evan's lounge were closed. She wondered unkindly whether they had been closed all day. Opening the curtains was always the first thing she did, a matter of pride, if she were honest. Specially if she was a bit late rising, she hastily opened them as if afraid people would think she was lazy. What a stupid way to behave, as though anyone else cared! But she still felt a little smug to think Sophie had still not opened hers. More evidence that she had got out of bed very late and gone straight out for milk.

The dogs were soon sniffing around in the back garden as she approached from the cliff path. As she approached the door with the pile of letters ready to push through the letter-box, she heard the sound of quarrelling.

'If you won't take me out I'll go on my own,' she heard Sophie shout. This was followed by low and indecipherable words, obviously Evan. She pushed the letters through and was about to walk away when she heard Sophie scream her name.

'Meriel, Meriel, Meriel! That's all I hear, Meriel wouldn't do this, Meriel didn't need to enjoy herself. If Meriel was so perfect what are you doing here, with me? And what about that watch? Who did you really buy it for? Planning another change of residence, are you? Someone younger than me?'

Meriel ran down the path, deeply ashamed of both her eavesdropping and of the doubt she had placed in Sophie's mind.

Churchill's Garden was quiet when Meriel walked in the following morning. Assistants were busy rearranging the various shops. They were dismantling the seasonal displays that had become drab and shabby once the celebrations were over. The muddle of the Christmas aftermath, followed by the usual sales, had left the place looking far from its usual orderliness. There was a low murmur of conversation from behind the net curtains of the hairdressing salon, and the few customers in the cafe were whispering, as though subdued by the sober activities. Of the usual group of friends, only Cath was there, sitting in her usual table.

'Are you ready for another coffee, Cath?' Meriel asked after depositing her shopping to claim the table.

Cath stood up and moved to the larger table and handed Meriel a piece of paper. 'These are the dates and venues of all the sales for January,' she said. 'Not many, and some of these are miles away. It's always quiet after Christmas.' When their coffee was in front of them they studied the list and decided which of the events they would attend.

Vivienne was the next to arrive. 'My Toby is with Helen and Reggie,' she said, glaring at Cath as though expecting her to ask.

Cath smiled and said, 'I'm sure Helen enjoys that. She misses her children, no matter how bravely she copes without them.'

Mollified, Vivienne turned to Meriel. 'Your Evan's new woman is a lively one! You should have seen her the night before last. Star of the dance floor she was. Drunk enough to abandon all her inhibitions and just sober enough to stay upright. I went to a new club in town and she was there with another woman and they picked up a couple of lads. Having fun they were, was it a celebration? A birthday?'

'How on earth would I know? And he isn't *my* Evan!' Meriel said firmly. 'He lives with Sophie and I don't care what she gets up to.'

'Got up to plenty she did, mind.' Vivienne said, taking a bite of a cream doughnut. 'I don't think she went home at all.'

Remembering the untidy appearance of Sophie when she saw her the previous morning, walking up the road carrying a bottle of milk, Meriel was confused. Her emotions twisting and weaving so it was impossible to analyze her feelings. She felt slight sympathy for Evan, then spiteful satisfaction that burned inside her. There was also bitterness and, although she tried to ignore it, a tiny tinge of hope.

'Would you go back to him if he and Sophie separated?' Vivienne asked watching Meriel's face and the cavalcade of thoughts flitting across it.

There was a lack of certainty in Meriel's, 'No.'

On the beach with the dogs later that day Meriel was surprised to see Christian, Ken and Evan. She walked on, having decided to ignore him.

106

'Don't tell me you've got time to stroll along the beach in the afternoon,' she teased Christian.

'He's looking for that cave I and my friends used to dare each other to go into as kids,' Evan told her.

'Rupert and Oliver came home covered in mud one day and I suspect they're doing the same as Evan did,' Christian explained with a grin. 'Even though they promised not to.'

'I don't think it's as deep as it used to be,' Meriel said. 'The dogs sometimes go in there but the opening seems to stop a few yards in. The stream that ran through the middle became a torrent for a while but it's nothing more than a trickle now.'

'Perhaps I was wrong then. They must have been somewhere else.'

'The dogs get muddy here sometimes,' Meriel explained. 'I think the bank above is sodden after the wet autumn we've had and the soil is being washed into the sea.'

'The boys did say they were muddy once after a swim.'

'And you didn't believe them,' Ken teased. 'Sign of a misspent youth when you suspect your kids of doing forbidden things!'

Christian looked up at the bank of earth above the rocks. 'I think you're right, Meriel, the soil is slipping after the rain.'

Joanne had a visitor that afternoon. She hadn't appeared at the cafe that morning and no one had seen her for a few days, so Cynthia, on the way back from one of her charity lunches, parked in her drive and walked to the front door. The door was open and to her surprise she saw Joanne on her knees, polishing the stripped oak floor in the hall.

'Oh dear, don't tell me your cleaning lady's let you down again?'

'Why are they so unreliable?' a flustered Joanne said, as she got up and disposed of dusters and polish. 'It's Fifi, she loves to play in the garden and the ground is so wet. So as I had to wipe it up, I decided to polish it as well, just to remind myself I still can,' she tilted her head towards the kitchen, her face flushed from her exertions. 'Coffee? Decaffeinated of course.'

'Of course.' Cynthia guessed from this occasion and several others that Joanne did her cleaning herself. What she couldn't understand was why she lied about it. Meriel did her own, and so did a number of her friends. She had done so herself for years and had never found it in any way shaming. So why the secrecy? And more seriously, what else was she finding it necessary to lie about?

She drank the coffee and complimented Joanne on her delicious cake.

'I'll give you the recipe if you like?' Joanne offered. While she was finding it, and copying it out, Cynthia went to the bathroom to replenish her make-up, leaving her bag lying on the couch.

Seeing the bag was open, with her wallet so temptingly on show, it was seconds only for Joanne to open it and remove two ten pound notes and replace the wallet exactly as she had found it.

Eight

The five boys still went out secretly at night whenever the weather and circumstances allowed. With winter making the prospect less attractive, Joanne's boys would sometimes wait in vain for the call to let them know the Sewell boys were there.

With growing confidence, they began to go out on their own. If Rupert explained that they were unable to get out, Jeremy and Justin waited until they were certain their mother was asleep, and took the car for a few turns around the lanes. They didn't go far and they were never tempted to drive fast.

Justin was now tall enough to reach the pedals and see enough through the windscreen to avoid trouble but he only took over when they were in a place safe from being observed. They learned that the gates of the sports club were broken and one night they went in and drove around the field, leaving tyre marks to mystify the groundsman. They practiced manoeuvring the car around corners, both forward and in reverse and they would creep back to bed unable to sleep after the excitement, coming down for breakfast bleary-eyed and weary.

Joanne gave up checking the mileage on her car during the cold, dark weeks following Christmas. There were no other incidents to make her suspicious on the occasions that she did check and gradually her curiosity faded. The boys settled down to their school work and apart from occasional arguments about the amount of time spent on home projects, and constant requests for extra money from John, life had no serious problems.

She did take the boys to the doctors to ask if there was a physical reason for their unusual tiredness, but the doctor found nothing wrong.

Before she had married, Joanne had worked as an assistant cook. She was not fully qualified but she had real flair for sugar-work. She began to specialize in desserts and, as a side-

line, she had on occasions decorated wedding and other celebration cakes. In recent years she did this very skilled work
only rarely for friends but she still enjoyed it, so when John
asked if she would make a wedding cake for one of his
colleagues she was pleased.

'It's a man who supplies me with bacon and sausages and
all that, at a very reasonable rate,' he told Joanne. 'Divorced
he is and marrying a woman who worked for me for a time,
in the OK Cafe I sold a month ago.'

The wedding was arranged for Easter and Joanne rang the
prospective bride and made an arrangement to meet to discuss
what was required. The result of the initial phone call was to
promise to make the desserts and the starters as well as the
cake and Joanne was quite excited.

'I've been idle so long, what with having the boys and being
involved in their upbringing, now this request to do the cake
and the rest, well, it's made me suddenly realize that I have
time for myself at last,' she told Cynthia and Meriel and
Vivienne one morning when they met in Churchill's Garden.
'I'm going to meet her later this morning to discuss the style
of cake she requires and I've bought a few magazines to help
her decide.'

'I'm so pleased,' Cynthia said. 'You're very talented and
it's a sin to waste a talent, isn't it, Meriel?'

'Yes. I've wasted mine, such as it is, for too long.' She
smiled at Joanne saying innocently, 'Some extra money for
you too and we can all do with that.'

'There's that too,' Joanne said as though it wasn't important. 'I've no idea what to charge!'

They decided to visit the local bakery and get a few prices
and phone others in town before Joanne left for her appointment. The result cheered her enormously. If she could develop
a reputation for this, she would soon have her finances under
control.

An hour later she stood near the counter in Boots cafe looking
around for the woman who was to marry Carl Davies, John's
colleague. A young girl stood near by and they exchanged
comments about friends who were late, before realizing that
they were in fact waiting for each other.

'I'm Dolly Richard. I didn't realize you were John's wife,'
Dolly said. 'I expected someone – er – different. Long hair

and—' she thought 'younger' but decided it was wiser not to say so.

Joanne smiled. She couldn't admit that on seeing this girl who could hardly be older than seventeen, she too had been expecting someone, er, different! Carl was John's age, at least forty!

Disapproval faded as she talked to the girl, who was obviously very much in love with Carl. What she began to feel was sympathy. What was this young woman thinking of, tying herself to a man more than twice her age? Then came the second shock.

'It's so kind of you to make the cake for me and do the desserts and starters. I haven't any parents see, and I can't afford anything very grand. If it wasn't for your offer to do this as a wedding gift, I would probably have to make do with a Marks and Spencer's celebration cake,' she said.

'Isn't Carl paying for your wedding?' she asked, her spirits sinking. 'I mean, in the circumstances he's better able to afford it than you.'

'It's the divorce you see. His wife has been very bitter, and she's taken so much, that Carl hasn't recovered. Unless we do everything on the cheap, we'd have to wait years and,' she blushed prettily, lowering her eyes, 'Now, with the baby an' all—'

Joanne waited for John that evening, her fury making it impossible to sit still. She opened the front door the moment his car stopped and demanded, 'What are you thinking of, telling this Carl Davies that I'd do his wedding cake for nothing? And the starters and the gateaux! I don't care how you get out of it, but I'm not doing it! You refuse to give me the money to buy the boys what they need for school and yet offer to pay – with money we can ill afford and with my efforts – for this man's wedding to that poor innocent child. It's not on.'

John walked past her into the house and turned angrily.

'Don't shout out my business for all the world to hear! If you *have* to act like a shrew at least wait until I've closed the door!'

The two boys stood at the kitchen door, curious to know what had happened to make their mother so angry. She had been walking up and down like a caged tiger ever since they had come home from school and had snapped at them for no reason.

'Go to your rooms.' John said.

'No! Stay and listen to this. You aren't children. You're old enough to understand why I am angry.'

'Your rooms,' John said threateningly, and they hung around the newel post unable to decide who it was most politic to obey. John gave a growl that made them shoot up the stairs, but at the top they stopped and leaned over the banister rail, hoping to hear enough to understand what had happened.

'D'you think it's another woman?' Justin whispered.

'It won't be another man, she's too old,' Jeremy replied sadly. 'Pity mind, I wouldn't mind a stepfather, your real dad spoils you rotten then.'

'John,' they heard their mother say, 'I would willingly make this wedding cake, even though I think it's an embarrassment to be associated with such a travesty. I would make the cake and do what I could to make that poor child's day as successful as possible. But I won't do it as a favour.'

'Why not?' John said in exasperation. 'It's something Dolly couldn't manage but it would be nothing to you.'

'Nothing? I do have an idea of what my skills are worth and I want my fee. Surprising as it might seem, I do have some self-esteem left!'

'It's a favour for a business associate, who's in a position to do me several favours in return.'

'None of which will reach me or the boys!'

'What are you talking about? You live in this house and you and the boys have what you need. It's my business that keeps us here and for once, instead of always moaning and complaining, you can help!'

'Not with this.'

Joanne wondered afterwards what had given her the strength, but she adamantly refused to do what he asked. It was as though her training, her experiences as a cook had been all she had left and John was stripping her of that, reducing it to a casually requested favour, like minding someone's dog.

John slammed the door and the boys heard the car drive away. Creeping down the stairs they went into the living-room, peering around the door, preparing to retreat if their mother was crying. She was not.

'Come in, Jeremy and you, Justin. Sorry you had to hear that, but what your father was asking me to do was unreasonable.'

'To make a wedding cake for nothing?' Justin tentatively asked.

'To reduce my skills to something worth nothing, a very different thing.'

'Is he really marrying a girl?' Jeremy asked. 'How could she marry an old man?'

'Money and security,' Joanne said bitterly. She looked at her sons and decided it was an opportunity not to waste. 'You see, this girl, she is going to have a baby. And that is something you two have to be wary of.'

'Mum!' Jeremy gasped. Justin, his face reddening, looked at his brother for guidance.

'Sex is so pleasurable,' Joanne warned. 'Be prepared for how urgently you'll want to succumb. Pleasurable, desirable and so very easy,' Joanne went on, oblivious to their embarrassment, 'But the results of it are not.'

'Is succumb the same as seduce?' Justin wanted to know as they crept back up the stairs, lecture over.

'Oh yes,' Jeremy said airily. He was thoughtful as they gathered their books and began to settle to their homework once again.

'D'you think it's serious and we'll have to move out of this house?'

'No, but Dad might have to leave.' He grinned then. 'Sex education from Mum. Weird.'

In Churchill's Garden the following morning, Joanne tried to explain to Meriel how she felt.

'I can understand,' Meriel told her. 'After all, I had a small business. Art teachers sent their students to me, knowing I was reasonably priced and reliably stocked, and it was really successful. But I sold it to start Evan in business. It wasn't even mentioned when we divorced. Yet, for me, it was a big commitment in our marriage. It was enough to pay Evan's fare to Thailand to make contacts with the makers of the furniture and fancy goods he wanted to sell. It paid for the first two consignments. We lived in a small flat above the shop I had once owned and I worked in a supermarket for a year to keep us while he got the business off the ground. All that has been forgotten. It's no longer important. So, yes, I do know how you feel when John regards your skills as something to casually give away as a favour from him to one of his business friends.'

'And you don't think I was wrong to refuse?'

'I certainly do not.'

'Thank you.'

'Joanne, why don't you pick up that business again? You won't need premises to start, just to decorate a few cakes, make gateaux and lovely stuff like that. I'll bet that once you start, the requests will come rolling in.'

'I couldn't. The boys take so much of my time.' Joanne waved a hand brushing the idea away. But something had happened when John had shown such disregard for her abilities, and the idea of earning money, for herself, from something she had once enjoyed, was already beginning to grow.

It was a few days before John spoke to her civilly and then it was only to tell her that another arrangement had been made regarding the cake and that, in spite of her churlishness, she was invited to the wedding. 'And,' he said firmly, 'We are going and no excuse will be acceptable. Right?'

'I'll need money for a decent dress,' she said defiantly. 'And suits for the boys of course.'

'The boys aren't invited. It's a small affair, only a dozen guests. You'll have to ask one of your friends to have them for the day.'

'And the money for my clothes?' she insisted.

He took out his wallet and handed her eighty pounds. 'That will have to do, there's no more so don't ask for a handbag or matching shoes. That is it.'

'Do I have to buy you a shirt and tie out of this too?' she asked sweetly.

Cynthia was careless with her handbag and she often left it on the table while she went to the ladies, or to order more coffee. There was a fold of ten pound notes just inside it one morning and as Joanne was the only one there besides Cynthia, and Meriel, who went with Cynthia to choose cakes for them all, she slipped a note off the roll and into her own bag. She was looking at a magazine for brides with a special feature on cakes when they returned.

Later that day, Cynthia called the bank and asked if there had been a discrepancy in one of the tills. 'I cashed a cheque for fifty pounds when I came to pay in some money for my husband,' she explained, 'But when I got home, I only had forty.'

The bank assured her they would be in touch if they found a mistake had been made, but when they telephoned it was to say that none had been found.

Cynthia was thoughtful. Only Joanne had the opportunity to take that money. It was at Joanne's house that a previous twenty pounds had gone missing. The wallet containing fifty pounds had been taken from Churchill's Garden and again, Joanne had been there.

She knew Joanne lied about having a cleaner and had boasted about arranged holidays that never materialized, so were her money difficulties so serious that she had resorted to stealing from friends? How could she ask Meriel or Helen or Vivienne? And how could she accuse Joanne without experiencing terrible embarrassment if she were wrong?

Buying an outfit for the wedding of Dolly Richard and Carl Davies was not something Joanne was looking forward to. The eighty pounds John had given her wouldn't buy anything like she would have chosen. Shoes alone would cost at least forty. She wondered wickedly whether she might get away with finding something in a charity shop, and announcing the provenance of her purchases, loudly, at the wedding ceremony. It would serve John right, but she knew she couldn't embarrass him in front of his business acquaintances. But, if she could find a second-hand outfit at a 'Nearly New' place, the rest of the money could go towards the pocket money for Jeremy's school trip.

Cynthia spoilt it by asking, a few days later, when she was intending to go to town and choose her clothes.

'Oh, I thought I might go this afternoon,' Joanne said airily, convinced she was safe as it was Thursday, one of the days on which Cynthia 'did lunch' with a friend.

'I'll come with you!' Cynthia announced, much to her dismay. 'I'm free as my friend is in Gstaad for a couple of weeks. Walking on an Alp or something,' she said with a smile. 'So? Shall we go straight from here?'

'I did intend to go back home first.' Joanne tried desperately to think of a reason why she should, but one was supplied by Cynthia.

'Your cleaning lady is there?'

'Yes, I have to check she has done all I ask and, of course, to pay her.'

'Phone her.' Cynthia handed her her mobile. 'Tell her you'll call in with the money later.'

Joanne picked up the phone and walked outside into the small courtyard and dialled her own number. She smiled back at Cynthia and pretended to speak into the mouthpiece. 'She's managed to get the bed stuck awkwardly, I'll have to go back,' she reported.

'I'll come with you and wait!' Cynthia smiled. Joanne recognized the determined challenge glowing in her green eyes.

'Oh, it's all right, I won't bother. She said she would try and sort it out herself,' she said. 'Your car or mine?'

It was difficult to find reasons not to buy some of the beautiful clothes Cynthia urged her to try. But confessing that she was tired and undecided, they at last drove home.

Cynthia had been looking at her oddly all afternoon and Joanne knew she had guessed that her finances were not as rosy as she tried to pretend. Should she carry on with her pretence? Or should she take Cynthia, a friend from whom she had stolen money, into her confidence? Once again Cynthia took the initiative.

'You're having money worries, aren't you?' she said as she pulled up beside Joanne's car in the car park. 'Is John's business in trouble? You can tell me and I promise it will go no further.'

'Of course John's business isn't in trouble.' Joanne's voice was harsh and Cynthia thought for a moment that she had been wrong to ask. But Joanne went on, 'John's business is fine, but he keeps me short of money. Increasing his businesses at the expense of the boys and me. There. Now you have it. I haven't had a cleaning lady for months and months. I simply can't afford to pay her. I'm at my wit's end wondering how I can buy the clothes Jeremy needs for this damned school trip and then John gives me eighty pounds so we can go to this wedding.'

'Borrow something of mine. He'll never know, and use the money for something you'd really like.'

Joanne stared at her, a muttered 'thanks' drowned by choking sobs.

'There's something else,' Cynthia said, ignoring the tears, which she suspected were tears of remorse, flowing down Joanne's cheeks. 'You can use our chalet in Tenby if you wish, no charge of course, give the boys a couple of days away?'

'I couldn't.'

'Regarding the wedding outfit, I don't think you have a choice. Not unless you want to wear M and S! No one else will know. There are a few dresses I took to Paris and never used. People don't dress up like they used to, more's the pity, so you can try them and take which ever you like best.'

'Thank you,' Joanne tried to hold back the sobs that were filling her throat.

'Friends aren't only for the good times,' Cynthia said. 'And think about the chalet, you haven't had a holiday for almost two years, have you? It's yours whenever you want it. I know it's early, but with a bit of luck with the weather you'll enjoy a change of scene. Now, we'd better get home and see our children, hadn't we? And Joanne, dear, think also about Meriel's suggestion about starting your cake making and decorating service.'

Getting back into her own car, Joanne felt stiff and aching as though heading for a dose of flu. She sat there for a long time after Cynthia had driven off, guilt and humiliation towards herself, anger and bitter disappointment towards John, and affection for Cynthia, all changing places like a crazy nightmare in her head. Her one thought as she went into her neat and orderly house was, it was time to stop the pretence. Time to stop covering up for John's meanness.

'Jeremy, Justin,' she called, waving the eighty pounds in the air. 'I have a surprise for you. I'm going to book a weekend in a chalet down in Pembroke. What d'you think of that?'

'Cool,' was the reply.

'It probably will be,' she laughed.

The boys quirked eybrows in surprise. Sex talk and now jokes?

'Good one Mum,' Justin said approvingly

At Churchill's Garden, the next time Joanne met Cynthia, she waited until Helen and Cath and Vivienne had arrived, then said loudly, 'Cynthia has kindly offered to lend me one of her gorgeous dresses to wear at this wedding. Isn't that kind?'

Cynthia stared at her, then smiled, fully understanding what Joanne was doing.

Meriel saw nothing odd in the arrangement, but was puzzled that Joanne, who was normally so boastful about her husband's wealth, was admitting to it. She was even more surprised when Joanne went on, 'I can't really afford the kind of clothes I'd like to wear, what with the skiing trip and one thing and another, so Cynthia generously offered to lend me something of hers.'

'With a business continually expanding the money is often tight,' Meriel said. 'There are times when even the most well run firms have to be extra careful.'

'I don't think it's that,' Joanne said, 'I think John is simply too mean to enjoy giving money to his family. Now, any cakes this morning? My treat.' She tip-tapped in her fussy way to the counter to replenish their supplies.

'I don't want to go to this wedding,' she said later as they demolished the fresh cream doughnuts, 'But as I have to, I intend, with Cynthia's help, to knock-'em-dead!'

The wedding of Dolly to Carl Davies was indeed a small affair, with no one on the bride's side except for a girl who looked about fifteen, who was introduced as Dolly's friend, Marlene. Dolly wore a white dress that strained slightly across the front, with a short veil and a flowered head-dress. The dress was supported by a hoop that was clearly visible under the thin material of the dress. But in spite of the inferior quality of the clothes, Dolly looked happy and it was this that people would notice and remember long after they could recall what was worn. She had been made-up by an expert and had the look of a shy, fresh-faced young girl that was very appealing. Joanne told her she looked lovely and meant it.

Marlene wore a soft pink dress and carried a posy that matched Dolly's. They both wore their hair loosely curled and falling wildly down their backs.

Not knowing anyone except her husband, whom she coolly ignored, Joanne was relieved when it was time to leave the brief wedding breakfast in an hotel room near the register office. Carl shook her hand and told her he quite understood about the cake, 'John explained that you're out of practice and afraid of not doing a good job,' he said. The stiff smile on Joanne's face threatened to crack it.

'You're coming to the do tonight, though,' John said as they prepared to leave.

Aware that they would have a serious quarrel if she argued further, still seething about Carl's condescending remarks, Joanne could only agree.

The party was in the basement room of a public house and there was a small band which was too loud and too large for the size of the room. She knew no one there and, apart from a smiling welcome from Dolly and a brief nod from her new husband Carl, she spent most of the time on her own.

She stood in a corner wearing shoes that had cost two pounds in a second-hand shop and were too high and too tight, longing to ecape. She didn't see John after they had left their coats in a small room leading off the dance floor. He was smoking cigars, drinking whisky and introducing himself to those who might be useful. Business contacts. It was obviously the reason they had come.

Seeing people getting more incapable and unable to join in the foolish laughter that increased in ratio to the amount of alcohol swallowed, Joanne felt utterly miserable and lonely and realized she had felt that way for a very long time.

A man appeared beside her and asked if she would like a drink. 'Something long and cool? It's uncomfortably hot in here isn't it?' he smiled. In the depth of her loneliness, his smile was warming. He was taller than her by almost twelve inches and he touched her shoulder lightly as he bent down to hear her reply.

She hesitated and he went on, 'To be honest, you look as bored with the whole thing as I feel.' He led her to the crowded bar, a hand on her elbow. 'A wedding should be a celebration of the new life beginning for Dolly and Carl, not an excuse to talk business and do a few deals.'

'It's certainly an unusual party,' Joanne agreed. 'I don't think the happy couple have spoken a word to each other.' She looked around while the man bought drinks: at John who was laughing and talking with a group of men, his face red with the heat of the room and the drinks he had consumed. At Carl who was writing down something in a notebook. Some useful telephone number she guessed. At all the strangers gathered in groups which formed and reformed as people drifted around, seeing a face they recognized, stopping to exchange a greeting. Joanne wondered just how many of these people were Dolly's friends. Voices called, raucous, trying to make themselves heard over the music to which no one was dancing, and which Joanne decided was nothing more than a damned nuisance.

Dolly had a group of her own in a corner. Young girls dressed in skimpy dresses and heavy make-up. Dolly was still wearing her wedding dress and Joanne noticed it was torn at the hem, as though someone had carelessly trodden on it. There was a shriek of laughter as someone else did the same thing and a large tear appeared. Joanne tutted in disapproval at the lack of concern.

'What does it matter?' her companion said, having followed her gaze. 'It has done its work and can go out with the rubbish tomorrow.'

Joanne laughed. 'You sound more cynical than me!'

They talked with difficulty, standing close to hear each other to reduce the need to shout. He smelled clean and fresh in spite of the overheated room. They exchanged names and their connection to the wedding-party and Joanne learned that the man was Dai Collins who owned a chain of cafes called Gingham.

'I know them, repro early thirties, wooden tables and chairs, waitress service, aiming at comfort and style and good traditional food,' she said.

'No plastic, no freezer-to-microwave, and, no music!'

'Wonderful,' she breathed.

John called to her after a while and she followed him to where he wanted to introduce her to one of Carl Davies's associates. When she was once more left on her own, Dai Collins said, 'If you wish, I could run you home. It's obvious that, like me, you're only waiting until it's polite to leave.'

Thanking him, she found John and explained. He waved a 'thank you' to Dai, promising to 'give him a bell', and turned back to his friends. It was only ten o'clock but her feet felt as though they were welded into her shoes. Her strongest need was to get home and kick them off. She had difficulty walking to Dai Collin's car. She didn't invite him in for coffee and he didn't seem to expect it. Unlocking the door, she kicked her shoes off and stood in utter bliss on the cold floor tiles in the porch, allowing her coat and handbag to fall beside her.

Cynthia told her husband that she had lent Joanne a dress and offered her the use of the chalet in Tenby.

'I didn't think you were that close?' he frowned.

'I'm not. Not really, but I have a feeling that things are not well with John's business and she is short of cash. She actually admitted it today and was relieved. Keeping it to herself was destroying her.'

Christian looked at his wife's face, seeing an expression he knew well. 'There's something else?' he coaxed.

'Darling, I'm almost certain she has been stealing from me.'

'And you want to help her?'

'I can't prove it, but three times I've lost some money and on each occasion she was the only one who could have taken it.'

'So why help? I'd have thought it better to avoid the woman after giving a hint that you know what she's been doing.'

'She's trying so hard to cover up her difficulties. She's talked about her cleaning lady, and I guessed she was imaginary weeks ago. And then there was the holiday that they cancelled. It had never been booked. Clothes that appear but aren't new. Once I became suspicious, other things fitted too. I don't know why, but I had to offer help. If she tried stealing from someone else, or from a shop, can you imagine what the shame of it would do to her?'

'She isn't your responsibility, Cyn.'

'I know, but she is a friend, of sorts. And we had help when things were desperate. Ken's mother saved us from a life of utter misery. Poor dear lady. If I've made Joanne admit to being short of money it was worth letting her use a dress and the chalet, don't you think?'

'I'll ask around, see if I can find out if John is in difficulties or overreaching himself, or just being mean with his family.'

'Thank you, I would like to know.'

'Don't get involved in family arguments, mind. If you get between man and wife, you *always* end up as the villain!'

'Thank you, darling.' She paused. 'There's been no more talk about subsidence?'

'No, but two of the houses are up for sale, dammit. To be honest, Ken and I are a bit worried about these stories. This contract we're trying for, which would give the workforce security for two years, maybe more, is needed badly. If someone has started the rumour to make sure I lose it, I'll find out who if it's the last thing I do.'

'Do you know who else is tendering?'

'Ken's trying to find out. There aren't that many firms big enough to cope with it. He's going to see someone this evening, trying to get some information.'

Ken left the pub where he had been playing in a darts match and walked towards home. He hadn't brought his car having decided he would enjoy a few drinks. It was late and the roads were quiet. When he reached the corner of his street he was surprised to see lights on in the house. His mother was usually in bed by this time. He groaned. One of the neighbours must have called for what he called tea and sympathy. His Mam was good at that.

Without expecting anything more, he stepped through the door and called to his mother.

'There you are at last. Come in Ken, there's some friends waiting to see you.'

He went in to see the two men who were theatening him, and his Mam making them tea! The scene was so incongruous he laughed. His luck just never seemed to change, just like when that lad at work never placed that winning bet for him. You have to laugh, or else you'd cry.

'Time you came to a decision, Ken, old lad,' one of them said.

'Yes, time you sorted it all out,' the other replied. There was a serious threat implied as they smiled and looked from Ken to his mother and back again.

Meriel and Cath attended several Collector's Fairs and Antique Fairs during the early months of the year and towards the end of April, they booked a table and prepared to sell some of their stock. They had taken tables at some of the smaller events, getting rid of unwanted items and to practise their selling skills, but this was a big one.

'Even if we lose money, we have to start somewhere,'

Meriel said as Cath showed nervousness at the expenses they had incurred. 'This is a practice run and whatever trade you are in, you have to pay for experience.'

Although not officially antiques, Meriel took some of her fifties pieces and to her surprise, had sold most of them before lunch on the first day.

They took turns to go to the cafe and when Cath was due back after lunch, Meriel saw her standing at a stall selling children's toys. She saw her pick up a teddy bear and then watch a toy train that whistled and sent smoke through its funnel. There were several dolls, many of which were not intended to be played with by small hands. Cath ignored these and handled the soft, cuddly ones, a faraway look in her dark eyes. Meriel turned away, not wanting Cath to know she had seen her.

Had she lost children of her own? Or been close to children who had moved away? Or perhaps she was unable to have them. Something important had happened to make Cath such a sad person and whatever it had been, children were central to it, that much was certain. Perhaps, she thought again, with less hope, she still might trust me enough to tell me one day.

They were getting very tired by four o'clock on that first day, the preparations and the worries about whether they should be doing it had kept them both awake and besides, the actual setting up of the stall, carrying their goods from the van they had borrowed had been physically exhausting.

'Will I be glad to get home and flop into a bath and dressing-gown!' Meriel said. A woman was looking at a cup and saucer in the black and white Home-makers china, black sketches depicting all the things needed for the home, like vacuum cleaner, tables, lamps etc. Smiling as she wrapped it while Cath took the money, she was startled when Cath suddenly said, 'Look, isn't that Toby?'

A girl no older than fourteen was strolling through the aisles, looking at one or two items, and vaguely keeping an eye on the youngster who constantly wandered off.

Cath handed the change to Meriel to finish serving and watched the child. The girl was making an offer for a heavy glass milk jug and after looking around and not seeing the child, Cath heard her say, 'Can you hurry please? The little boy I'm looking after has wandered off again. Little devil he is, mind.'

Cath ran to where Toby was half hidden between the toy stall and a large chest of drawers from the next display and took his hand. She waited until the girl completed her transaction and began looking for him.

'Are you supposed to be looking after this child?' she demanded angrily.

'Oh, thanks, I wondered where he'd got to,' the girl smiled, apparently unaware of Cath's anger.

'Who are you? What are you doing with Toby?'

'My auntie usually looks after him but she had to go to town so she asked me to. What business is it of yours?' The girl at last awoke to the realization that Cath was not pleased.

'Your aunt is—?'

'Millie Rees, she works for Mrs Sewell, if it's any of your business! Any other questions, or can I go?' She stared at Cath her head tilted, one hip forward as though preparing for a row.

'Just make sure he's safe. Don't let him wander around in this crowd. He'd be frightened if he got lost.'

'I am looking after him, not that it's any business of yours!' She turned to Toby who was looking from one to the other with great interest. 'Come on Toby, love, let's get you that burger I promised you.' With a glare of disapproval she pulled Toby through the dwindling crowd towards the exit.

'Vivienne is so careless with her baby,' Cath said sadly when she returned to the stall. 'If I had a child I'd never let him go off with anyone who'll have him, like she does, would you?'

'I can't imagine doing so, no. But I don't have this craving for crowds and dances and music that Vivienne does.'

John told Joanne that he wanted her to organize a dinner party for the week following the wedding of Dolly and Carl. 'Eight people and here's twenty pounds to get the extra food,' he said, handing her the notes.

She was tempted to refuse, but didn't want any more confrontations. Things had not yet settled since the wedding, so she simply nodded agreement.

Jeremy and Justin were to spend the evening and night with Cynthia, as John had insisted it was a very important occasion. Even with John hardly being civil to her, she was looking forward to demonstrating her skills and the prospect of some small talk while the men talked business.

The first guest to arrive was Dai Collins and for a moment she failed to recognize him.

'That isn't very flattering!' he teased as she took his coat and hung it in the cloakroom. 'I'd have known you from miles away, even though you're smaller than I remembered, now you've taken off those ridiculous heels.'

'They're in the rubbish bin,' she confided.

'Joanne, your guests need you,' John called, and she hurried forward to greet Carl and three other men she did not recognize.

'Where's Dolly?' she asked, looking through the door expecting to see her.

'Men only tonight,' John said, and her spirits fell. So this wasn't going to be a social occasion. She was to act as hostess through the meal then disappear.

It was as she was in the kitchen preparing the tray of coffee that Dai found her.

He had 'accidentally' spilt cream on his coat sleeve and made the excuse of finding a cloth to clean it.

'Will you come and see my latest acquisition?' he asked her, handing her a small card. 'Bring a friend and the typical Welsh tea is on me. Wednesday?'

She thanked him, hardly taking in the address of the cafe advertised on the card. The way she felt at the moment she'd have accepted an invitation to fly to the north pole!

It was Cynthia she invited to go with her to the Gingham Cafe the following week and Dai was there, looking very different wearing, instead of a smart suit, a white apron and a gingham hat. The tables were immaculate with white cloths covered with a square of gingham. There were fresh flowers on every table. Gingham framed studies of Victorian children covered the walls and dried flower arrangements filled the corners. No harsh lights but far from gloomy, the place offered a quiet peace that fell over them like a mantle.

They were greeted like VIPs and offered a generous choice. Sandwiches (various), toast or scones with jams (various), cakes (various) and a large china pot of tea. The cups and saucers were delicate floral china matching the teapot. They settled for what Dai called Lady's Selection and it came on a huge oval tray, the contents of which filled the table.

As they left, thanking Dai and promising to recommend the place to friends, he took Joanne on one side and whispered, 'If you ever need a friend, I'll be here. Please remember that, will you?'

'What can he mean?' Joanne asked, repeating his words as they walked towards the car.

'Nothing,' Cynthia reassured her. 'He was just trying to be friendly. Probably fancies you. What's the matter, is that so unlikely?' she demanded as Joanne laughingly protested.

'Fancies me!' Joanne smiled. 'As if he would.'

Cynthia was thoughtful as they got into the car to drive home. Something Christian had told her made her think that the concern Dai had shown was not misplaced.

Nine

Joanne was surprised when John asked her to arrange a luncheon party only a few days after the dinner. She didn't like lunches, the evening felt like an anticlimax. Whereas with a dinner party, the evening was filled and drifted quietly towards bedtime with a glowing feeling of success and the warmth of congratulations surrounding her.

She arranged it for the following Wednesday and asked for a list of guests. If it were to be a business lunch, she would like to know in advance and not be disappointed at the insignificance of her role. She was pleased to learn that this time there would be some women and surprised to hear that two of the guests would be Meriel's ex-husband Evan and his partner, Sophie Hopkins.

How would she cope with being polite to Sophie Hopkins, a woman who had split up Meriel and Evan? Being formally polite would give her the opportunity to be quite cutting without actually being rude, she decided.

'What is their connection with you?' she asked John as she wrote down the names. 'I didn't think you had business connections with Evan?'

'I have decided to furnish one of the cafes in cane furniture as an experiment. A sort of sixties revival, with a chrome and glass counter, lots of bright red fittings, and coffee machine and a balcony, and palms in pot. Plastic of course.'

'Of course.' Joanne groaned inwardly at the prospect, remembering the tasteful ambience of Dai's Gingham cafe.

'Evan is going to quote me for chairs and tables, cane bases and cheerful plastic tops and seats.'

'Lovely,' Joanne breathed, hiding a shudder.

'He's promised a friend's discount. The hand of friendship is a powerful one. We never know when we might need it ourselves.'

'Hand of friendship? Evan? You hardly know him.'

'If I get a better deal by giving the illusion that we're friends, then we've been buddies for years! Glad of the pretence he is. Not many around here have much sympathy for him and Sophie.'

'I don't for one,' Joanne said sharply. 'Meriel didn't deserve what he did to her.'

'Then you should. Falling in love can happen to the most unexpected of us.'

Joanne remembered Dai Collins and his gentle, warm smile and said no more.

As she was uncertain how long the luncheon would last, she arranged for the boys to go to Cynthia's after school from where she would collect them.

'Don't worry,' Cynthia assured her. 'Millie will be here if I'm not and she'll get them something to eat.'

'The gannets that they are, they're looking forward to clearing what's left of the luncheon,' Joanne laughed, 'But thank you. You are very kind.'

Sophie and Evan were the first to arrive and, removing her coat to reveal a very short black skirt and red, low-necked blouse, Sophie looked around the room with interest.

'Very nice,' she said finally. 'I thought you'd live in an old-fashioned place. Dark furniture, good-but-boring ornaments and heavy curtains. Funny isn't it, how wrong you can be about people?'

'So glad you approve,' Joanne breathed politely.

Dolly and Carl Davies were among the guests and several other couples whom Joanne had met only briefly at the wedding.

Sophie's voice was the one most heard throughout the meal and instead of being irritated, the others seemed to enjoy her sometimes silly remarks and her almost boastful displays of ignorance. Whatever the subject, she had some input and if it was obvious she didn't know what she was talking about, the laughter was instant and far from unkind. She saw Carl staring at the young woman with an interest that was clearly upsetting the obviously pregnant Dolly.

Joanne was thankful when the party broke up at three. At least her compliance with John's wishes had meant Jeremy had gone on his school trip without further argument. Leaving the dishes to be dealt with later, she walked over to Cynthia's about an hour later, to give Fifi some exercise and to collect the boys.

Christian answered her knock and said at once, 'They aren't here.'

At once Joanne began to panic. 'Not here? But—'

'They're out on the cliffs playing hide and seek. Come on,' he laughed, 'I didn't mean to frighten you. I'll come with you and find them, shall I?'

They let Fifi off the lead and she led them across the field, along narrow paths through the tufted grasses and wild flowers. Voices guided them to the cliff path, and below it, they saw Justin and Marcus squeezing out of a fissure in the rocks on the beach below.

'Call the others, will you, Marcus?' Christian shouted. 'Time for Jeremy and Justin to go home.'

They watched as the two boys climbed back up the cliff as nimble as goats.

'We don't know where the others are,' Marcus said. 'We all went to hide ages ago but they haven't come to find us, even though we called and whistled.'

'Determined to hide until the very end,' Christian laughed. 'Let's see if I can find them.'

Leaving Joanne to walk back to the house with Justin and Marcus, he set off across the rough ground, stopping to listen occasionally. He hoped to creep up on them and frighten them, so he didn't call. In fact he almost fell on top of two of them. His son, Rupert, was in a freshly formed hollow, the grass at the bottom surrounded with an almost complete circle of reddish earth as though formed by a tunnel entrance collapsing below the surface. Almost beneath his son, eyes closed and deeply lost in a kiss, was Henrietta, Helen's young daughter.

For a moment, Christian said nothing, there was something quite beautiful about the scene, then he heard the swish of grass and looked behind him to see Joanne approaching.

'Time to come back down to earth I think,' he said softly and like clockwork dolls, with stiff jerking movements the two separated and sat up. Christian walked away with a chuckle, and led Joanne back towards the house. 'I've found Rupert and he can find the others. Come on, I think we might persuade Millie to make us a cup of tea.'

That evening, when his sons were in bed, he spoke to Rupert about Henrietta. 'Be careful, young man. She's only fifteen, and you could find yourself in a situation you can't handle.'

'She's all right, Dad,' Rupert mumbled.

'More than all right, she's a looker, even though she's still at school. Just don't get carried away, that's all I'm saying.' Christian went downstairs feeling uneasy. Talking about sex and its fascination was not something that came easily to him.

'I hope I said enough,' he muttered to Cynthia.

'I'm sure you have, darling. Too much advice, whatever the subject, and you make them rebel.'

When Sophie and Evan left Joanne's luncheon party, Sophie was unusually quiet. Putting it down to the wine she had consumed, Evan said nothing. Back at the small semi, not far from the large property of Cynthia and Christian, he started preparing coffee. Sipping it, still looking subdued, Sophie said, 'Evan, I want us to get married.' Startled but trying to hide the fact, Evan said simply, 'Why?'

'It's time you made a commitment. I hate living with you and everyone knowing you don't love me enough to marry me.'

'That's nonsense, Sophie. What more commitment can I have shown? I left my wife, and bought this house with you. I divorced Meriel. You and I share everything. We don't need a ceremony to prove to everyone that I love you.'

'Even Carl Davies married that poor little girl when he got her pregnant. She doesn't fit into his world at all, and never will, but he married her.'

'Is that what this is about? Dolly expecting a child? You know how I feel about us having children. We don't need another person. Our relationship is perfect as it is. You wouldn't like having to stay in night after night, and look after a baby for twenty-four hours day after day. Dealing with the messy side of child-rearing. Admit it, you don't really want that any more than I do.'

'I think you do want children. But you don't want them with me.'

'Sophie, you're drunk!' He kissed her and tried to coax her out of her mood with laughter. 'Good lunch, eh? And you, my darling, were the star.'

'You can't let her go, can you?'

'What nonsense is this? You can't mean Meriel? I divorced her for God's sake! Would I have done that if I'd had any doubts?'

'You still can't let her go. How many times have you been over there this week? Twice? Three times?'

'I cut the lawn. That's all. When she eventually decides to sell the house, I want it looking its best.'

'You're working harder than you need, just to make sure she doesn't go without. It cuts you up to see her working on someone's garden. You watch her, afraid that she will find someone to love. Why else did you buy us a house so close to her?'

'You're jealous,' he teased, 'And I am flattered. Come on, you need a lie down.' He kissed her gently, 'In fact, we both do.'

When Evan went to shower ready to go out to a night club later that evening, Sophie dialled Meriel's number. 'Let him go, you jealous bitch,' she spat into the phone. 'He doesn't want you any more. It's me he loves, so get dignified. Stop hanging on to him. Give him some peace.'

'The cracks beginning to show?' Meriel said softly, before gently replacing the receiver.

Meriel couldn't decide how she felt about Sophie's anxiety. An unkind part of her wished them to fall apart. The pain of being told Evan was in love with someone else, then the devastating moment when he walked out of her house, was something that still brought her to the verge of tears. Hearing from others about how happy they were, and about the house they had bought close to the boundary of Cynthia's garden, was still too fresh for her to be kind enough to wish their happiness to continue.

A part of her wanted Evan back, but in calm moments she wondered whether she actually would take him if she had the choice. Would she ever rebuild the confidence to believe they were together for ever? Or would there always be doubt, if he was late, or when she couldn't reach him on the phone?

She was walking the dogs the following Sunday morning and saw Ken, Christian's friend and partner, standing looking at something on the ground. Curious, she walked over, wading through the tall grasses, intending to cross the field and continue her walk down the lane. He saw her and walked towards her heading her off.

'I thought I'd found an unusual bird's egg,' he laughed. 'Then I realized it was a partly covered golf ball!' He walked with her a little way, asking about her gardening job, and talking to her about Rupert and Oliver and Marcus, whom he loved as though they were his own, he told her proudly. But Meriel sensed that he wanted to avoid the area he had been studying with such interest.

She felt hustled. Hurried away from the place where she had intended to walk. Was he making sure she didn't see whatever he had found? A golf ball was hardly something to protect. So what could it have been?

She allowed herself to return to the cliff path and excused herself by telling him she intended to walk along the beach a little way before going back.

'The dogs love a run on the sand,' she explained as she began to scramble down the precarious earthen path to the rocky shore.

'You be careful, the soil there is far from solid.' He watched her for a while as though making sure she was safe, then waved a hand and disappeared.

An hour later, Meriel climbed back up and headed for the place where she had seen him standing. She was still a long way off when she saw that two men now stood there. Calling the dogs to her and snapping on their leads she watched and slowly recognized the men as Ken and Christian. More curious than ever, she waited until they had gone before walking across to see what had held their interest.

The bowl-like indentation in the ground looked freshly done. It was as though something circular far below the surface had collapsed, and she frowned. There were dips and bumps all over the area close to the cliffs, so what was so secretive about this one?

She called to see Cynthia a day or so later and when Christian walked in to collect some post, she asked,

'Christian, what is that fresh indentation out there near the cliff path? Are there mine shafts around here? There used to be iron ore workings, didn't there?'

'Years ago that was. No, it's probably our kids. Sometimes I despair of them ever growing up. Playing hide and seek they were last week. Ask Joanne, she came to collect them and they were all out of sight, hiding like ten year olds.'

'This looks like a fresh fall,' she said.

'They used to build dens over there when they were younger. They'd dig deep holes, then cover them with old corrugated iron or wood or something, and put the turf on top. Plenty of evidence left of the childhood of Rupert and Oliver.' He laughed. 'Imagine the fun some archaeologist will have at some future date trying to understand the mysterious earth-works, eh?'

Cynthia saw some uneasiness in her husband's expression and she added to his story, making a joke of it all. 'Christian's right. I remember how frightened I was once, when I knew nothing of these dens. I went out to call them in and there was no sign of them. Then up from the ground came three mud-stained boys. Funny afterwards, but at the time I thought of some invasion of aliens from a flying saucer.'

Meriel didn't believe them. They were covering up. 'Surely Rupert and Oliver don't play in dens now? They're almost sixteen,' she said doubtfully.

'Of course not, but the damage is still there. The rain shifts a bit more soil from time to time, that's all. And besides,' Christian leaned forward confidentially, 'When I found Rupert, he and Henrietta were making more adult use of the hiding place.' He glanced at Cynthia encouraging her to share his amusement.

When Meriel left to walk home, Christian offered her and the dogs a lift.

'Thanks,' she said, 'But the reason for bringing them was to give them a walk. They'd feel cheated if I accepted a lift.'

One evening a few days later, while walking the dogs she saw black rain clouds moving towards her with remarkable speed, driven by the warm air from the land moving towards the cooler sea. Visibility was reduced as the rain began to fall and the houses on the Sewells' estate were lost from sight. She was walking along the path, head down, wishing she had turned back earlier, or had had the foresight to wear a heavier mac and wellingtons. She knew that no one living in the houses would see her and as she was so wet that a few more minutes outside would hardly make any difference, she left the path. She walked to the soil disturbance that had caused

133

such concern to Christian Sewell. The place had been filled, dug over and the place no longer showed a clear depression, just an area of disturbed soil and dead foliage.

Unaware that her car was being used occasionally by Rupert and Oliver and her sons, and also ignorant of the fact that her son, Justin, at thirteen, could now drive as well as her older son, Jeremy, Joanne no longer checked the mileage. She did notice how tired they still were, and that she had to chase them out of bed some mornings. But the doctor still claimed they were healthy.

John told her to stop fussing. He was still very irritable with her sometimes and once, when she had used his car when it had blocked hers in the drive, he was unreasonably angry. She was gradually less tolerant of his short-tempered reaction, and, when he came home one evening, very tired and went to bed before she had collected the boys from the cinema, she found her car blocked in again, and didn't hesitate to use his.

The alternative was to wake him and she decided that using his car, even though for some reason he didn't like her doing so, was the most sensible of the two alternatives. Driving off she didn't see the bedroom curtains move but when she returned, chatting to the boys and hearing about the film they had seen, she was startled to see him standing by the open door, waiting for them.

There was something about his stance that made her feel nervous and she spoke to Jeremy and Justin as though they were babies. 'Run in, Jeremy and Justin, get yourselves washed, teeth cleaned, undressed and ready for bed,' she chanted the repetitious instructions without thinking about them.

'Mum!' Jeremy protested. He and Justin were outraged at the affront to their maturity. But their mother was unaware.

Anxiously wondering whether John would be angry, or would accept her explanation, she fumbled to reach her handbag and found instead a mobile telephone, still in its box, half hidden by magazines, between the seats.

Surely John hadn't bought one without telling her? How many times had she begged him to get one so she could reach him if there was an emergency? She looked at the number determined to memorize it.

'John?' she called, waving the phone in a questioning

manner. With a bit of luck she could show anger over this and make his remarks about her borrowing his car appear trivial.

'Put it back, it isn't mine,' he said. 'Someone I gave a lift to forgot it.'

'Are you sure it isn't yours?' she accused, chanting the number in her head as she walked towards him carrying the phone aloft.

'Do any bills come to the house?' he said sarcastically. 'You don't get one for nothing you know. Put it back, it isn't mine.'

She did so, looking at the number displayed on the box again and again, as she committed it to memory. Going inside, pushing past John, she ran up the stairs talking to Jeremy and Justin, but heading towards her bathroom where she wrote the number down in her diary. She didn't stop to wonder why she no longer trusted him, she only knew that she didn't.

Meriel had arranged to help in Joanne's charity shop one afternoon, when a volunteer was unable to do her shift, and to her surprise, Evan came to see her there.

'How did you know I was here?' she demanded. 'Don't tell me someone told you, because Joanne only asked me this morning when a last minute appointment came up and she couldn't get here to do her hours!'

'Steady on with your suspicions,' Evan laughed holding up a hand in mock protection. 'I was walking past and saw you, nothing mysterious, love.'

'I still feel you're watching me and checking on what I do,' she said only slightly less suspicious. He hadn't looked in, but had walked up the street and straight into the shop. She had watched him from the window where she was displaying a summer suit.

When she went home she looked around for a sign that Evan had been there. But nothing had been touched. Her diary-cum-calendar beside the phone had all her appointments noted, clearly seen. She put it in a drawer, then, realizing she was becoming paranoid, she took it out again and replaced it next to the phone. Perhaps it was time to sell up and move on, away from Evan, where he wouldn't find it so easy to watch her.

On her way to Churchill's Garden the morning following her discovery of the mobile phone, Joanne dialled the number from a phone box, putting 141 before the number so the number from which she was calling would not be available to whoever answered. The phone was picked up by John.

She was thoughtful as she walked in to greet her friends. Perhaps John had spoken the truth, and the phone did belong to someone else and was simply still in his possession? She decided to try it again from somewhere she did not usually go, and this time not use the 141 code, so he would not be suspicious.

'Is something troubling you?' Cynthia said as she approached the table in the garden, where Meriel and Vivienne were waiting.

'Troubling me? Good heavens Cynthia, that sounds serious. Of course nothing's troubling me, apart from my usual lack of money,' she joked, taking out a fan of ten pound notes and putting them more tidily into her wallet-cum-purse. She had regretted her confession that John did not give her enough money and whenever she had the chance, she showed a full wallet. That the money was to pay a bill for one of John's business purchases, and not hers at all, she didn't bother to explain.

Cynthia smiled understandingly, then said to Meriel, 'Remember the hole that the boys had dug? Christian got one of the labourers to fill it in. He was afraid someone would fall into it, you see. I don't think they really want to play such childish games any more, do you?'

'Why do you think I look troubled?' Joanne wanted to know. Cynthia looked down with deep concentration at the cake she was eating.

'No reason, Joanne. You looked a bit serious, that's all.' But Joanne noticed that she didn't look at her when she spoke. Did she know about the vases she had taken from the charity shop for two pounds and sold in one of the antique shops in Cardiff?

'John gave me some extra so I can buy a few extra clothes for the boys,' she explained quickly. 'If you were serious about us borrowing your chalet, Cynthia, we'd like to go next weekend as part of summer half term?'

Arrangements were made and instructions on how to get there written on a page of Joanne's diary, while Meriel mused over the unlikely interest in the hollow on the cliff.

A few days later, while Joanne was in Tenby with her sons, Cynthia announced that she and Christian were considering selling their home.

'But why? You love it there and so do the boys,' Vivienne gasped. 'I thought you planned to live there for ever, start a dynasty, leave it to your sons and their sons and for always?'

'Christian has a chance of a large building project and we need to put everything into it that we can,' Cynthia explained sadly. 'I don't want to move, and I hated telling the boys, but if Christian is to build three large, top quality houses in an expensive area, he can't cut corners. They'll be wonderful properties. My Christian really is an exceptionally good builder you know and the architect he works with is at the top of his profession. They both have a good reputation. There'll be huge conservatories or Winter Palaces as the designer prefers to call them, and indoor swimming pools, and patios with canopied areas, lights and outdoor heating. Everything has to be of the very best, and of course, that costs. So, we'll probably be living in a small rented house for a couple of years, and then we'll be able to buy something like we have at present. Perhaps even better.'

They each described their dream home, Joanne loud in her description of the most modern designs. Vivienne admitted that she didn't want the work and organization involved in owning a grand house. 'I like to be free to go out and enjoy myself,' she said cheerfully. 'So a little cottage is all I aspire to.'

Helen admitted to wanting a larger place, 'So I can give Henrietta a room of her own when she comes with her brothers. My boys don't mind roughing it in sleeping-bags on the floor, but I do wish there was a room for Henri,' she sighed. 'She's fifteen now, and she needs a bit of privacy.'

Meriel said very little. She was thinking about the concave depression in the ground between Cynthia's house and the cliff path, and the stream that had widened, and the soil falling on to the beach, and wondering whether the possibility of subsidence, so close to the properties, was Cynthia and Christian's real reason for selling.

But thoughts of the hole that had been so quickly filled were forgotten when she walked into her house and became immediately aware that someone had been in her kitchen.

A drawer was hanging open, its contents disturbed, a cupboard door wasn't quite fastened and swung in the draught from the open window. Her hair stood up on the back of her neck. She must have a burglar! What should she do? Phone the police? Run out and get help? Thoughts raced around in her mind and she stood listening for a sound to confirm her fears.

Later she was unable to say how long she stood there but it could hardly have been more than half a minute before she moved forward and picked up a knife, then, shuddering at the ugly thought of using it, dropped it quietly back into its slot. She then lifted a steak tenderizer which looked like a hammer but would do very little harm and, holding it aloft, walked slowly through the hall and glanced into the lounge through the crack of the door.

Evan was asleep on the couch, a newspaper draped across his knees as though it had fallen from his hands as he slept.

'Evan!' she shouted and was gratified at the suddenness of his wakening. 'How did you get in!'

Recovering after a few seconds of confusion, he said, 'Sorry darling. I must have fallen asleep. I was waiting for you and it was uncomfortable sitting on the back porch so I came through the back door.'

'It was locked.'

'No, you must have forgotten.'

Her response was to hold out her hand, into which he slowly placed a back door key.

'Do you have any more?' she demanded.

'None, I promise.'

'You promised once before I seem to remember.'

'I really don't have another key. I forgot that one when I handed over the others and, well, it was in my pocket so I used it.' He seemed unconcerned by her anger, continuing to chat as though the occasion was a regular one. 'See any of your friends in Churchill's Garden?' he asked.

'I've decided it's time to sell this house and move on, away from you and your partner. I realize I should have moved a long time ago.'

'There's no need,' Evan said. 'There's plenty of time. You wouldn't like to move too far away from Cynthia and Joanne, and the rest of your friends, would you? Best we wait until you're sure what you want to do.'

'What about you, don't you want to sell and fully commit yourself to Sophie? Marry her? Say goodbye to this place?'

Ignoring her questions he said, 'Look, I'll make a cup of tea and we'll discuss what's best for you shall we?'

'No!'

'Or what about a bit of lunch? Do you have any goats' cheese? Sophie never buys it and I love it with a bit of salad. Greek style. Remember Crete, darling?' He went into the kitchen and opened the fridge.

Meriel didn't know what to say. Was this a sign that he wanted to come home? Was he trying to pretend he could step back through the door and carry on as though the past eighteen months hadn't happened?

Suddenly wearied by trying to deal with it she sat at the table and watched in a bemused way as Evan prepared a salad with feta cheese and olives, the way they both liked it, with his favourite salad dressing which she still used. He took crisp bread rolls out of the shopping basket she had brought in, broke them open and filled them with butter, then announced that lunch was served. Like an automaton, she allowed him to help her off with her coat and sit beside him at the small kitchen table.

Meriel and Cath were aware that besides selling, they had to buy, and collecting a few items at car boot sales and spotting one or two table top bargains was not enough. That summer they decided to try their hand at an auction.

'Nothing heavy,' Meriel promised a doubtful Cath. 'A house clearance for a start. Small things until we know what we're doing.'

'Will we ever?' Cath sighed.

At first they were taken aback by the speed at which the auctioneer went from 'who'll start me off at?' to 'sold' on the items he was selling.

'He didn't even look at us!' Meriel said. And they began to laugh nervously. A set of shelves they wanted, was sold for less than they had decided to pay, simply because they hesitated too long before getting into the bidding. 'That hammer comes down faster than I can think!' Cath moaned.

'Right! From now on I mean business!' Meriel said with greater confidence than she felt.

By the end of that first auction they had managed to buy a fifties vase, some cutlery, a box of oddments and two pieces of carnival glass. Both were convinced they had paid too much for them all.

'My Henrietta is coming to me to celebrate her birthday! What d'you think of that, choosing me and Reggie instead of Gareth and her step-mother for her special day. Good, eh?' Helen said when they were drinking coffee in Churchill's Garden one morning in late June. 'My Reggie and I want her to have a really good time. Any ideas about where we can take her?'

'If she's like most sixteen year olds, she won't want to be taken anywhere!' Vivienne said. 'Give her plenty of money so she can go shopping and have an evening out with her friends. That's the way to please a sixteen year old!'

They all laughed and Cynthia said, 'The twins are sixteen in two weeks' time and they'll be having a party. The last party in the house, so make sure Henri is free for that, Rupert and Oliver want her to come. Your boys too,' she said, turning to Joanne.

The conversation left Meriel free to think about the visit from Evan and the way he made himself at home in the house where he had lived until Sophie had entered their lives and ruined everything. She had made up her mind during that night, as she had sat in bed, pretending to read, trying to sleep, and she announced her decision to her friends.

'I'm selling the house and moving away, probably into the town,' she said.

Everyone congratulated her on finally coming to her senses.

'I'm not looking for a house,' Meriel continued, glancing at Cath who had joined them. 'I want a shop with a flat above.'

'What? You want to live above a shop?' Joanne gasped.

'Cath and I plan to start a small business selling both antiques and collectables and, while we learn the business, a section selling more modern second-hand items.'

'You're going into business? In a shop?' Joanne made it sound like a toxic bath.

'Like you were when you discussed the possibility of cake decoration,' Meriel frowned. 'What's wrong with starting a business?'

'Nothing I suppose, but as John pointed out, it changes your life so you don't have a spare moment, and makes every friendly gesture harden into a business deal.'

'You think I wouldn't have any friends?'

'Of course you would, but things are bound to change, aren't they? We'll always be there for you though,' she breathed.

'So you won't be advertising for catering work?' Cath said quietly.

'John doesn't think it's a good idea.' Joanne spoke in a clipped manner that made it clear that the subject was closed.

'Why are you and Cynthia both selling your houses now?' Vivienne asked, 'No trouble in the area, is there?'

Meriel looked away, alarmed, as Cynthia quickly – too quickly – asked if anyone wanted more coffee.

Late one night, Justin got out of bed and went to the window, he had been disturbed by needing the toilet, then, as he felt around for the bedside lamp, he heard a sound outside of a car door closing.

It was difficult to see clearly as there was only a sliver of a moon, but he could make out two shapes near his mother's Fiat and he quickly ran into his brother's room and woke him.

'Is it Rupert?' Jeremy asked, as soon as he woke. 'I didn't hear him call.'

'I don't think he did,' Justin said. 'I think he's going without us and he has that Henrietta girl with him.'

Jeremy leapt out of bed and grabbed his jeans, hopping about as he pulled them on.

'Quick, find my shoes! Where's my sweater!' Laces threatened to trip him up as he slithered down the stairs trying to hurry, trying not to wake his parents. He was through the back door with Justin, still in pyjamas, close behind him. A large shadowy shape was moving away from the house; the Fiat was being driven away and although he ran after it, Jeremy failed to catch up with it before it disappeared around the corner at the end of the long drive.

'Why d'you think he didn't wait for us?' Justin asked, reaching for the biscuit tin.

'He's got a damned cheek. It's our mother's car. Why doesn't he use one of their cars?'

'Too big and noticeable I suppose,' Justin said. 'Shall we have some hot chocolate?'

The following morning they woke early and went out to where the car was usually parked. It wasn't there.

'Best we say nothing, pretend we haven't noticed,' Jeremy said.

They ate breakfast and announced that they were going to see Rupert and Oliver and Marcus.

'Tell Cynthia I'll call in this afternoon, to discuss what I'm to make for the twins' party,' Joanne said as she popped some pale slices back into the toaster for John, who liked it well done.

'You aren't doing this as a business deal I hope?' John asked. 'You know how I feel about you working. I see enough of women cooks during the day without coming home to the chaos of you making cakes.'

'Where will you be today, John,' she asked, ignoring his remarks as she refilled his coffee cup.

'Doing the afternoon shift at the all-day-breakfast in town,' he said. 'One of the girls is off sick and another is new so won't be able to cope without help.'

'So you'll be home for dinner?'

'No, I don't think so, in fact, I might not be back until late tomorrow.'

She didn't ask why and he didn't offer any further explanation. She had arranged to meet Dai Collins at one o'clock and they were going to have drinks in a small village about eight miles away and discuss the possibilities of her starting a business. Smiling at John she breathed, 'You work so hard for us, darling.'

Going out to get in the car, she was so surprised to find it wasn't there, that for a second she stood there holding out the key as though it would miraculously reappear. Then she saw Justin and Jeremy running towards her.

'Mummy, your car. It's stuck over in the field near the path,' Justin called as he and his brother ran towards her.

'Where's Dad,' Jeremy said, 'He'll need to help get it out.'

John wasn't pleased to hear of the delay but walked across the rough ground towards the car, telling Joanne that she must have been careless. 'You forgot to lock it. Even though it's close to the house, you have to make sure it's locked.'

Joanne said nothing. She was certain she had turned the key, but until they made sure, she didn't want to argue. When they reached the vehicle it had been securely locked and when she opened it and got inside, the reason for its abandonment was clear. It had run out of petrol.

'John,' she said out of the boys' hearing. 'I think the car has been used once or twice before, and returned to its usual place.'

'And you didn't tell me? Or report it to the police? Good heavens, woman, it might have been used for a robbery! Why don't you make sure you lock it? Why are you so stupid?'

'I do make sure it's locked. I thought you had borrowed it.'

'Without telling you?'

He began walking back to the house, Joanne following close behind, wondering whether to say anything more about the unexplained mileage, or remain silent. She hated being called stupid. It was the one criticism that angered her more than any other.

Taking a petrol can from the boot of his car, he returned to the Fiat without another word. That he was angry was clear from the tight lips and the frown around his eyes. The boys had waited for them and were ready to push the car from its muddy resting place.

'Don't push it, Justin, you could strain yourself,' Joanne said, preparing to push beside Jeremy.

'I could steer it, Dad,' Justin suggested, 'I'm the lightest. Then you could push with Mummy.'

The car moved easily out of the mud and Justin steered it successfully on to the road. 'Can you show me how to drive it to the house, Dad?' he asked hopefully. 'I know what to do.'

John laughed. 'As soon as you're old enough and show me you have enough common sense, then you'll learn to drive, I promise,' he smiled.

'Fool! You could have given the game away!' Jeremy hissed when they were once more walking towards the Sewells' house.

'No I wouldn't. I watch Mam often enough, don't I? I didn't need you to show me.'

Justin and Marcus complained about the older boy's attitude when they were alone.

'It isn't fair,' Justin moaned.

Marcus tutted in sympathy. 'Big brothers, eh?'

Justin went on complaining, but the ever cheerful Marcus whistled as he went into the kitchen, lifted a bunch of keys from their hook and opened his father's large BMW.

A few minutes experimenting and giggling then the car burst noisily into life and rolled backwards, off the hard-standing, and shot straight across lawns and flower beds and into the bottom hedge, beyond which was the field and then the cliff path and a drop to the beach below.

'Lucky for you the hedge was there,' was Christian's only comment when he was called for help, 'Or we'd be scraping you two off the rocks!'

Wandering back from a walk on the sand towards lunch, the five boys saw a man in the distance and Rupert recognized his father's partner, Ken.

'Uncle Ken,' he called and, as an aside, told the others that, 'Uncle Ken's usually good for a couple of pounds to buy a can or some ice-cream. Uncle Ken,' he called again as he ran to catch up with him, with the others in a gaggle following on.

To his surprise, the man turned, saw them, then ran off.

As he slowed to a stop, Rupert said, 'That's funny. I'm sure it was Uncle Ken and he was covered in streaks of that red mud.'

Ken ran as fast as he could along the path, trying to think of an excuse for when he next saw the Sewell boys.

Meriel was leaving the house with the dogs, intending to walk to the next beach and buy a snack from one of the cafes and sit on the rocks for a while. She had a book in her hand and as she was looking at it, making sure she had marked her page, the figure suddenly appeared and knocked her flying into the bushes alongside the path.

She was scratched by the brambles and her hand sank into a muddy patch near where a small stream ran. Her clothes were torn and filthy and she felt the unmistakable trickling of blood down her face. She called the dogs and began to retreat back to the house. She was trembling with the shock of it and leaned on an old fence post to recover.

'Meriel?' She looked up to see Evan running towards her across the field and as she saw the concern on his face, she burst into tears.

144

He helped her across the rough ground of the field, to the back of his house. Sophie was standing in the kitchen, something – but not concern – making her frown.

'Some idiot of a jogger knocked her down and didn't stop to see if she was harmed,' Evan explained as he gathered a bowl of warm water and cotton wool and took down a first aid box from a kitchen cupboard.

He bathed her face and Sophie made some tea and rather reluctantly offered her some clothes to wear home.

'It's all right,' Meriel assured her. 'It isn't far.'

'It will be soon,' Sophie said, looking at her curiously. 'Evan tells me you're moving.'

'Yes, and the Sewells have put their house on the market so you'll have new neighbours.'

'The Sewells? I thought they were happy there?' Evan said in surprise.

'Cynthia said something about having to release all their assets so Christian can build these manorial halls or whatever they call them,' Meriel joked. 'So grand they have to put every penny they own to get them built, it seems.'

'I don't understand,' Evan frowned. 'That can't be the reason for selling. His firm is up for the contract to build them, it isn't his project. He won't have to lay out the money. The firm he will be building them for will pay him for his work.'

'Evan, if they're selling, I think we should too,' Sophie said. 'I've always said we're too near the edge of the cliffs.'

Meriel thought of the subsidence on the field and the red soil slipping down on to the beach, and the changing appearance of the stream and could hardly disagree.

Ten

Joanne's boys were at the Sewells' house, their regular venue during these summer holidays, and so Joanne felt no qualms at having arranged to meet Dai Collins for lunch, one day at the beginning of August. Jeremy and Justin had taken a picnic and planned to swim at the local beach. The weather was far from ideal, but the five boys took pride in bathing in the rain, when only dog walkers and occasionally surfers were there to keep them company.

Dai took her to a popular eating place called The Boar Inn, in a village about eight miles from home. He didn't call for her but arranged to meet her at the Inn at twelve o'clock. She sat in the car waiting for him, having arrived early, feeling rather self-conscious, hoping that no one she knew would see her and expect an explanation of why she was there. A village pub would not have been John's choice for lunch.

Dai pulled up beside her in his open sports car, leapt out and opened the door for her, touching her face, looking into her eyes with a hunger of longing. His obvious delight at seeing her was flattering and very exciting. Taking her hand he led her into the restaurant looking into her eyes with an expression that suggested love and desire. Her legs weakened making a chair a necessity.

'I've thought of this meeting to the exclusion of everything else,' he whispered as the waitress took their coats.

'So have I,' Joanne breathed. They both knew their relationship was going to take a big step forward today. They had met for drinks once or twice, but this was their first meal together.

The room looked full but they were given a corner table from where they could see the room but were not easily observed.

From the excellent selection offered they chose grilled Welsh

146

salmon, and sat apparently relaxed, but both unable to open a conversation as though a shyness had overcome them. The conversation gradually opened up, first about the venue and then developed into questions and answers about each other. The place filled up as they talked but they were so wrapped up in their conversation, they hardly noticed.

Joanne told him about her disappointment when John had told her not to start making cakes. 'He doesn't mind me doing it for friends, but he won't help me start a business. I did well before we married you know. I specialized in desserts: Tiramisu, gateaux and I made a pavlova you'd die for.'

'How happy are you and John, honestly,' he coaxed.

'I haven't thought much about being happy until recently,' she said. 'John works hard and I see less of him than I'd like. It also means I have to see to everything and he's never there when I need him. But besides the minutiae of the daily grind, I've begun to think that life should have something more than boring routine, and being hard up and pretending all is well. I thought that if I earned my own money and filled my time doing things I want to do, well, John would benefit too, wouldn't he?'

'I wouldn't advise you not to use your talents, I believe we should use whatever gifts we have, but I do wish you'd think about doing something for yourself and not to please John. That's where happiness lies, doing things for yourself, feeling fulfilled, and then your happiness spills over to the benefit of everyone close to you.'

She was aware of his hands over hers, smoothing her wrists, her lower arm and she wanted him to move further, to touch her body, make her feel alive as she hadn't felt for a very long time. Their starters arrived and he moved his chair to allow the waitress room to get to the table and his leg pressed against hers and didn't move away again. His hand returned to hers and he fondled it as though it was a most precious thing. His eyes stared into hers and her throat felt tight and she wondered if she would ever be able to eat.

'I have something to show you, if you have time after we've eaten,' he said as he picked up his fork and started on the melon.

'I don't know,' she said, 'The boys will be back from their swim and I like to be there when they get home.'

'So caring,' he smiled. 'Come on, let's eat and see if we

have enough time. It's a property I own with the cafe downstairs, and two rooms above that I don't really use. You could fit one up as a kitchen and maybe make that dream of yours happen.'

'No, I couldn't work out of the home, not for a few years, until Justin is older. That's why I thought making and decorating cakes would be a good start. I can do that in my own kitchen.'

'Come and see the place,' he whispered, 'It will give you some ideas—'

'Ideas about cooking?' She quirked an elegant eyebrow.

'We'll cook something up, I'm certain.'

She hardly tasted the meal, unaware of the plates coming and going as they talked in double entendre throughout the hour they were there. The rest was inevitable. He flattered her and it was something of which she had been starved. He didn't sound at all false to her, needing him so badly she heard what she wanted to hear, and he listened to her with such apparent interest, and admired the way she had thought out her ideas.

He told her she was highly intelligent and quite beautiful. He was considerate of her comfort and made sure she had everything she wanted while allowing her to talk, stopping her only to ask for a clearer explanation, being supportive of her ideas and plans. In a dream, she went with him to see the rooms he had described, only to find that one was furnished as a living-room, the other a bedroom.

He kissed her at once and she was so enamoured of his flattery and obvious attraction, she fell under the spell of him. He lifted her and carried her into the bedroom.

They met once or twice a week after that day, usually in the afternoon, mostly after lunch, sometimes before. They never met in town or anywhere near her home, except on one occasion when he was a guest at a dinner she attended with John.

John introduced them and Joanne found it hard not to laugh. 'We've met before, haven't we Dai? You came to dinner with us soon after Dolly and Carl were married. Don't you remember, John?'

'Sorry, I forgot,' John said vaguely, he was already leaving them and heading for Christian and Cynthia, who had just walked in, bronzed after a week in Greece.

'Any luck selling the house yet?' he asked Christian brightly.

* * *

148

'You look happy,' Helen said to Joanne one September morning, in Churchill's Garden. 'You and John had a making up or something?'

'John and I haven't quarrelled,' Joanne said stiffly. 'We never quarrel.'

'Funny, I thought – never mind, I must have been mistaken.'

'What have you heard?' Joanne demanded and she caught a glimpse of Cynthia warning Helen to be quiet. 'Tell me, Helen. What gossip have you picked up this week?'

'Nothing, I thought you had separated or something.'

'What on earth gave you that idea? You've seen me with another man, is that it? Well he's advising me on the possibility of starting a business, that's all.'

'I haven't seen you with another man, but I thought John must – have – sorry, I misunderstood.'

Irritated rather than alarmed, Joanne insisted on being told.

'Well, I thought it was him, but I was probably mistaken, I don't know John that well. A man put an advertisement in the shop window for a bicycle for a seven year old and he wanted a pink one.'

'Really, Helen! Why would John want a pink bicycle? Justin is nearly thirteen and he certainly wouldn't want a pink one!' She turned to the others to share her derisive laughter and was startled by the sorrowing expression in Cynthia's eyes.

'Cynthia?'

'Oh, sorry, Joanne, dear, I was just thinking of having to sell my lovely house,' she extemporized. 'A couple came to look at it yesterday and they seem very interested.'

The conversation drifted to buying and selling and Helen, fount of all knowledge said,

'I heard the other day that your Evan and that Sophie Hopkins are thinking of selling. Nothing wrong with the houses on the cliff, is there, Cynthia?'

'Of course not. And I'd prefer it if you don't repeat stories that have no basis in fact!'

Joanne went home feeling relief that Helen hadn't seen or heard about her meetings with Dai Collins. She felt guilty and decided that the affair had to end. She was shocked at the ease with which she had been persuaded to cheat on her husband. She was no better than Vivienne who went out to clubs looking for brief affairs, one night stands, and seemed unaffected by them. It was puzzling to imagine why John – if it were he – would buy a pink bicycle for a seven year old. He did see a lot of other women, most of his staff was female, and perhaps he was buying a present for one of them. Because he was mean with her and the boys it didn't follow that he was mean with others, she thought bitterly.

Cynthia went home a little upset. She would have to stop the rumours about subsidence or the sale of the house would be an impossibility and Christian would lose the chance of his important deal.

'Mrs Sewell! Thank goodness you're back!' Millie ran to meet her before the engine had been turned off and behind her the five boys were grouped around the door looking solemn.

'What's happened? Are the boys all right? Is Christian hurt?'

'It's this.' Millie pointed to the step on the back porch, which had dropped by about fifteen centimetres.

Cynthia took out her mobile and began to dial Christian's number.

'I was in such a panic I couldn't remember the number of your mobile, so I phoned him when I couldn't reach you,' Millie said. 'He's coming straight back.'

Calming herself, Cynthia looked again at the damage and standing up, said, 'I don't think we're going to sink into the sea just yet, Millie. The concrete under the paves has crumbled, that's all. Come on, boys, what about some lunch?'

'There's something else,' Millie said. She went inside and in the hallway close to the front door, several of the floor tiles had cracked. One had sunk slightly in the centre.

'There's a hole in the field again too,' Rupert told her.

Ken and Christian arrived within several minutes of each other. Together they examined each area of damage and spent a long time discussing the implications.

It was late that night before Ken went home, having listed the tests they needed to carry out. Christian said to Cynthia, 'We have to keep this as quiet as possible. If I have built an unstable structure, I won't get that contract.'

'Contract?' Cynthia said curiously. 'I thought you were the contractor, employing others?'

'You know what I mean,' he said uneasily.

'Are you the owner of this project or are you hoping for the contract to do with work, Christian?'

He sat with his head in his hands. 'All right, I should have told you, but I was worried by that land slip in the field. That's why I thought we should sell.'

'Why didn't you tell me?'

'If I'd told you, you wouldn't have agreed to my selling the house to some unsuspecting family until it was fixed, would you?'

'We've always been honest.'

'Until now, when the house we've spent so much money on building and improving could turn out to be worthless. Honesty isn't so easy when you think you might lose everything.'

'Ken knows?'

'Yes.'

'How long has Ken known there was something wrong?' Cynthia asked.

'Why? What does it matter?'

'The boys saw him one day coming up from the beach covered in that red soil. Had he been down that old cave the boys discovered? Is that where the problem lies?'

'It isn't a cave, it's a water course,' Christian told her. 'It's no longer used. The stream has diverted to another place, taking away some earth occasionally. We had every test imaginable done before we built here. The old pipe has perished, there's only a thin trickle of water seeping in occasionally and sometimes some soil slips. But these houses are built too far back to be affected. Damn it, Cynthia, this could cost me that contract and the sale of this house. We'd be finished.'

'What did Ken find when he went down there?'

'I don't know. He didn't even mention it to me.'

'He ran away when he saw the boys, or so they told me, and at the time I wondered why. If he wasn't investigating on your behalf, what was he doing? Why did he run when he saw the boys? And why didn't he tell you?'

'He probably didn't see them. And don't start putting more mysteries in my lap. I've enough to deal with, love.'

'I think it was Ken who knocked Meriel over that day a few months' ago when she went to Evan and Sophie's to clean up. What was he doing, pretending not to see her as well as not seeing the boys? He knocked her over. He could hardly say he didn't notice *her*.'

They decided to set tests in motion, getting one of the civil engineers who did the original tests to come in. 'But don't let's do anything for a few days,' Christian said. 'Keep it quiet, if we can, ask Millie and the boys not to discuss it, give me time to make a few enquiries of my own.'

'Our boys will agree but what about Jeremy and Justin? They'd find it hard not to tell Joanne and John.'

'Promise them something, a party, a trip to Ilfracombe on the ferry, anything, but keep them quiet for a few days.' Unaware they were too late, Cynthia agreed.

They went to bed that night too distressed to sleep, wrapped in each other's arms seeking comfort. Remembering his partner's enjoyment of gambling, and his desire to visit his family in America, Christian wondered whether a mild excitement had become an addiction. A man with serious debts was capable of anything. When he finally slept it was Ken and his daughters who peopled Christian's dreams. He said nothing of his suspicions to his wife.

Meriel and Cath took a table in an Antiques Fair early in September. They had amassed enough good quality items to fill a stall and hoped to cover the cost of the rent and make a profit to help towards the purchase of a shop. They had decided that Cath would continue to live in the chalet until she was ready to cope with sharing.

Still needing time on her own, subject to moods that isolated her, Cath was not an easy person to know, but Meriel hoped that she would gradually learn to trust her.

Looking at properties, she was always looking for a place in which Cath could have privacy, and one she she had seen just a week before the Antiques Fair looked a strong possibility.

One of the upstairs rooms had once been used as a bedsit and contained a small kitchen and a shower besides a single room which served as living room and bedroom. There were two other rooms besides, plus a larger kitchen and bathroom. Downstairs, behind the double-fronted shop was a store area and a yard with a building large enough to be used as a workroom for cleaning and painting and polishing.

In great excitement, Meriel arranged an appointment to see it after the fair ended at seven o'clock.

'You'll love it,' she told Cath. 'There's a complete bedsit, perfect for you if you want it one day. We can use it as an extra store until you're ready to move in, but I think you'll move sooner than you planned once you've seen it. There's even a view of the sea!'

With some trepidation they set up their stall. Meriel had sold her car and bought a transit van so they could transport the larger pieces and the marble-topped washstand with its pretty mirror and ornately carved drawers looked impressive as a centrepiece. They had several country chairs and stools and two dark oak bedside cupboards. They had chamber pots displayed in them as they stood with the doors open, to demonstrate their original purpose in the years before inside lavatories became commonplace.

Before lunchtime they had sold three tables, two stools and the two bedside cupboards. They were debating whether to accept a lower price on the marble-topped washstand when Cath announced she was hungry and went to find them some tea and sandwiches.

Meriel stood looking at the crowd, excited by being a part of this interesting business. She had begun to recognize some of the traders, and exchanged a few words with one standing near, when a man came up and asked the price of one of the rather primitive stools. They haggled amiably for a while and he eventually bought it. Writing out a cheque he asked,

'Will it be all right if I leave it here while I continue looking around? I might even have some lunch.'

Marking it with a 'sold' notice, and adding his name, Mike Thorpe, she chatted for a while before he left to examine the rest of the stalls.

It was while she and Cath were eating their snack that he returned. Cath had her back to him so she didn't see him until they were close.

'Cath?' he said curiously. 'Where have you been, we've all been desperately worried.'

To Meriel's alarm, Cath dropped her drink and shot off without a word. She ran from the room, followed by Mike Thorpe and, more slowly, by a frightened Meriel. Pushing her way through the arrivals they saw her heading for the van. Mike tried to head

153

her off but ignoring the no exit signs, she drove out through the entrance to avoid him, ignoring or unaware of the hooting of irate motorists and car park attendants.

'I hope she comes back,' Meriel said breathlessly. 'I don't think I could carry a washstand back to Abertrochi!'

'Is that where she lives?' Mike Thorpe asked.

Some caution stopped her answering. 'I don't think I should give you her address without her agreement,' she said.

'I understand. But will you take my address and give it to her? Her family are very worried about her.'

She took the card he handed to her and walked back. Worried about her friend as she was, the first worry was how to get home.

She returned to the stall to find one of the other stall holders clearing up the spilt tea and broken china. She didn't notice that Mike Thorpe had followed her.

'I'll wait if you like, I have a large car and I should be able to get most of this inside.'

'I don't want to lead you to Cath,' she said at once, aware of how ungrateful she sounded. She had already told him she lived in Abertrochi so there was nothing to lose. 'But, yes,' she added with a smile, 'I would be very grateful for your help. Thank you.'

'I don't wish her any harm,' Mike said as they struggled to get the last of the small furniture pieces into his car.

'I'm sure you don't, but Cath must have her reasons for not wanting to see you and as her friend, I have to respect them.'

'I'm her brother,' he said quietly. 'She ran away after a tragedy, about three years ago and we've never been able to find her.'

'What happened?' Meriel asked.

'Perhaps this is something on which I must remain silent. You're her friend, so if she hasn't told you, then perhaps I should respect her silence too?'

'Sorry,' she replied. 'I didn't mean to sound pompous. But Cath is so easily upset and she doesn't trust anyone. I said we're friends and I believe that. We're considering starting a business together but I don't feel secure about her working with me. I just hope that in time she will learn to accept my friendship. Whatever is bothering her, I have a feeling that it will be eased once she begins talking about it.'

'Some things are so painful that talking about them is rubbing salt into a wound.'

Mike chatted easily on the journey back to Abertrochi and, after helping Meriel to unload the furniture, agreed to stay for coffee.

In fact, Meriel had hoped he would refuse the automatic politeness. She wanted to go and find Cath.

'If Cathy doesn't re-emerge, give me a ring and I'll help with transport when I can,' he promised. She thanked him, although suspicious that he only wanted an excuse to call in the hope of finding Cath – or Cathy as he called her.

It was after nine o'clock before he finally left. She stood at the doorway watching as he turned the car and headed back to town. Waiting only a few minutes, she collected the dogs and a torch and set off on the long walk up to the chalet, where she expected to see the van and find Cath. It was time for some explanations.

It was dark when she reached the chalet and, although the others in the row were clearly occupied, and issuing the garish lights and discordant sounds of a television programme, the one at the end, tucked into the rock, was dark and silent. There was no sign of the van and, shining a torch through a window she had the impression that the place was more than unoccupied, it had that indescribable look of being abandoned.

Clothes were scattered across chairs, books had fallen to the floor, boxes that looked as if they had been partly filled with foodstuffs then forgotten, were on the couch, from which cushions and covers had been removed. Cath had gone.

Late that night, Jeremy couldn't sleep and in the eerie moonlight, he went out. Justin didn't hear him and for once he was glad to be alone. His mother's car was there but he ignored its tempting presence. Earlier that day he had heard his parents arguing about it, his mother accusing his father of using it without telling her. Best they forget their night-time rides for a while.

He walked to the cliff end and wandered along the path towards the house where Meriel lived. Not far from the path, a large shape loomed and, seeing the transit van he was curious. It hadn't crashed, it looked in good order, and as he leaned against it to look inside, he saw that the keys were swinging gently in the ignition. He opened the back. It was enormous, and empty apart from a few blankets folded and piled in one corner. Temptation was rising by the second. He didn't need Rupert to tell him when he could drive.

He hesitated, panic touching him and making him start as though to run back to home and safety. Had it been stolen? Would he be stopped and accused of the theft if he were seen? He could surely outrun any policeman? He knew the fields and paths better than most, they had been his playground since he could walk.

He turned on the engine and moved off. It was very different from driving the Fiat. The van, with its lack of windows made driving it seem as though he was being followed by a brick wall.

Reaching the Sewells' house, he left the engine running and threw some gravel up at Rupert's bedroom window. Aware of someone running towards him, he prepared to run but, just in time, recognized his brother.

'Why didn't you wake me,' Justin panted angrily.

The four boys drove along the quiet lanes, laughing, comparing their skills with those of the few other drivers they passed.

'Whose van is it?' Oliver asked.

'I think it belongs to Meriel, Mum's friend.' Justin said.

'Funny place to park it then,' Jeremy laughed.

Because the van was more of an adventure, they didn't take much notice of where they were driving, going down the narrow Gower lanes, further and further from home, stopping sometimes and changing places, taking it in turns to drive. It wasn't until the number of cars on the roads increased and dawn began to show over the horizon, that they began to panic about getting back in time to be back in bed before their parents missed them.

Taking a road they didn't know in the hope of a short cut was a mistake and when they came to a village they didn't recognize, their alarm increased. A detached house was showing lights and Oliver got out and asked for directions.

A woman answered the door with a little girl at her side, both dressed in night clothes. Before he could ask directions, a man appeared.

'What is it, darling?' he asked, picking up the little girl and hugging her. Then he recognized Oliver. 'What the hell are you doing here?' he demanded. 'Who told you about this place?'

156

'I – er – we're lost, Mr Morgan. We want to be put on the right road, that's all.' Oliver stared at Jeremy and Justin's father, with wide, startled eyes.

'Just get out of here and don't discuss this, d'you here? You don't understand and I have no intention of explaining it to you. Say nothing, are you clear about that?'

The child in his arms asked, 'What is it, Daddy?'

'Nothing to worry about, pet, let mummy get your breakfast, eh?' He handed the child back to the woman and, stepping out of the gate, gave brief directions on getting back on to the right road. If he had looked into the van, he would only have seen Rupert. His sons were cowering in the back.

When Oliver got into the van he was trembling. Justin was crying.

'My dad is leaving us,' he sobbed, 'He's living with another woman.'

'I didn't say definitely,' Jeremy said, also choked with misery, 'I only said it looked like it. Perhaps he broke down too and stopped to ask the way.'

They drove home, less worried about being caught and more worried about what they had discovered.

The house was filled with lights when Rupert and Oliver reached home and running up the stairs they saw with relief that their mother was just going into the bathroom. Forty minutes was the time she took, before emerging perfectly groomed.

The two boys showered together, arguing about the soap and the towels, and they quickly dressed. At intervals they told Marcus to 'Shut up!'

Although they had been out most of the night, they were too hyped up to feel tired. They were very hungry and ate a breakfast that pleased Millie, who insisted that a good hearty breakfast was the sure way to good health.

Leaving the van more or less where they had found it, Jeremy and Justin were in their beds as Joanne's alarm clock began to rouse her. They got up without being called, and ate their breakfast in silence. Justin was still trying to hold back sobs. They dared not say anything and both badly needed to be reassured.

Joanne seemed distracted and Jeremy whispered to Justin,

wondering if she knew and was hiding it from them. Justin was desperately trying to convince himself it hadn't happened. If he managed to forget it, perhaps everything would be all right, so he kicked his brother every time Jeremy tried to discuss it.

When the boys left for school, Joanne noticed how red Justin's eyes were. She watched him as he set off a long way behind Jeremy, kicking the ground, not wanting to leave, afraid that nothing would be the same when he returned.

'Justin? Is something wrong?' she asked and he shrugged his shoulders, lowered his head and hurried on to catch up with his brother.

'I hate Dad!' he called back.

'Come here, tell me what's wrong,' she called but Justin ran faster and soon he and Jeremy were too far away to hear her.

'I can't think what's upset Justin today,' she told her friends as they sat with their first cup of coffee. 'He was angry with John but wouldn't tell me why. They do get some funny ideas sometimes, don't they?'

'The twins were so tired this morning that they didn't look fit to go to school,' Cynthia said. 'I worry that they aren't getting enough sleep. I know they wake up sometimes in the night and talk and play games. I've even seen them slipping out of the house. I wondered whether they met Jeremy and Justin. What could they be doing?'

'Nonsense. When I tell Jeremy and Justin to go to bed they stay there!'

'Why don't you ask them for heaven's sake, Cynthia?' Vivienne asked. 'They're young to be wandering around at night, aren't they? I'm sure I'd want to know where Toby was if he started leaving the house at night, even at the age of fifteen.' The others exchanged looks of amusement. Vivienne was not the most anxious of mothers.

'Did the Antiques Fair do well?' Joanne asked Meriel, to change the subject.

'Yes, we sold a few items, covered our costs more or less, but Cath seems to have disappeared. Have any of you seen her?'

'What d'you mean, disappeared?' Helen said.

'She saw someone she knew while we were eating our lunch and she just ran off. I've been to the chalet several times and she has definitely gone. She took the van too and if it hadn't been for Mike Thorpe, I would have been stranded.'

'Who's Mike?' Joanne, Cynthia and Helen chorussed, sensing a budding romance.

Meriel explained that he was the man from whom Cath had run.

'Thank goodness I didn't trust her to look after Toby,' Vivienne said. 'It just shows that you can't tell what people are really like. Who'd have thought she'd behave like that?'

'You did ask her, remember, and she refused. You might have had a narrow escape there,' Helen said warningly. 'Perhaps you'll be a bit careful who you ask in future.'

'Definitely,' Vivienne agreed.

The others weren't surprised, however, when, as they were leaving, she was seen asking one of the girls serving at the counter if she would Toby-sit for the following Saturday evening.

Vivienne had a serious decision to make and dancing was a way of forgetting it for a while.

Joanne had arranged to meet Dai Collins that afternoon. She sat in her car in the lay-by as arranged but although she waited an hour, he didn't come. She wondered whether she had misunderstood. They met at so many different places she could easily have got it wrong. Driving slowly, still hoping to see him, she made her way to the Gingham Cafe where they had first met, and, opening the side door leading up to the rooms above, she went in. The place was the same as when she had last visited, but there were ornaments and some photographs on the room divider separating the dining area from the lounge. She picked one up idly and saw a pretty young woman. A sister perhaps? Then on another one the same girl was shown head to head with Dai, the expression on their faces no longer giving the impression of brother and sister. She shrugged. She couldn't expect him to have a past without women. She was married and hardly in a position to be jealous. But she was.

It hurt her to imagine him making love to another woman. He was in love with her and it was now, the present moment on which she should concentrate. He was going to take her away from her miserable life with John, he had said so many times. It was no longer just an affair, an arrangement that could end at any time. There was deep and mutually involving love.

She sat there for a while, wondering what had happened. Then her thoughts drifted to her sons and the odd behaviour of Justin that morning. John hadn't been home for three days, so what had he done to upset Justin? He hadn't forgotten a birthday or been unable to attend some event at school. She could think of nothing to explain Justin's anger.

A glance at her watch told her it was time she left. Going quietly down the stairs she went to where she had left the car and drove home. An affair could hardly be expected to continue without a few hiccups.

Justin was subdued as she prepared their meal. When Jeremy went upstairs to do his homework, she asked her younger son what had been the reason for his outburst that morning.

'Why are you angry with Daddy?' she asked, neatly dicing carrots and adding them to a pie filling with the meat and onions. 'He'll be home tonight and you can sort it out with him, whatever it is, can't you?'

'I don't want to talk to him. I won't talk to him.' Tears threatened, and he turned away to follow his brother.

'Justin.' Joanne caught hold of him. 'Tell me what this is all about, now, at once.'

'He's leaving us for that fat woman and her kid,' he shouted and, pulling free of her, he ran up the stairs.

Joanne called them both down and, sulkily, they stood before her, Jeremy holding Justin's arm and squeezing it as a warning to say nothing more.

'What is all this?'

'Nothing!' The lips came forward in a pout and the stubborn, closed down expression warned her that little would be achieved at that moment.

'Homework,' she said firmly, 'Then I'll talk to you one at a time. Right?'

A car pulled up outside and she looked up in relief. John was early and he could take over the inquisition since he appeared to be the cause of the problem.

She explained briefly that the boys were in a funny mood and seemed to blame him.

'What's the matter?' he demanded irritably when she had called the boys down once more.

'That woman and that girl!' Justin shouted, struggling to be free of Jeremy's painful grip. 'You're leaving us for them and we'll be a one parent family. That's what.'

'What woman? What are you talking about?' Then he guessed that the van on that previous evening hadn't contained just Oliver and Rupert Sewell. 'Were you two joyriding last night when you should have been in bed?' he demanded. He turned to Joanne and said angrily. 'What are you doing that you can let these boys wander about at night in someone else's van? I stayed with Dai Collins and his wife last night and presumably, these two saw me. That's what happened. They saw me with Dai's wife and daughter. Are you incapable of looking after two boys while I go out and earn our keep?'

'Dai Collins and his wife?' she said, trying to control her voice. This couldn't be true.

'I went to the door when those irresponsible boys of Cynthia's knocked to ask for directions. These two must have been in the van with them. Where were *you*? How could they wander about under age, driving a van at that time of the morning without you knowing? You must be more stupid than I thought!'

He turned to sit at the table. 'I'll let you sort this out. Any further details you want can wait until we've eaten, or do I have to go out and find myself a takeaway?'

'Oh, do what you want!' Joanne snapped. 'Do what you damned well want.'

John didn't stay and as soon as he had driven off, Joanne turned to the boys and asked them to explain the night time excursion in someone's van.

Taking a lead from Jeremy, Justin supported the story that it was a once only event and they had been persuaded into it by Oliver and Rupert. Joanne sat looking at them in silence for a long time while they squirmed and wondered how long they would have to manage without pocket money.

Then she surprised them by offering no punishment. She hugged them both, told them they were wonderful boys and she loved them dearly.

'Weird,' Jeremy whispered when they went upstairs to their rooms. 'Seriously weird.'

Eleven

When Christian opened his post one morning, he looked ashen.

'Darling? What is it?' Cynthia asked.

'We've lost the contract to build the houses. And,' he threw a letter across the table at her, 'there's little chance of us selling this house.'

She read the letter with growing alarm. The estate agents advised that, until the problem of suspected subsidence had been dealt with, they would not attempt to sell the property. It was politely worded, but the meaning was clear. They had an unsaleable house on their hands.

'What will you do?' Cynthia asked.

'I've been in touch with a civil engineer, not the one we usually deal with but a different firm, one from outside the area.'

'You think there's something odd about all this?'

'Someone seemed to have made sure I didn't get that contract.'

'You can't mean it. Who would do that?'

'It's a valuable deal. In all there'll be seven very large, high quality houses, within an enclosing wall. Three in the first stage then four more. It's a damned good contract and there aren't that many builders able to do the job, apart from the real big boys. And the specialist work involved means most of *them* wouldn't be able to take it on. I have those specialists. Oh yes,' he went on bitterly, 'those who wanted this contract wouldn't hesitate to deal in dirty tricks to get it.'

'And you think one of your rivals is discrediting you?'

'I can't think of any other explanation. When we built these houses, we followed every guideline to the letter, I put down footings far stronger than the regulations require. There's no way a building like this can subside. The ground was checked thoroughly by both my people and the council before building permission was granted.'

'I'll phone Ken. You need to discuss this.'

'*No!*' he shouted as she reached for the phone. 'Not Ken. I don't want to talk this over with anyone until I've made my own investigations.'

Cynthia stared at him. 'Not Ken? You can't think he's involved? You and Ken built this business. You've been partners from the beginning when you built that tiny bungalow together and we lived in a caravan until you were paid. We weren't even married then, d'you remember? We ran from our families and started living our own lives, and Ken was our friend. Please don't let it be Ken.'

'Say nothing. Pretend you haven't heard any of the rumours. I'll get on to this today.'

Christian spent much of that morning on the phone. When Ken rang with a query, he made an excuse not to see him and he said nothing about the damage to the house. They had discussed it previously and debated on the possible cause but he didn't want to discuss it further, he didn't even want to see Ken until he had some facts.

Cynthia didn't go out. She did some paperwork and arranged meetings with the committee of one of her charities but she couldn't really concentrate. The thought that someone was trying to destroy them filled her mind like a bubble, expanding, tightening, becoming more painful as the day went on.

The agony didn't stop. The surveyor inspected the property but explained that nothing could be done until the following morning and even then, it might be a week before a full report came through.

The surveyor had tried to be reassuring but his expression was grave. Christian waved him off and ran in to tell Cynthia.

'Nothing official until the results of all the technical stuff comes through, but he agrees it might be deliberate and misleading damage. It's possible someone removed the tiles from the side of the steps, dug out some soil below the concrete and probably put something weighty on it. He wouldn't have needed to do anything more.'

'But who? And what about the cracked tiles?'

'That wouldn't be difficult with a bit of care and a hammer! We were in Greece when it happened, remember? Millie was visiting her sister. Ken had the keys to the house. If he is as short of money as I suspect, he had motive and opportunity. Isn't that the suspicious combination?'

'Not Ken. I don't believe it.'

'Like me, you don't want to believe it. But if not Ken, then who?'

'And the holes in the field? They have happened over the past weeks. Were they made deliberately too?'

'We'll have to wait for the results before we know the answer to that one.'

She looked thoughtful. 'Could this be anything to do with that old cave, or water pipe or whatever it is, that the boys once explored? It's a long way from these houses but it must pass under the field, it comes out through the rocks above the beach?'

He stood up suddenly, a positive expression on his weather-beaten face. 'I don't know, my darling girl, but I'm damned well going to have a look.'

'No, Christian! Please don't. It isn't safe. If there is subsidence it could go at any time. Be sensible and wait for the report.'

'I have to know, love. I have to know now.'

He took a camera belonging to Oliver, a couple of powerful torches and some extra batteries. Wearing a waterproof suit, and with a coil of rope across his shoulder, he set off with Cynthia watching the clock and promising to raise the alarm if more than forty minutes passed without seeing him safely returned. He knew that if he did meet trouble, forty minutes would be too long, but giving her something to do, helped her to cope with the danger he faced.

Walking into the blackness was daunting and he almost turned back. He wasn't even sure what evidence he was looking for as he shone the strong beam of light around the narrow entry.

He tied the nylon rope to a rock near the entrance, and returning the coil of it to his shoulder, released it as he walked. A flimsy enough precaution but there was little else he could do to ensure his safety.

There were remnants of the old pipe, rusted and misshapen, embedded in the wet soil, and he could see a trickle of water down the sides, settling in the centre of the floor and slowly making a way to the entrance.

In some places the tunnel was lined with a solid mass of rock with wet, gleaming surfaces showing in the wandering beam of his torch. In other spots there was gravel and soil forming a slide, with some larger pieces of rock showing between the patches of reddish soil.

After a minute or so he came upon a fall of soil that alarmed him by its size, containing rocks from very large down to small gravel, and soft, damp earth. It had fallen in an ever widening slide. He passed it, forcing himself to ignore how easily he could become entombed. Then he saw another, mostly soil, and he stood trying to imagine where he was in relation to the surface above. Was he in the area where the mysterious hole had appeared? He looked for evidence that someone had damaged the roof and caused the fall but everything looked natural, no marks of a tool, no footprints on the freshly fallen soil.

He was more nervous after he passed the falls of earth imagining their suffocating embrace, and when he saw another and then a fourth, he decided to make his way back. Before he did so, he looked with greater thoroughness at the area around the fall of soil and spotted a metal bar almost hidden by the gravelly soil.

He wrenched at it to pull it free but soil fell like heavy rain all around him burying his feet and ankles in seconds. He stumbled towards the entrance but stopped and went back. He had to be thorough; he didn't want to do this again.

He waited until the soil stopped slipping, his heart racing with the reminder of how easily he could be buried alive, then, with extreme caution, he scraped the soil from around the metal bar, disturbing it as little as possible. Pulling the bar free, he saw that it was a scaffolding pole. There was no sign of deterioration. It was shiny and very new. He stared at it as though asking for its explanation of how it got there.

Looking up he could just make out one or two indentations where the pole had been used to poke at the roof, encouraging the already friable gravel and clay mixture to cave in. He also saw marks that were clearly made by a spade, neat cuts as though someone had stood there and stretched up to bring down some of the roof. More soil fell as he stood there and he took a few photographs, hoping they would be clear enough for the marks to be seen before another, more serious fall destroyed the evidence.

165

As he turned in relief and headed back to the entrance, he wondered cynically whether a member of the council or a surveyor could be persuaded to do what he had done, and go down to look at it. He thought not. He stopped and took more photographs, marking the rope as a primitive measure of the distance from the adit on the cliff.

When he emerged into the startlingly bright sun, he heard Cynthia call. Looking up to the cliff path he saw her waving at him and pointing at her watch.

'Five minutes to go on the longest forty minutes of my life!' she said, tearful with relief.

There had been no sign of Cath since she had run from the Antiques Fair but Meriel found the van parked near her house. She was relieved. She was due to work that morning for Tom and Ray and she didn't fancy walking. She inspected the van looking for damage but found none. Opening the back doors she saw that it was completely empty. Even the blankets which she and Cath used to protect their cargoes were gone. She did find a used contraceptive thrown carelessly aside and wondered whether a couple had taken the opportunity the vehicle offered of a comfortable place to make love.

Without really understanding why, she went to the house and, carrying a bucket of soapy water and trailing a hosepipe, she washed the van thoroughly. After phoning to tell Tom that she would be late, she drove it to a garage and filled it with petrol.

Before starting work on Tom and Ray's garden, already late, she detoured and went to the chalet to see if Cath had returned. The place was deserted, the desolate emptiness more marked than before. She was aware of a deep sense of sadness.

Cath had returned at some time, though. Or she had been burgled. Much of the furniture was gone, including the pieces on which she was working in preparation for selling.

When she stepped through the back gate of the house on Holly Oak Lane she was startled to hear raised voices. Tom and Ray were quarrelling, she thought, as the voices rose higher, ceasing suddenly as a door was violently slammed.

She knocked with some trepidation, just to let them know she was there, determined to pretend she had just arrived and had heard nothing. To her surprise it was Vivienne who opened

166

the door for her. 'Hi yer,' she said casually, before dragging an obviously upset Toby down the garden and out of the gate without another word.

Meriel went to the shed and took out the hoe with which she intended to do some weeding. She worked in silence for an hour, then Tom came out and handed her a cup of coffee. He carried a second one and sat beside her to drink it.

'Ray has left,' he said.

'Oh well, it's probably nothing more than a wrong word at a wrong time. Quarrels are often only opinions spoken at an inopportune moment.'

'More than that,' Tom said. 'He and I – well, you've probably heard the gossip, Ray and I are partners. We've been living together since we were twenty-two.'

Meriel didn't know what to say. Then she remembered the hasty departure of Vivienne. 'Was a friendship with Vivienne the cause of the trouble? I don't think jealousy is the prerogative of mixed couples, is it? We can all suffer from insecurity.'

'My parents don't know. They think Ray and I are simply friends who share a house and live separate lives.'

Meriel's thoughts were different from how she imagined. No embarrassment, only sympathy. 'It must be difficult to tell people the truth, specially those you care about. "Coming out" doesn't affect only the person making the statement. Like any decision, there are always others to consider. Perhaps one day, you'll know they're ready to accept who you really are.'

'It's far easier to pretend,' he said sadly.

He talked about their life together for a while, reminiscing about past holidays, and the fun of buying the house and furnishing it, then he stood up and offered her his hand. She took it, somewhat bemused, half expecting him to tell her he no longer required her to work for him. Instead he said, 'Thank you for listening and understanding, Meriel. I'm very grateful.'

'Any time you need a listener, call me,' she said, and meant it. 'Losing someone you love is very painful.'

She was thoughtful on the way home and when the phone rang later she expected it to be Tom. But it was Mike, Cath's brother, and he wanted to know whether she had any news of his missing sister.

'Sorry, but she seems to have gone right away. The place

where she was living has been emptied of her things. Even the furniture she was working on has gone. I'm worried but I don't know what I can do. I have no idea where to look for her.'

'I have a few ideas,' Mike told her. 'If you don't mind, we could compare notes and try to out-guess her.'

'She's so secretive, I don't have a clue where to start.'

'She might be on a camping site. She's done that before, mingled with the holiday-makers, using a tent.'

'Like looking for a needle in a hundred haystacks!'

'The holiday season is nearly over,' he comforted.

'Fifty haystacks?' she teased

'Shall we talk about it? What about dinner tonight?'

Meriel felt a warmth flood through her. Meeting him again was a pleasant prospect. Then foolishly, Evan sprang into her mind, bringing an overwhelming feeling of guilt. It was as though he were still her husband, and she was being disloyal. The fleeting hesitation made Mike add, 'Just a drink if you prefer?'

Pulling her thoughts back from the abyss of unwanted loyalty, she replied, 'Dinner would be wonderful. Thank you.'

Mike had guessed correctly. Cath had taken her old car and was travelling around camp sites using a tent. She felt safe, the chances of meeting someone who would recognize her were very slight and besides, she would be miles away before they could tell anyone. She avoided becoming involved with the entertainments offered on some sites, staying most of the time on farms, sometimes the only person staying in a field in some of the more remote places.

She didn't stay long anywhere and remained in her tent whenever possible, shopping in the towns and wandering around second-hand shops and antique shops – the only clue for someone attempting to follow her. But no one would. She knew the police wouldn't get involved with searching for someone who had chosen to disappear and was not in any obvious danger.

She was surprised at how lonely she felt. After wandering around for months before settling in Abertrochi, she had begun to enjoy the growing friendship with Meriel. It was harder than she had imagined to go back to a solitary, wandering existence.

Several times she started to dial Meriel's number but always replaced the receiver before the number was complete. She would have to wait until Mike had given up hope of finding her. Autumn and early winter would be spent travelling, and only when the frosts and winds made her present way of life impossible, only then would she feel safe enough to contact Meriel and perhaps talk about her private nightmares.

Joanne was trying to contact Dai Collins. She had spent several nights and days trying to think of a reason for his not telling her about his wife. It must be that they were divorced. Otherwise, why would he not have been seen by the boys when they had inadvertently knocked on his door? That led her to another worrying thought. If Dai no longer lived with his wife and daughter, then what was John doing there at night? No, the explanation must be simpler. The boys had made a mistake. Exhausted with trying to fathom out the truth – or a version of the truth that would be comfortable for her to live with, she set about once more trying to contact Dai. If she couldn't reach him by phone, then she would sit outside one of his cafes until he turned up.

She tried each of his cafes several times, and after the third try to reach him at his office, and being fobbed off by an office girl, she knew she must face the fact that he was avoiding her.

Before, when she had phoned, even if he was not available, he would phone her back within a few minutes. She was being given the brush-off, no doubt about it. An end to the affair was something she had prepared herself for in the early days. Over the more recent weeks she had gradually accepted that this was for real, and her future was with Dai Collins, a partnership made in heaven. Now, his leaving her without a word, ending it so unkindly, so casually, distressed her more than she had expected.

This had been a promise of a real romance, being loved by someone who would appreciate her and want to spend every moment with her, not someone who would stay with an estranged wife only a few miles from Abertrochi rather than spend the evening and the night with her.

She felt ugly, and old and foolish. Two men had told her they loved her, and neither really cared. She wouldn't again wait outside one of his cafes like an abandoned dog no one

169

wanted. She had more dignity than that. She drove home hardly aware of how she got there, and reached the bedroom before she succumbed to tears.

Mike Thorpe called for Meriel as arranged at seven and took her to a restaurant close to the sea. He said very little until they had ordered and then said, 'I don't think I would be breaking a trust if I told you some of Cathy's story.'

'She's a very private person. I don't know whether she would approve of my knowing things she hadn't told me herself,' Meriel replied doubtfully.

'You know nothing? She didn't tell you about the children?'

'I guessed children were involved. I've seen her hugging dolls and other toys, and she became very angry once when she thought our friend Vivienne was neglectful of her three year old, Toby.'

'She went out, leaving the children with a neighbour, a young girl called Sylvia. Sylvia went back home to collect a video she wanted to watch and while she was out, a fire started. They think it was an electrical fault. A worn flex on an old lamp Cath had bought at a car boot sale. She always loved old things.'

'And the children?' Meriel asked, a pulse beating furiously in her throat as she waited for the words she dreaded to hear.

'Megan aged three and Gareth aged just six months, were suffocated.'

Meriel felt an icy cold chill envelope her, imagining Cath's home-coming and having to face the fate of her babies. How could she have survived the tragedy, the horror of such cruel deaths? It was enough to send a person insane. 'How do you live with such a tragedy?' she muttered. 'She clearly blames herself and there aren't any words that would help comfort her.'

'It wasn't her fault.'

'How can she not take responsibility for it? I can't imagine anyone not blaming themselves, even though they had done what was necessary to ensure the children's safety. Not to be there, out on some errand and coming home to that. I don't know how she manages to function at all.' Meriel whispered sadly.

'She didn't for a while. She was treated for shock but she

signed herself out of hospital and just disappeared. No one heard from her. Her husband, Bryan, was left to grieve alone. I find that hardest to accept, that she left him to deal with everything.'

'Where is he now?'

'Waiting at home for news of her. Every holiday, every day off work, he spends searching. Me too whenever I can.'

'I suppose the need to run is an attempt to forget it, but I don't suppose she'll start to recover until she stops, turns around and faces it, will she?'

'That's what we all think, but we can't find her to talk about it. Please, if you do hear from her, will you tell me? I only have her interests at heart. Bryan doesn't blame her. He was out too, celebrating someone's birthday. Not important as you say, a trivial reason for leaving two precious children in the care of a young inexperienced girl.'

'I haven't any children, but I don't think there's a woman alive who wouldn't sympathize with Cath and Bryan.'

Mike took her home after the meal and she invited him in for a coffee. Leaving the painful subject of his sister, they talked about themselves, with Meriel explaining her plans for opening a shop. 'I'm going ahead with it, but I'm disappointed not to have Cath with me,' she told him. 'We work together so well.'

Mike worked for a telephone company and hesitantly offered to go with her when she looked at properties if she needed a second opinion. 'I know that knowledge of telephone systems isn't an advantage when looking at properties,' he laughed, 'but sometimes a second input helps.'

'There is one place I am interested in and one of the reasons I like it is because it has a small bedsit which might suit Cath, when she comes back.' Taking out the details they talked about it for a while and agreed to go and look at it the following weekend.

'And if I hear from Cath I'll call you,' Meriel promised. 'I can't promise to let you know where she is, that will be up to her, but at least I can tell you she is safe.'

He stood up to go and leaning forward, placed a kiss on her cheek, near her lips.

'Thank you for letting me talk about it,' he said. 'You've no idea how it helps. My parents can't discuss it any more, it's too painful.'

'Any time,' Meriel said, 'If you want to talk about it, just phone me, I'll always be here to listen.' Suddenly remembering how she had promised the same to Tom, she smiled.

'I said something funny?' he asked.

'No, Mike, I did.'

Cynthia was looking thoughtful when Meriel arrived at Churchill's Garden. She was sitting alone and had a half empty cup of coffee in front of her.

'If that's cold, can I get you another one?' Meriel asked. She was about to order when Joanne and Helen arrived, closely followed by Vivienne. Adding to the order, they made their way to the table, Meriel glancing towards the chair they now called Cath's seat. It was occupied by an elderly man.

'No news of Cath then?' Helen said as they shuffled chairs to make room around the table.

Thinking that the reappearance of Cath's brother was hardly a secret, Meriel said, 'Her brother called to see me yesterday. In fact, he took me out for a meal last night, hoping that I had some information that would help him find her.'

'Nice, is he?' Vivienne asked, her eyes widening with interest. 'About time you had some fun, Meriel.'

'He was charming, but he only wanted to ask about his sister,' Meriel smiled. But deep inside her there was a jerk of pleasure as she remembered that gentle kiss.

'You couldn't help him?' Helen looked quizzically at her. 'If anyone could guess where she went, and why, then it's you.'

'I've no idea where she went. She did leave the van, though, so that's a relief. It was parked not far from my back gate on the field.' She leaned towards them and added, 'I suspect that a courting couple made use of it before I found it, so I gave it a really good scrub.'

'You look a bit distracted, Cynthia,' Helen said. 'Anything wrong? How is the sale of the house going, any prospects?'

'Not yet,' Cynthia said brightly. 'It's in the top bracket and there aren't many buyers around at that price level. We have to be patient.'

When Helen went to buy more coffee, and Vivienne went to help carry it, Cynthia said to Meriel and Joanne, 'Confidentially, I am worried. Christian thinks someone is trying to destroy us. Not a word to Helen, mind. We don't want gossip spread all over the county!'

It was on the tip of Meriel's tongue to offer to talk to her if it would help but she stopped the words from escaping. She was beginning to act like an agony aunt, someone without a life, needing the problems of others to fill in her empty hours.

Parked in a lay-by, wondering whether she would ever have the nerve to go back to Abertrochi, Cath watched the moon riding the night sky. It was late. Far too late to find somewhere to spend the night. The lane was quiet, on the outskirts of a village and with little prospect of being disturbed, she settled to sleep in the Saab. A not unusual occurrence.

She had hardly closed her eyes, hugging the thick blanket around her, when she heard the sound of a car approaching. It was moving slowly and she shrank down.

The car was a small one and it stopped just in front of her own. Three boys got out, one urinated in the hedge, the others laughing at some unheard joke. Another boy got out and helped a girl to alight. She crouched down near the hedge, while the boys made silly remarks. It was as they clambered back in, arguing about who would drive that she recognized Cynthia's oldest boys with Joanne's two sons, and the girl, her face just visible in the moonlight, was Helen's daughter Henri.

Cath's first reaction was anger that their parents didn't take greater care, but then her face softened to sadness. Everyone took chances, parents and their children. She did many stupid and potentially dangerous things when she was young. Danger and risks were part of life. Most survived unscathed, but for her, on that terrible day, luck had turned away from her.

Christian's investigations were leading nowhere. He didn't believe children, especially his own, were responsible. His thoughts turned reluctantly to Ken. But why would Ken try to harm the firm that gave him a generous income? They'd known each other all their lives. They had built the business together by hard work and determination. How could he think for a moment that Ken would want to ruin it? Because there was no one else. He had to make some effort to get to the truth, so he tried to look at Ken as though he were a stranger.

173

They were no longer close, sharing so many hours together as they once had, both at work and socially. With the death of Ken's wife, there had come a divergence of their paths. He and Cynthia had become a part of the local scene, always going out to theatres, dances, clubs, dinner parties. They involved themselves in fund raising. Christian was a governor of the boys' school. He played golf.

Ken had given up those things. He went to the local pub and played darts, visits to the racetrack being his only treat. Yet he lived as a lodger with no visible evidence of the wealth he must have accumulated. He insisted he couldn't afford to visit his daughters in America. A worm of unease wriggled in Christian's stomach. Something didn't add up.

Then he realized that much of Ken's money must have been spent keeping his sick mother in a comfortable home. That would explain it, he thought with relief.

Ken was very loath for Christian to visit the house where he now lived. With his two daughters grown up and living in America, it had seemed sensible for him to sell his house and move into a B and B accomodation. He had implied at the time that the money from the sale of his home had been invested for his daughters. No one had ever questioned that.

He always made an excuse for Christian not to call for him, even when they were going off together in the camper van. He insisted on meeting Christian at a crossroads some distance from the house, explaining that his landlady was strict and didn't encourage callers, adding that she was elderly and set in her ways and that visitors bothered her. Always too busy to think about it over much, or think it unusual, Christian had never seen where his partner now lived.

He hadn't seen Ken's mother for many years and for a long time had rarely questioned that. Now, he began to wonder if Mrs Morris was a greater part of the mystery. Perhaps she had run up debts or needed expensive medical treatment that was keeping Ken short of money? His head ached trying to make sense of it.

Restless, and desperate to solve the mystery, he phoned Ken that morning and, when he couldn't reach him, he decided it couldn't wait and drove to the last address at which Ken's mother had lived.

No one knew of her there. He knocked at several of the

smart houses but she had been gone too long for anyone to have news of her. He was about to give up when he saw a corner shop and stopped to buy some chocolate. Without much hope he asked the elderly lady serving him about Mrs Morris and was told the address to which she had moved.

He checked the address he'd been given three times, not believing the directions when they led him to a small, neglected property set back from the road on the edge of town. He knocked on the door, convinced he had been mistakenly sent to another Ken Morris. A woman of about seventy opened the door. Neatly dressed and with a brightness about her, he was convinced he was in the wrong place. This attractive woman was not the shy, nervous individual Ken had described.

'I'm sorry, I've come to the wrong door. I was looking for news of a Mrs Morris but you aren't the person I was expecting to see.'

He was stepping away from the door when the woman smiled and said, 'Christian? Don't you remember me? I remember you very well, even if you are too grand to ever visit me these days. Many's the plate of bread and jam you've had at my kitchen table years ago.'

'Mrs Morris? Ken's mother? But I don't understand!'

'Come in and I'll make us a cup of tea. Good heavens I can't think how many years have passed since you came to see me. Cynthia well, is she? And you have three wonderful boys, so Ken tells me.' She chattered on as she led him through the dark passageway and into a small, rather overfilled room looking on to a long narrow garden.

'I didn't come – we didn't come – because Ken told us you were ill, and then said you didn't like visitors.'

'Don't like visitors? Why, the house is always full of them. Neighbours calling and leaving the children while they go shopping, coming for a chat, and for help with their knitting or cooking. Grannie Morris to them all I am. Me, ill? I never have a moment to think about being ill.'

She went through the room to the small kitchen and talked to him while she prepared a tray of tea. Her voice with its gentle, sing-song Welsh lilt brought tears to his eyes with its touching reminder of his childhood when he used to go to her house to escape from the misery of his own. He only half listened to what she was saying. He looked around the shabby room and wondered why Ken allowed himself and his mother to live in such a place. What had made them move from the attractive house they had owned, to come here and live like this?

The room was spotlessly clean but everything was worn and colourless. There was linoleum on the floor covered in places with rugs. The curtains at the window were thin and misshapen with too many washes. The wallpaper was falling away from the wall in one corner where damp had penetrated. The chairs were wooden, the cushions neatly covered with material which, like the curtains, was well washed and faded.

Curiously, he stepped towards the kitchen door and saw more of the same. A belfast sink, a wooden draining board, oddments of shelves and mismatched cupboards. The cooker was ancient, there was oilcloth covering the wooden table. A mop and bucket stood near the back door still steaming, Mrs Morris had obviously been washing the stone floor when he had knocked. What looked like a wooden box stood on its end, partly concealed by a curtain, inside it were stacks of soaps and powders and other cleaning materials.

'Why are you living in a place like this?' he asked softly as Mrs Morris placed the lid on the teapot, turned and saw him standing in the doorway.

'It's only temporary, Christian. Ken wants to design and build a house with a flat on the side for me, a grannie flat but for a grannie with no grandchildren. Why did the girls have to go to America to live, eh? Did you know one of them is a teacher?' she went on, 'And her husband is—'

Refusing to allow her to change the subject, Christian interrupted and asked again. 'Why aren't you living in a decent home? Ken can't be short of money. We're partners, equal partners, and Cynthia, the boys and I don't live like this. Far from it. Is he gambling more than I know about?'

'Gambling? No, no, not really. Just now and then, a bit of excitement.' She poured tea and offered him a plate and a serviette and gestured for him to help himself from the plate of home-made cakes.

'What's going on? I only want to help,' he said.

'Have a welsh cake,' she said. 'Or what about a piece of bread pudding, dear? That used to be your favourite.'

Refusing to be put off, Christian put down his plate and

stared at her. 'Please, tell me what's going on. I'm not the enemy, I want to help – if it's needed.'

'All right then, he had a bit of bad luck, made some foolish investments. Ill-advised he was and him so trusting of everyone.'

'How long ago? This place looks as though it's been like this for years. You should be living somewhere modern and comfortable. Please, Mrs Morris, what's going on?'

He was having bad thoughts about the attempts to discredit him. If Ken was in serious trouble, might he have succumbed to the temptation of having debts paid? He wouldn't be the first to give in to such pressures. Ken did gamble, he didn't hide the fact, but perhaps he had been hiding from him just how deeply he was addicted. It wouldn't be difficult to get into this state if he kept increasing his stake in the hope of solving his problems. More importantly, having reached this state, he was vulnerable to a bit of persuasion.

Something else clicked into place to add to his growing fears that Ken was the one responsible for his problems. A man, who his sons believed was Ken, ran from them when they called after him one day. They said the man who they were all convinced was Uncle Ken, had climbed up from the beach not far from the tunnel. Presumably it was the same man who knocked Meriel over a few minutes later and didn't stop.

'Ken has been saving to go to America,' Mrs Morris said, interrupting his unpleasant thoughts. She lifted the cake plate and coaxed him to eat something.

'About time he went to see his daughters,' Christian said. 'I've been telling him for years.'

'He's paying for me to go too,' she said. 'I can't wait to see them, lovely girls that they are. Never been on a plane, mind, I'm a bit anxious about that, but better than a long trip by sea. More time to spend with them, isn't it?'

When Christian discussed his thoughts later that evening, with his wife, Cynthia didn't believe him.

'You can't think that Ken would do something like this? He's a partner in the firm, he'd lose everything too. It doesn't make sense.'

'From what I've seen today, I don't think there's anything

left *to* lose. I think he's gambled everything away. If he's in debt to some of the clubs then he'll probably be desperate enough to do whatever they ask and if that means creating a situation where I appear to be a dishonest builder, and lose this important contract, then I'm afraid he'd agree.'

'I didn't know his mother had simply moved. Why did Ken tell us she was mentally ill and in a home?'

'Why indeed,' Christian said ominously.

'The poor dear lady. And all these years she thought we didn't care.'

'The house she owned was a good between the wars semi, wasn't it?'

'Yes. So why did she end up in a place like you describe?'

'That's something I didn't feel able to ask.'

'Surely Ken hasn't robbed her of her home?'

'What other explanation can there be?'

Cynthia went to Churchill's Garden and put on a brave face, insisting that everything was wonderful, 'Christian is building some fabulous houses,' she told the others proudly. 'He's such a remarkable man. Someone tried to embarrass us you know, but it's all sorted. Christian has a reputation that can't be tarnished. Jealousy and greed made someone try to discredit him but it didn't work.'

'You aren't selling because of the subsidence?' Vivienne asked doubtfully.

'There is no subsidence. Someone tried to make it look like there was but the buildings Christian puts up are built to last.'

'Evan and Sophie Hopkins have put their house on the market,' Vivienne insisted.

'I think that's because she wants to move far away from me,' Meriel said. 'She still doesn't feel secure with him. And he doesn't help, constantly calling to see what I'm up to!'

'And what are you up to, Meriel?' Joanne asked. 'Anything interesting?'

'Well, I have seen Cath's brother Mike, a few times. He's rather nice, but whether it will be anything more than a mutual concern for Cath, I'm not quite sure.'

'I do find it odd that she isn't in touch with her family,' Helen frowned. 'Fancy running away from her brother like that. Quarrels and fights happen in most relationships, but with family, you usually fight to the bitter end, get all your anger out and sizzling, then get back to normal. I couldn't bear to lose my sisters or brother.'

Meriel hadn't mentioned Cath's husband, or the tragedy of the lost children.

'I can understand why she might avoid him. I haven't seen my sister Samantha since I married John,' Joanne reminded them. 'She and I fell for the same man, and the vindictive way she tried to keep him, well, I don't want her back in my life, even after all these years.'

'She must have changed. She's probably married now and any feelings she had for John will have been forgotten. I'd have to seek her out,' Helen insisted.

'I've managed without Samantha in my life for so long I hardly ever think of her,' Joanne smiled airily. 'And I doubt if Samantha ever thinks of me. Best we leave it like that.' She turned to Helen to change the subject. 'Are your children staying with you at present?'

'Only Henri. She loves coming, but her stepmother tells me I spoil her. Give her too many treats. She has put on a bit of weight, mind, but teenagers often do, don't they?'

'Of course. I was plump when I was fifteen,' Cynthia said. 'My darling Aunt Marigold who brought me up after Mummy died, used to say it was the bloom of youth and gave a promise of beauty.'

'As long as it isn't the wrong kind of weight,' Joanne said warningly. She was shocked when Helen stared at her, the colour draining from her face.

Twelve

Helen thought about Joanne's flippant remark about the weight her daughter, Henri, was showing and the more she thought, the more clear it became. Henri, not quite sixteen, was pregnant. Henri's listlessness and her occasional dislike of certain foods, the sickness. Why hadn't she recognized the signs before this?

Her hand trembled as she drew the telephone towards her and began to dial her ex-husband's number. She wasn't necessarily to blame, she comforted herself. Henri wasn't here for very much of the time and she must have boyfriends near her home. Yes, this has to be down to Gareth and his new wife. They were responsible for not taking proper care of her daughter.

The phone rang and rang and Helen wondered whether Gareth's wife had recognized her number on the display panel and was refusing to pick up the phone. She allowed it to continue to ring. She had to let Gareth know her suspicions. Gareth and his new wife couldn't blame her. She only saw Henri when they allowed a weekend visit. It was at home that there would be a regular boyfriend. She had almost convinced herself the fault lay with her ex-husband and his new wife when the telephone was picked up and a voice said coldly, 'Helen?'

'I hope you know that Henri is unwell?' Helen said. 'She was sick a few times and I think you need to get her to a doctor, fast!'

'What are you saying?' the cold voice asked. 'Are you suggesting we don't look after your daughter properly?'

'I think she should see a doctor, that's all.' Her suspicions were no more than that. How could she tell this woman that she suspected that her daughter was carrying a child? Lots of teenagers put on weight. It was the age of weight problems.

The age when girls blossomed and panicked and became paranoid about overeating. Everyone knew that. She muttered a repeat of her words and replaced the receiver.

She mentioned it to Reggie when he came home from work and all day she worried about it. If she was right and Henri was pregnant, then the sooner she saw a doctor the better. Her ex-husband called at the flat that evening.

'Come in, Gareth,' she said, unable to hide her pleasure and relief.

'I gather you're worried about Henri,' he said after the social politenesses. 'Any particular reason? She seems fine to us.'

'She was sick and a bit lethargic,' Helen said.

'She's fifteen, they grow so fast they often suffer from tiredness and a bit of awkwardness.'

'You've noticed her putting on weight?' Helen said, twisting her handkerchief in her hands.

'Normal for a fifteen year old I'd say. Hardly a reason to panic,' Gareth replied.

'You don't think—' she hesitated then, after glancing at Reggie and acknowledging his nod of encouragement, she went on, 'You don't think she's expecting, do you?'

'What? Don't be ridiculous, Helen! She's fifteen!'

'Sixteen in a few weeks.'

'All right, sixteen, but what you're thinking is crazy. She's a tomboy, not some slinky siren chasing boys instead of doing her homework!'

'She spends a lot of time with the Sewell boys while she's here. And Joanne's two. I'd say she likes the company of boys.'

'Yes, she does, but only for the fun of more adventurous games than her girlfriends prefer. I repeat, Henri is a tomboy, not a girl to play adult games.'

'I'm not asking you to believe me, I'm asking you to check. Get her to a doctor.'

'I'll talk to her first.'

'Let me know what happens, will you?'

'I certainly will. It's apparent that if she is in this sort of trouble, then it's happened while she's been with you!'

Meriel and Mike met often, sometimes to go to the cinema or

a meal but they occasionally preferred to stay at Meriel's house and walk the dogs before cooking supper together and talking. After a while the talk and growing attraction led them to bed.

The first time they went upstairs together, Meriel didn't close the curtains or put on the light. Mike put it down to shyness and told her so. But she knew it was that niggling guilt, that ridiculous fancy that she was still married to Evan that made her want to keep her growing attraction to Mike a secret. Realizing what she was doing, the next time she switched off the downstairs lights and walked with him, hand in hand, up the staircase, turned on the lights in her bedroom and welcomed him into her room and her heart with joy.

One Saturday morning that autumn when they were walking along the beach with the dogs, they noticed a lot of activity around the area where water once flowed out of the land-drain pipe. It was a wet morning; a drizzly rain darkening the air and making the scenery gloomy. Uniformed men were gathered around the adit, men in protective clothing, bright against the grey rocks. Some were crouched on the rocks above it and as they grew closer, they heard and then saw a small digger in the field. Policemen, firemen, first aiders, and there were several men in smart suits and hard hats carrying the inevitable clip board to show they were in charge.

There were swarms of children milling about and several adults trying to persuade them to stay out of the way. Cynthia and Christian were there with their boys and Joanne's two.

'What's happening?' she called up to Cynthia, and Cynthia beckoned, inviting them up. With Mike's unnecessary but welcome help, Meriel made her way up to join them, climbing across the rocks to where Cynthia was standing on the cliff path. 'What's happening?' she repeated, breathlessly.

'There's been an attempt to discredit Christian by making it look as though there's been some subsidence. We reported it to the authorities. They're down there now trying to decide on the best way of making that tunnel safe. It's about time it was filled in. Children go in there, I've had to warn our boys about it. It's a miracle no one has been killed.'

'They're going to open it up from above if they can and then fill it,' Christian said as he approached them. He held out a hand to Mike and they were introduced.

182

'It isn't level soil below the surface. There are areas of solid rock down there so it will be difficult to open it up,' Christian went on. 'They're doing a survey to decide if they can get at the soil between the rocky parts. They want to make sure it's solidly packed.'

'Where does it lead?' Mike wanted to know and Christian and he went to examine where the surveyors had marked out the route of the underground watercourse. An attempt had been made many years before to drain the land and control the stream, but after meeting rocks and finding the stream was too widely dispersed, and too far away from where it found its access on to the beach, the scheme had been abandoned.

'It doesn't go anywhere near the houses,' Mike said when they returned. 'No wonder you were suspicious. Do they know who was responsible?'

Christian and Cynthia exchanged glances but Christian shook his head. 'Suspicions but no proof so we can't say.'

They walked back to the Sewells' house, stripped off their cagoules and wellingtons and went into the porch, where Christian explained about the attempt to make it appear that the house suffered from subsidence.

Millie brought them coffee and home-made biscuits. Christian explained about the lost contract and they discussed it for a while. Then Meriel asked, 'Where's Ken? I thought he'd be here to see what's happening. He must be as disappointed as you at losing that valuable contract.'

'Oh, he is,' Cynthia said, and there was something in the tone of her voice that made Meriel look at her and frown.

'Ken isn't involved in the business any more,' Christian said shortly. Meriel said nothing, it was not her business and from the expression on Cynthia's and Christian's faces it was something they didn't want to discuss.

Avoiding the activity around the entrance to the old pipe, Meriel and Mike walked back to the cliff path and headed for the next bay. The path was filled with people coming to see what was happening near the estate of expensive houses. Several stopped them and asked what they knew but Meriel, following Mike's lead, simply said, 'We don't know, we haven't been that far.'

Going down on to the sand once more they started to make their way back, the dogs exploring the pools and the small

183

cave-like structures in the rocks along the shore, oblivious of the rain which was increasing in ferocity. Above them in the distance, the path was still filled with people; the weather didn't deter the inquisitive. The brightly coloured weather-proofs added a little cheer to a miserable day.

Before they returned to the area where the men were working and half of Abertrochi was gathered, the sound of voices and the hum of machinery reached them. They were past the spot where the stream fell out of the rocks in its new place, almost directly in front of Evan and Sophie's small semi, which was situated between the large grounds of Cynthia's house and the home of Joanne and John Morgan. A large quantity of soil had come down with the water and was spreading across the beach, discolouring the sand with red soil and a great deal of gravel.

'It seems to me that it's here they should be investigating,' Mike said curiously, stopping to look.

'I'm sure they will, but their priority now is to make sure the area around the old drain is safe.'

'Is it always like this?' Mike asked, staring at the steady flow of water.

'I don't remember it before last year. It was then that water coming through the old pipe slowed to a dribble. I suppose the underground stream must have found an easier route. It's certainly much faster than usual. I wonder what happened to reroute the stream?'

'Perhaps building Sewell's houses changed things. They might have blocked the stream in some way and caused it to find another way out to the sea.'

'I doubt it. Wouldn't a survey have picked up on that?'

'Not if it was deep underground and it had changed route before the survey for that phase of building took place. Christian told me the landward side of the estate was built first.'

Christian was still there when they passed below the scene and they called up to him.

'What about the stream further down, is that going to be investigated too?'

'Probably,' he called back, 'But they don't think there's any danger. There's plenty of rock below the soil, a good foundation. Solid as a rock, eh?' he joked. But he wasn't laughing.

* * *

184

Dolly's baby was born, Joanne was informed by John and she sent a small gift. The baby talk spread to Churchill's Garden where Helen told her friends that her suspicions were confirmed and Henri was expected to have her baby early next year.

'Henri refuses to consider adoption,' Helen said, 'And I'm glad about that. But she also refused to tell us the name of the father.' Helen didn't add anything further. It was too difficult. She met Cynthia's gaze and they both looked away, unusually agreeing not to talk about their recent painful confrontation. For, after exhausting discussions that ended with Henri and Helen in tears, Gareth had decided that the father must be either Rupert or Oliver.

'You're joking!' Henri had laughed. 'They aren't interested in anything but cars.' Taking her adamant and sneering response as proof that she was covering up the Sewells' involvement, Gareth, Helen and Reggie had gone to see Cynthia.

Cynthia was shocked but remembering how much time the young people spent together, she said nothing. She had gone up to the boys and asked them to come down.

'This is very embarrassing for us all,' she began, 'But it seems that Henri is pregnant. Do either of you know anything about this?'

The twins stared at each other, a half grin on their faces, which was part shock part embarrasment, but which Helen took for guilt. A long discussion followed during which the boys both denied having exchanged more than a kiss with Henri. Threatening to involve the police, reminding them that their daughter was underage, Helen and her two husbands left and Cynthia faced her sons.

'Honestly Mummy, we haven't done – that – with Henri or anyone else.'

'Do you know who did?' she asked, hugging them to assure them they were believed.

They shook their heads. 'No idea. It must be someone she knows from school. She isn't here that often, is she? Just on visits to her real mum.'

Joanne hadn't seen Dai for weeks, until she opened her door one evening in November just after seeing the boys off to the cinema with the Sewells, to see him standing there, soaking wet and asking for her to spare him a few minutes to explain.

'I've been waiting for the boys to leave,' he said.

'You'd better come in,' she said formally. She stood in the hall, watching water dripping from his clothes on to the wooden floor, refusing to do anything to remotely suggest she was pleased to see him.

'I had a visit from John,' he said, taking off his hat and looking around vaguely for somewhere to place it. Joanne said nothing and made no attempt to help him so he shook it against the doormat and put it back on his head.

'He told me to stay away from you,' he said. 'He found out about us meeting and, well, he warned me off. I'm sorry I did it in such a cowardly way, Joanne my darling, but I am old-fashioned enough to accept a husband's warning.'

'Nothing to do with your wife and daughter?' she asked primly.

'My wife and daughter? *My* wife and daughter?' he said. 'I don't have a wife and I certainly don't have a daughter.'

'My boys were driving, I mean, er, out with friends, one evening a couple of months ago and they called at a house to ask directions. My husband was there and he told me that the woman and the little girl were yours. Why deny it? I can hardly complain about you being married when I'm married too. I do complain about your not telling me.'

'Joanne, I am not married and I never have been.'

Her mind went blank, she didn't know what to say and couldn't formulate another question.

'Can we talk about it? I want to see you, but if you and John are happily married and you were exaggerating your difficulties, well, I want to know.'

'I didn't lie to you,' she said finally.

'I didn't lie either, so who has?'

'I think you'd better go, I don't think we have anything to say to each other.'

'I hoped we had. I saw John the other day, and something he said made me think he'd been wrong to tell me to stay away. I thought you knew – I mean, I thought you and he had decided to part. I was wrong and I'm sorry I came.'

Joanne had the strongest feeling that something was not being said. A question was being formed, but just then he moved his head and a stream of water poured noisily out of his hat brim to drum on the floor. Forgetting the question, she began to laugh. 'I can at least provide you with some dry clothes,' she said.

They went upstairs and she handed him some trousers and a sweater and he came out of the bathroom wearing them. The sleeves reached hardly to his elbows, the trousers ended halfway up his calf. The fly was stretched open as wide as it could go. 'A shade too small, don't you think?'

Helpless with laughter, she helped him undress and gathered his clothes ready to put into the tumble drier.

'Later,' he said, removing the last item of clothing. 'Much later.'

The For Sale board outside Evan and Sophie's house had gone. Cynthia and Christian had joyfully taken their property off the market and as winter set in, life returned to its normal pattern. Cynthia boasted about her husband's integrity whenever an opportunity presented itself, Joanne admitted that she had a lover and that life was truly wonderful, Meriel quietly admitted that for her, the arrival of Mike, Cath's brother, had added to her happiness. Vivienne was spending a lot of time with Tom, now Ray had gone for good, and she said that having a devoted 'uncle' was making Toby a very happy child. It was only Helen who was brave enough to admit that life for her was not perfect.

'Henri went for a check up yesterday,' she said one morning. 'I went and of course Gareth's new wife went too. She was so domineering, insisting she was the one to be told what was happening and I came out feeling like an interfering nuisance of an aunt. She's my daughter for heaven's sake!'

'How does Gareth feel about it? Doesn't he share this with you?' Joanne asked.

'He tries, but he's soon out-gunned. "I have responsibility for the girl on a daily basis so I have to deal with this", she keeps telling him.'

'Has she found out who the father is?' Meriel asked.

Helen shook her head. 'Henri still refuses to say.'

Cath had rented a holiday chalet for a couple of months. She couldn't settle or consider it a home. One of the neighbours was extremely inquisitive, and was constantly calling for a 'chat' which was a euphemism for a grilling.

The chalet had two bedrooms but Cath lived and slept in the small living-room-cum-kitchen, using the rest of the small place as storage for the furniture and oddments she had bought.

She had some larger pieces which she was painting, some with flowers, some with seascapes and some for children. The latter were difficult at first. She kept picturing her own babies, imagining how they would have looked if she could see them now, counting their ages in years, months and days and hours, half planning the birthday parties they would never see.

Gradually it became less painful. Guilt softening into sadness. The pictures became more colourful and happy. It had been a kind of therapy.

Ken no longer worked for Christian Sewell. He had not admitted he was responsible but by no longer working with Christian any more, seemed to be indicating at least an involvement in the affair. Stubbornly he refused to talk about things, and managed to evade Christian, but one day, Christian managed to find and confront him.

'Just tell me why you did it,' he pleaded. 'I want to understand why you did this to me. I could have lost everything, the house, the business, I'd have been back where we started, only without you to give me the strength to start over again. Why?'

'I want the partnership dissolved but I don't want to take out my investment,' Ken said, repeating the words with which he responded to every question session. 'I want you to treat me as an investor, a sleeping partner if you wish.'

'Tell me why, Ken. I need to know. You owe me that, surely?'

'All right. I tried to ruin your chance of that contract, and I was well paid,' he said. 'But don't quote me. You have no proof and I'll sue you for slander if you say a word to anyone. Right?'

'I have no intention of accusing you,' Christian said sadly. 'Like brothers we've been. We've been friends since we were first able to walk and I toddled into your house for a bit of love and comfort from your Mam. How could I accuse you?'

'I'm going to America in the spring.'

'Your mother is going too, I understand.'

'She told you that? When did you see her?'

'I called when I was trying to get in touch with you after the subsidence scare.'

'I told you not to call.'

'Didn't want me to see what you've done to her?'

'I got into difficulties and she sold the house and bought a cheaper one to help me out.'

'She's looking forward to going to see her granddaughters.'

'She isn't coming. I'm going alone and I'll probably stay there, if I can get work.'

Outrage filled Christian at the way Ken was behaving, but he waited until he had calmed down then said quietly, 'I'll see she's all right. Cynthia and I will take care of her.'

'Thanks,' Ken muttered.

'She was good to me when I was a scruffy little sod living off scraps and wearing other people's cast-offs.'

'She deserved a better son than me.'

'Yes,' Christian agreed. 'She did that.'

Christian saw very little of Ken after that confession, but he wrote to try and rescue the lost contract. In the letter he gave details of what had been done to convince the authorities that he had built on unsafe ground. He also enclosed the findings of the survey of the field about the water-weakened cave. If they accepted his story he would be safe. If they did not, then no one else would trust him either and he was finished. He wrote to Ken following up the suggestion of a legal end to their partnership but received no reply. Where Ken went Christian didn't know but he was never seen in any of his usual haunts. Letters addressed to his mother's house were unanswered and neither were they returned. Needing him to sign some papers and sort out pensions, Christian even called on the various bookies and clubs where he had regularly spent his time and money and asked for news of him. No one had seen him.

Christian hadn't gone back to see Mrs Morris. He felt ashamed of his long absence even though it had been at Ken's request. How could he explain to Ken's mother what had happened?

'Why don't we both go and see his mother again? If he hasn't answered any letters, and they haven't been returned, she must be sending them on. She'll tell you where he is, won't she?' Cynthia suggested.

'You'll come with me?' Christian asked.

'Of course.'

'We'll have to avoid being too specific when we explain why we have lost touch. Somehow, though, I have the feeling she's guessed, from the little I said before I understood, and I don't think she'll ask.'

He had told Cynthia something of Mrs Morris's situation but she was not prepared for the state of the place where she was living. He parked the car and allowed her time to take in the depressing state of the house, far worse than its neighbours.

'Why has Ken been living like this? He was a partner and had the same income as us,' she whispered.

'Ready to go inside?' he asked, giving her a hug. 'Try not to show your dismay, love. She's proud, and refuses to believe that her son has failed her so badly.'

'What does she think we've done to him? He must have blamed us.'

'No, she thinks he made some bad investments, a bit close to the truth really, he invested in horses and gambling clubs, didn't he?'

Cynthia tried not to look around her as a delighted Mrs Morris invited them in. She kept her eyes on the smiling face of Ken's mother and marvelled at her air of contentment.

'Don't look at the place, darling girl,' the elderly lady smiled as she went into the kitchen to prepare tea. 'My Ken is so full of ideas but he's so busy. But he'll be starting on the work here very soon.'

'Let me know how I can help,' Christian said. 'Where is he by the way? I have some papers he needs to look at. You do know he and I have dissolved our partnership, don't you?'

'Fool that he is,' Mrs Morris sighed, placing a tray of tea and cakes on the table. 'He told me he needs a rest and didn't want to leave you without help, so he decided to leave the firm and allow you to find someone else to share your worries. Said he's had enough of running a business.' She stared at Christian, her blue eyes sharp and intelligent and wanting an answer as she asked, 'What's the real story, Christian? What sort of trouble is he in? He is in trouble, isn't he?'

'No, of course not.' Cynthia added her voice to Christian's and the chorus, so prompt, sounded as false as the denial was untrue.

'I see. You aren't going to tell me. But I know something

isn't right. The police have been here twice asking for his address. I don't know where he is, but I do know something is wrong.'

'Nonsense. It's probably to do with a parking fine or something.' Christian looked at Cynthia and said, 'The reason we're here is because he left some money for you. A new kitchen he said.'

'Thank you, Christian love, but don't try to lie to me. I know you too well, even though you are grown up and living in a posh house. Remember when you broke that vase and you told me the cat had knocked it off?'

'Too high for the cat, wasn't it?' Christian grinned.

'Not too high for a catapult! So no fairy stories about Ken leaving money for me, right?'

'I would like to fit a kitchen for you though. You're so fond of cooking it seems a shame you don't have a modern place to work. I often get one cheap, so is it all right if I send a couple of lads down to fix it for you?'

'Say it's for past debts, including that vase!' Cynthia laughed.

'It is hard to say no to a proper kitchen—' Mrs Morris smiled, her eyes shining, as though she were imagining the transformation.

Shortly after, Mrs Morris had more unexpected visitors, including a policeman whom she had seen before. This time it wasn't to question her son Ken; he asked for permission to look in her house and garden.

'What for?' she asked, reaching automatically for the kettle.

'I can't really say, Mrs Morris, it's just that we'd like to question your son, Kenneth Morris and he's nowhere to be found. You haven't spoken to him since we last met?'

'Not a word. I told you, he was very tired and needed a rest. He's probably gone to an hotel for a break. Nothing sinister I'm sure, he just needed a rest. As soon as he gets in touch I'll get him to ring you.'

'And you don't mind us looking in his room?'

'Come in and welcome,' she said. 'Cup of tea? Coffee? How many of you today?'

'There are three of us and coffee would be very welcome, thank you.'

She showed them her son's room, then, while the kettle

boiled, she watched through the kitchen window as one of the men, using a stick, lifted nettles and other weeds and looked underneath them. She saw him pick up a spade and place it into a plastic sack.

'What are you taking my spade for?' she laughed. 'I'm not suspected of burying treasure, am I?'

The man walked towards her and asked, 'Is this yours, Mrs Morris?' He opened the sack for her to look inside.

She shook her head, frowning. 'No, that isn't mine, it's too big. I use a border fork and spade, small and easy for me to manage they are, a matching pair. You'll find them both in the shed if you look. I couldn't use one that size,' she laughed. 'I wonder where it came from?'

Christian came later that day with a kitchen fitter, to measure up for the units they would need and to discuss ideas with Mrs Morris.

'The police were here earlier,' she told Christian. 'Funny thing, they took away a spade they found among the nettles. It wasn't mine. Why would they want a spade, d'you think?'

'Mrs Morris, is there any way that I can reach Ken? Or leave a message for him? Do you know of any place where he sometimes goes for a night or two? Someone he visits maybe? Please,' he said as he saw her hesitate. 'It is important.'

'Well, I'm not certain, Christian love, but I suspect he's got a woman friend somewhere on Gower. I've overheard a couple of phone calls that ended sudden like, and there was a letter once that he snatched away off the table as if afraid I'd see it. Not that he's normally shy about telling me of his conquests mind,' she smiled.

'And you don't know where she lives?'

'No, but I think I know where they meet. I found an address once when I took his jacket to the cleaners. It was a receipt for a couple of nights in an hotel, called Sea Haven.'

Leaving his men to discuss plans for her kitchen, Christian drove down the coast and knocked on the door of the small hotel called Sea Haven.

Cath had grown tired of wandering. She had settled for a while in a small town near Tenby, and had found work as a cleaner, work she hated but which was anonymous and brought sufficient money for her simple needs. Now, with the darkest days of winter upon her, she missed Meriel and the strange comfort she had found on the periphery of the group at Churchill's Garden.

She gathered the coins she would need and dialled Meriel's number. She was surprised when a man answered and at first she thought it must be Evan, but the man who asked, 'Do you want Meriel?' was her brother, Mike. She was about to replace the receiver when the man added, 'I'll call her, what name is it?'

'A friend,' she replied. 'If she's busy—' She waited until Meriel announced herself then said, 'What's Mike doing there, Meriel?'

'Cath! How marvellous to hear from you,' Meriel said and Cath could hear the smile in her friend's voice. 'Where are you? When can I see you? Oh, it's such a relief to know you're all right.' She laughed then and said more slowly. 'Sorry, I'm not giving you a chance to speak, am I?'

'I want to come back to Abertrochi. But I don't know whether I'm ready to meet Mike.'

Mike had been listening, his head touching Meriel's and he now spoke into the phone. 'It's all right, Cathy. I promise I'll stay away until you and Meriel have talked. No one wants to rush you.'

'Where can we meet?' Meriel asked. 'Will you come here?'

'I'll drive up tonight. I have a few ends to tie up first,' Cath said. 'I'll be late, will it matter?'

'I'll be here, looking forward to seeing you. Oh, what a relief, I've missed you so much, Cath.'

'We all have,' Mike added, as the call was cut off by Cath, to hide the sound of her tears.

It had been a very wet summer and autumn and now, as winter was here, the weather worsened. There had already been several severe storms, uprooting trees, one had even blocked the road near the Sewells' house. The night Christian decided to go looking for Ken there was a 'Serious Weather' warning, and people were advised to stay in their homes. The tide was expected to be high but Christian was determined to go.

There were several hotels called Sea Haven, but Christian's guess regarding the whereabouts of Ken Morris was correct.

He was staying at the first hotel he tried. Ken was out when he arrived so he sat in the small bar, drinking coffee and wondering how long he dare wait. The weather was worsening, and he didn't want to be on the roads once darkness fell.

He telephoned Cynthia to make sure the three boys were safely inside.

'They wanted to go over to see Jeremy and Justin but I advised them to stay put,' Cynthia said. 'I want us all to be safely locked indoors tonight. Hurry, darling. Leave what you're doing and come home.'

Christian decided to leave a message for Ken and go home. Ken was in danger, but he could warn him just as easily by note and phone as by sitting here listening to the storm increase in fury. If he waited much longer, he might have to stay overnight. It was really hazardous to drive along tree-lined lanes through this, he thought, looking out at the swaying trees in the hotel garden, and imagining how much worse it would be on the coast beyond the town.

Ken and his companion came in as he was writing the note, laughing companionably, both windblown and dressed in outdoor clothes that suggested long country walks. Corduroys and heavy walking boots and good quality jackets with hoods.

'I'll go to my room, Ken,' the woman said. 'Come up when you've finished and we'll decide where we'll eat tonight.'

Christian had the impression they were good friends and nothing more. He felt a fleeting embarrassment for spoiling their evening but once the woman had closed the door behind her, his anger returned.

'Did you use that spade to pull down some of the soil in that tunnel?' he demanded after telling Ken about the police taking a spade away from his mother's house. When Ken hesitated, he said irritably, 'Come on, Ken. This isn't a time to be evasive. If you did, then I hope you cleaned it of your fingerprints!'

'Yes, I used it, but I didn't clean off my fingerprints. It was one I use occasionally, it would be odd *not* to have my fingerprints on it.'

'Of course it wouldn't! If someone borrowed it that's what they would have done!'

'I did clean off all the soil that came from the tunnel though.'

'Fat chance of that! They only need the faintest smear and

they've got you!'

'What shall I do?'

'Face it and plead ignorance. They can't prove it was you who used the spade in the tunnel, can they?'

'I can't face it. I'll disappear for a while, see how things go. After all, it isn't a hanging offence. What could they charge me with, malicious waste of police time? An attempt to make a hole in a field I half own?'

'You'll never get a job after this, but staying and denying everything is the only way to deal with it.'

'I'm leaving.'

'What about your mother? What do I tell her?'

'Tell her what you like!'

'You're a fool!'

'I can't deny that.'

Not wanting to waste any more time, Christian left. Why had he come? Only a distorted sense of loyalty. Now he no longer cared what decision Ken made, he had warned him and that, after what he had tried to do, was where their friendship ended.

Meriel was on her own. Mike had gone, leaving her to welcome Cath when she arrived. As she looked out of the window at the dark night, and listened to the horrifying sounds of the storm, Meriel wished he had stayed. There was something she wanted to tell him and the interruption of Cath's phone call had prevented it. She glanced at the phone. Perhaps she could tell him now. But then, she wouldn't see his face, and know his true reaction.

She hesitated a while longer, sitting alone, listening to the howling wind and the occasional clatter as something was dislodged by its fury. Then she dialled his number and said at once, 'Mike, I think I'm pregnant.'

'But, Meriel,' there was that tell-tale hesitation before he went on, 'That's wonderful.'

'Is it? You really think so?' Her heart raced as she waited for his reply.

'Darling Meriel. I couldn't be more thrilled. Honestly.'

There was a draught as the back door opened and she thought it was Cath, as she had left the door unlocked so she could walk straight in. 'I think it's due some time next July. I don't know whether I'm pleased or scared. My having a baby, it's

195

unbelievable. You are pleased, Mike?'

'Darling girl, I'm breathless! Can I come back so we can celebrate?'

'Get off that phone!' Meriel turned her head to see Evan standing there, white-faced, water dripping from his clothes, fury greater than that of the storm gleaming in his eyes.

'I'll talk to you later, when Cath is here,' she told Mike, sounding calm, but with her heart beating furiously within her. She listened for a moment then said, 'It's all right, it's only my ex. Come to see if the house is safe I expect. Bye, darling. Yes, see you very soon.'

'You bitch!'

'Please go. This is nothing to do with you. *I* am nothing to do with you. I'm selling the house and then I'll be out of your life for good.'

'Who is he, this Mike? A casual pick-up is he? First there's Tom, where you go and pretend you're working in his garden, and now Mike. How many more?'

'I've lost count,' she said flippantly.

She walked towards the back door that faced the cliffs and the sea, and as she opened it to tell him to leave, it was snatched from her hand by the gust of wind and banged against the wall. Glass shattered and Evan ran to pull her away from the danger.

'I'll get something from the shed to make a temporary repair,' he said. Ducking down to dive through the storm, he quickly disappeared, swallowed up in the wild blackness. Meriel collected a dustpan and brush and began to collect the shards of glass from the floor. He reappeared carrying a piece of hardboard, which he intended to tack over the hole.

'It won't fit properly, but it should hold until the morning,' he said.

She helped, first by holding the board in place, then by passing him nails, and all the time the wind threatened to burst through the house and out on the other side. They were both breathless when they finally closed the door.

'You'd better get back to Sophie,' Meriel said, aware that he was staring at her and waiting for the outburst that was hovering around the tight lips and angry eyes. Also aware that, in spite of carrying another man's child, she still loved him. But was it love? Or was it the need to win against the voluptuous Sophie Hopkins? Remembering Mike's voice, knowing he was waiting for her call before hurrying back to her, she felt the disappointment and pain of Evan's rejection of her fly away on the howling wind. She knew that, at last, she was free.

'I came to see if you were all right,' he said. 'But I needn't have bothered, you have plenty of men to look after you.'

'Plenty,' she said. 'Thank you for fixing the door, but please go.'

'How did we get like this, Meriel? We had such dreams, a beautiful house, a couple of children and "happy ever after".'

'Sophie happened,' she said harshly. 'You left me for her, remember?'

She turned away so didn't see him leave. He held on to the door as he opened and closed it, the noise of the storm was too loud for her to hear his footsteps walking away. And besides, she wasn't listening.

Thirteen

Cath was driving through the storm becoming more and more frightened. Trees were swaying threateningly and on two occasions she thought her way was going to be blocked as a branch dropped touching the side of the car. The sound of the engine obliterated much of the noise but when she opened her window to check her route the moaning of the wind filled her ears and made her wish she hadn't started on her journey.

Taking her mind off the dangers she faced being on the road in such weather she turned her mind to Meriel. Was she too late to become Meriel's partner in the business they discussed? She hadn't shown herself to be reliable, running away as she had, leaving Meriel to find a way of getting the goods home when the fair ended.

Meriel was very kind and they were obviously friends, but would she resist her pleas for understanding after this? She accepted the reality of it and knew that if Meriel had doubts she could hardly complain. It had been her own fault, her own inability to cope.

She would have to face meeting her brother, Mike, and then her husband, Bryan. Poor Bryan. How could she have treated him so badly? She had shown no understanding towards him when their children had died, so how could she expect understanding from him, or Mike or Meriel for that matter? She was so busy berating herself that she lost concentration for a moment and didn't see the huge tree that had fallen across the lane.

She clamped down both feet on the pedals, feeling the bite of the safety belt across her chest. The squeal of the brakes seemed to go on for ever. Leaves on the smaller branches covered the bonnet of the Saab and the miraculously intact windscreen before she stopped.

* * *

Sophie had the lights off and was looking through the window wondering where Evan had gone and when he would be back. She had foolishly offered to look after Toby, while Vivienne went out with friends and he was crying, and wouldn't be comforted. Not that she had tried very hard. So he was frightened of the storm? So what, there was nothing she could do about it. She put him into bed and let him cry, covering her ears when his wailing penetrated the sound of the storm.

Irritably, Sophie looked at the clock, squinting at the dial in the darkness. She couldn't see and that irritated her more but she didn't switch on the light, she hoped that with continuing darkness, Toby would eventually sleep. It must soon be time for Vivienne to collect him? And where was Evan? Impatient, bothered by the little boy's distress which she had no idea how to deal with, she grabbed a coat ready to go out. Evan was sure to be with Meriel, she decided with growing anger.

She was aware of a low moaning sound and to add to her alarm a window cracked and broke. Slivers of glass tinkled down on to the floor and the wind burst through the house. Pictures fell from the walls, shelves slithered to the floor. The staircase twisted with a fearful groan and banisters popped out and threw themselves across the hall like champagne corks. The whole building was out of true, up was no longer up, and the house seemed to shudder before slipping sideways.

She started up the stairs to fetch Toby but her nerve gave out as the house shook under the onslaught of a violent blast of wind. She ran to the door but it wouldn't open. Screaming she tried the door at the side which resisted but finally gave way and she almost fell from the house. She ran away from the shelter of the damaged building where the wind buffeted her, throwing her playfully against a wall. Leaving Toby in the bedroom, she ran across the field to find Evan.

The sound which began as a low murmur increased until the air around her seemed to be a part of it, making her stop and crouch on the ground, afraid but with no idea of what. The sound became a roar and filled her ears so she couldn't think. When it slowed, then built up again as loudly as before she knew she had to run. But when she stood up and looked about her, everything was dark and she had lost her sense of direction. She tried to go back to the house, guessing by the direction of the terrifyingly powerful wind, which way to turn, but the ground in front of her had disappeared, she was on the edge of a gaping hole. Screaming but with no hope of being heard, she ran first one way then another, until she recognized the path leading to the drive of Meriel's house, from where she could hear the barking of the two dogs.

Meriel was standing listening to the furious storm when there was a loud banging on the back door. Thinking that this time it had to be Cath, she ran to open it, thankful that the hardboard had remained in place. It was Evan.

'What are you doing back?' she demanded ungraciously.

'Come and listen to this,' he said.

In the distance, fearful in the darkness and the fury of the storm, there came a sound like thunder. But it didn't stop, it went on and on, so loud that it was clearly heard above the wind that lashed the trees around them.

'I don't think that was thunder,' he said.

'What can it be?'

'I don't know. Perhaps lightning struck a building?'

'It sounded more like a dozen buildings.' Then she added in alarm. 'Evan, what about Sophie? It's coming from the direction of your house!'

'And Joanne's and Cynthia's. Could this talk about subsidence have been real?' He turned to go inside. 'I'll have to phone to see if Sophie is all right.'

'I'll phone Joanne.' Then she added. 'You first.'

The door swung wildly as they re-entered the kitchen and the bottom panel dropped, making it difficult to close it. They were panting when they finally made it secure.

The telephone produced no reply. 'The lines might be down,' she said. Not knowing what else to do, she pulled on an anorak and prepared to follow Evan out into the night.

'No,' he said firmly. 'You wait here. There's no point in us both walking into danger.'

The night was torn with the sound of distant sirens approaching and, as they stood undecided, they saw the flashing lights coming along the roads from several directions.

'Police, fire and ambulance. I have to go!' Evan tightened his jacket around him when someone appeared at the door which was being held open with difficulty, by Meriel.

200

'Cath?' Meriel said, as the figure loomed out of the darkness. But it was Sophie.

'The house,' she shouted. 'Come quickly. The western side of the field has collapsed!'

'Where's Toby?' Meriel demanded.

'I was just about to leave the house to look for you,' Sophie sobbed, ignoring Meriel's question. 'Then everything went wild.'

'Where's Toby?' Meriel shouted.

'The house has fallen sideways and Toby is upstairs,' she sobbed, 'And you'd left me on my own.' Afraid to admit that she had been too scared to go up the damaged staircase to rescue him she went on, 'I came to fetch you, before going with him to find Vivienne, I didn't want you to be worried by finding the house damaged and me not there.'

Meriel didn't wait to hear any more. She squeezed her way past them, pushing unnecessarily hard against the cowardly woman, and ran, almost oblivious of the gale, across the field to the houses on the cliff.

Sophie tried to stop Evan from following her. 'Stay with *me*. Why is she always your first concern!'

'Out of my way you selfish bitch!' In a frenzy, Evan ran into the violence of the night calling for Meriel, pleading with her to wait.

The storm was at its height and when Meriel and Evan reached the cliff path they were soaked several times by the waves crashing abnormally high. In a panic, worried for the little boy alone in a damaged house, they ran on.

Cath was walking. At first she tried to look for danger from falling branches but soon realized it was impossible to see clearly enough to save herself from anything in the darkness. She walked as fast as she could, heading for the houses on the cliffs. On the far side of the estate was Meriel's house and to her that was sanctuary. Then she saw the flames.

Memories came flooding back. The fire, her children dead, then running and running and running. Now she pulled her thoughts away from that tragedy with difficulty and wished she had a mobile phone.

A car approached, and she flattened herself against the hedge, wishing she had chosen the ditch on the other side. The lane was narrow at this point and gave very little room for a car to pass.

Ken was driving too fast. He was unable to see much of the road ahead, but hoped that there wouldn't be anyone about on such a night. The headlights shone on the startled face of Cath and he turned the wheel too far and ended with the front wheels in the ditch.

He got out prepared to shout at the figure still standing against the hedge, but seeing her face and aware that the fault had been his own, he asked instead if she was all right.

'You won't be able to move that without help.'

Switching on a torch he had taken from the car, he shrugged and replied, 'This won't be the only road blocked tonight. Where are you heading?'

'I'm trying to get to Meriel Parry's.'

'I'll walk you there. I won't be going anywhere tonight. Not in this,' he said looking at his car, tilted at an angle, front wheels in the ditch.

Bending low against the wind, they linked arms for strength and pushed past the car and continued along the lane. Stopping for a rest when a heavy shower made walking difficult, she said quietly, 'I've been running away, and tonight I decided to come back and face it all. What a night to choose, eh? I wish I'd waited a while longer.'

Ken turned his head to peer at her in the gloom. He said nothing for a moment, then said slowly, 'That's what I was doing, running away, but perhaps in my case the storm helped. I know now that running away won't solve anything.' They continued on, linked like friends, Cath to face Meriel and Mike and her husband Bryan, Ken to face Christian and Cynthia, and the police, but nothing more was said.

During that walk through the wildness and danger of the storm, clutching the arm of a woman he did not know, Ken made his decision. He wouldn't run away. He had to face the people he had tried to destroy. At least that way there was a time in the future when he would be free, having taken his punishment. To start again was sobering but he had a feeling that Christian wouldn't completely abandon him. One day he would get everything sorted and be able to hold his head high.

Meriel and Evan reached the pair of semis and saw that Sophie had not exaggerated. Both properties were damaged but rescue teams had arrived incredibly quickly. In the glow of floodlights, with shadows of rescue workers adding their eerie presence to the scene, Meriel ran panting to one of the policemen and asked about Toby.

'Toby who, madam?' he asked. 'We have only two names for this property, an Evan Parry and a Sophie Hopkins.'

'Toby Robertson is in there! He's three and was being looked after by Sophie!' She tried to push past him but he held her back.

'You're mistaken, Miss. The place has been searched and there's no one there. No,' he added firmly as Meriel tried to pull away from him, 'You can't go in there I'm afraid.'

'I have to! Toby is there I tell you. He must have hidden in fright when this happened.'

Still holding her firmly, the policeman called to someone and told them to search through the building again. 'This time,' he added, 'Look in every place big enough to hide a mouse. There's a child missing.'

The shout about a missing child passed around the rescue workers and investigators and a team went in to search with greater care but they came out shaking their heads.

'There's a camp-bed in the back with the covers thrown back as though someone has just got out of it, but no sign of the child.'

Henri had called to see Rupert and Oliver and Marcus earlier that evening and, without telling Cynthia, who might have been worried, the twins had set off to walk her home. Marcus, listening to the howling wind that was increasing in ferocity, lay in his bed watching television, thankful that they had refused his request to go with them.

He heard the telephone and listened as his mother spoke to his father but didn't take notice of what was being said. He hoped his father would be home soon, though. It sounded dangerous out there. Then he heard his mother shouting and realized that their conversation had been inexplicably ended. Then the lights and his television went off. The sudden darkness and loss of sound was alarming and he ran down to see his mother.

'Daddy has broken down,' she told him. 'He's somewhere on Gower, but the phones went off before he could say any more. His car went into a branch of a tree that had fallen across the hedge and jutted into the road.'

'He'll be all right,' Marcus said, reaching out and clambering on to her knee.

'Yes, it's only this old storm that's pulled down the line I expect.' She kissed him then stood him down. 'Go and call your brothers and we'll make some hot chocolate.'

'No we won't, Mum.' He was about to tell her that the twins were out but instead, said, 'No electricity is there?'

They sat together listening to the storm raging around them, then they heard the roaring sound that had signalled the collapse of the cliffs near the semis, only yards from the end of their garden.

'What on earth was that?'

They looked out but could see nothing, and began to think it had been thunder, although the sound had been different from the usual crackling and thumps.

They were standing at the window looking towards the cliffs, from where the terrifying sound was continuing, when they saw the first of the flashing lights telling them something serious had occurred. Cynthia looked in the direction of the phone, wishing she could be told that Christian was safe.

'I'll have to go and see what's happened,' she told Marcus. 'You stay here with your brothers.'

'Mum, they aren't here,' he said, his eyes wide with anxiety. To reassure her he said, 'They won't be long, any minute now they'll be back and you can tell them off. They didn't want Henri walking home on her own.'

Cynthia felt the cold chill of fear. Something terrible was happening out there, and Christian and the twins were out in it. She hugged Marcus and, in a choked voice, said, 'We have to be brave, darling, and wait for them to come home.'

Vivienne was listening to the radio in Tom's house on Holly Oak Lane and was alarmed to hear the announcer say, 'Reports are coming in of a landslip near Abertrochi—'

She didn't wait to hear more. She reached for her coat and Tom grabbed his car keys.

When they reached the scene, it was quickly established that Toby was missing. The police assured her that every policeman available was out searching. 'He couldn't have gone far. He must have woken when the house was damaged and ran off to find you. He'll be found soon, I'm certain of it.'

Tom and she went to the cliff path. It was the way she and Toby often walked when they went to see Meriel and she had an idea that was where the little boy would have been heading. They heard someone calling her son's name and recognized a distraught Meriel on the same errand as themselves.

'That stupid woman left him alone after the house was damaged to come and find Evan. Oh, Vivienne, when will you learn that it's *your* job to see that he's safe!' The necessity to raise her voice to be heard added to the anger she felt.

'We couldn't have foreseen this,' Tom said, with a calmness he didn't feel. 'Now, where have you looked?'

'Only on this stretch of the path. I dodged the police and tried to clamber down the fallen area to make sure he isn't down there. I went as far down as I could and called, but I doubt he could hear me in this storm.'

'Wouldn't he have cut across the field?' Tom asked.

'We could try there but much of it is already cordoned off and in any case, several people have already looked, with more powerful torches than we have,' Meriel said, still shouting. 'We should separate. I'll try the rest of the path and—'

'No,' Tom said. 'We have to stay together. It's safer, and we stand a better chance of our voices being heard.'

Joanne wasn't worried by the storm at first. Apart from the rattle and clanging of a dustbin outside she had no presage of disaster. Jeremy and Justin had gone to the cinema with friends straight from school and should be home soon. She was enjoying the solitude, aware of the storm increasing, comfortable in the sensation of being safe from its fury.

The television went off and the lights failed but it seemed nothing more than a mild inconvenience. Then she heard the rumbling roar as the semis were damaged, the sound of the path shifting and rocks and gravel falling into the sea. The sound went on for what seemed an age and whatever had caused it was close at hand. Very close. She looked up as a trickle of plaster fell from the ceiling and a crack appeared.

Subsidence! Christian *was* guilty of a cover-up. He had lied and they were going to be killed. Oh, where were the boys? She felt her way to the telephone to try and phone the cinema and the parents of the friends they had gone with, trying to remember the number as she couldn't read the phone book.

205

The phone was as dead as the television and the lights. Where was John?

Leaving a message for the boys, she went out to see what had happened. Perhaps she'd be lucky enough to find a telephone still working and ring the cinema, then John. Feeling through the drawers, she found a notebook and took it with her; it contained most of their regularly used phone numbers.

The car started first time and she sighed with relief. She had to drive right into the village before finding a telephone box that was working. There were several people waiting to use it, anxious to report the loss of communication to the outside world. When it was her turn, she telephoned the cinema and they promised to flash a message on the screen telling the boys to wait for her to arrive and not go home with anyone else.

She tried three numbers but couldn't contact John. Crying with frustration and anxiety, she fumbled in her handbag for the notebook which she had grabbed before leaving the house. It was John's. In her frantic haste she had picked up the wrong one. She had to shine a torch to read the pages and couldn't find any place listed where he might be found at such time of night. There was a number without any explanatory name beside it. It wasn't a number she recognized. It was worth trying. Anything was worth trying, to reach him and tell him what was happening.

People outside were getting impatient and were knocking on the glass and miming for her to hurry. She opened the door a crack and said, 'I need to get in touch with my husband, our boys are out in this.' The faces relaxed with sympathy and they resigned themselves to wait. She dialled the number.

At first, she didn't recognize the voice. It was one she hadn't heard for many years.

'Is that you, John, darling?' the woman asked. 'Where are you? There's a report of a landslip near Joanne and the boys. You ought to go there and make sure they are all right.'

'Samantha?' Joanne whispered. Her mind whirled with questions. Why did John have her sister's phone number? Why was she calling him 'darling'?

'Who is this?'

'Joanne,' she said quietly. 'It's Joanne, Darling John's wife!' She replaced the receiver and stumbled from the box, reeling with the shock of what she had just learned. She got into her car and sat staring at nothing, trying to make sense of what she'd heard. It had to be her John Samantha was expecting. She had referred to herself and the boys. It explained a lot, but not enough. How could she find out where the woman lived?

A sudden gust of wind hit the car and it swayed back and forth in the aftermath. First of all she had to find the boys.

The road into town was full of debris as the storm had shattered windows and sent slates winging from roofs. The streetlights were on and visibility was normal as she parked outside the cinema and waited for the boys to emerge. Another car stopped behind hers and she thought it might be the parents of the friends calling to collect them so she got out to explain. The passenger door opened and Christian got out thanking the driver for the lift.

'Joanne, can you take me home?' he asked when he saw her. 'I don't know what's happening but I'm afraid for Cynthia and the boys.'

'It seems the stories about subsidence weren't exaggerations after all,' she said. 'I don't know the full story, but before all the electricity went off, and the telephones, there was a report of a landslip.'

'God help me, I haven't an idea how it could have happened.' In the poor lights from street-lamps and the garish display outside the cinema he looked wretched. Joanne decided she would say nothing more until she had the facts. She didn't want to say something she might regret, besides, she had other things on her mind. John's absences and his meanness, were they down to his affair with her sister? How long had he been Samantha's lover? She had no evidence, other than the phone call, but the certainty of his guilt was growing.

She opened the car door and Christian sat with his face in his hands and said nothing. She could only imagine the turmoil of his thoughts.

Rupert and Oliver were with Helen. When she couldn't get through by phone to tell Cynthia they were safe, Reggie phoned the police and they promised to let their parents know immediately.

Away from the severity of the storm, Helen watched her

daughter with the twins, trying to guess from the way they were with each other, whether one of them was the father of Henri's unborn child. She saw nothing more than friendship.

The insane fury of the storm subsided as the tide passed its peak and began to recede. As Joanne drove home, having collected Jeremy and Justin, the wind calmed down and only the occasional gusts were left of its violence. The house appeared little damaged but when they went inside, the boys shone their torches and they saw to their alarm that the walls had suffered severe cracks and one of the windows which had unfortunately been left ajar, had been thrown right out of its opening, complete with its frame.

'I think we'll sleep downstairs tonight,' Joanne said, going up to collect sleeping-bags and extra covers.

There was a knock at the door and two policemen stood there. They explained that because of the possibility of more damage, they couldn't stay in the house and offered to escort them to an hotel for the night. Joanne argued, insisting she needed to stay in case her husband returned.

'We'll let him know where you are and that you're safe,' the constable assured her.

'If you have an address for him we could send someone—'

'That won't be necessary!' Joanne snapped. How could she explain his absence to a stranger? And in front of the boys?

Cath couldn't get near Meriel's house. Police and firemen were everywhere, keeping people away from the cliff area. Barricades had been placed on the path and no one was allowed near the houses, even though Meriel's, far to the west of the landslide appeared to have escaped damage.

'I have to make sure Mrs Meriel Parry is safe, and besides,' she added pleadingly, 'I don't have anywhere to sleep tonight.'

'Sorry I am, Madam, but you aren't the only one. Just go and see the man over by the van there and he'll arrange for you to go to an hotel.'

Appearing to obey, she slipped past him in the dappling shadows of the activity and went across the field. The wind was subsiding but there were still occasional blasts and she staggered once or twice as she crossed the open ground.

She stepped carefully, having overheard shouts from the

rescue workers that the field had sunk in several places and the edge of the cliffs had fallen into the still roaring sea.

The sound, when it came, was nothing more than any other of the thousand unexplained sounds of the terrible night, but it was so small, little more than a squeak, that she stopped and listened. 'Is anyone there?' she called, and was answered by a repeat of the small sound. The wind was distorting the sound and she made a few false moves before she found the source. Then she almost fell over the scared little boy.

'Toby? What are you doing here?' She gathered him up and held him close.

'I was frightened,' he told her. 'All those funny men.' She hugged him tighter as she explained about the strange uniforms worn by the rescue workers, as she made her way to tell the police he was safe.

The police eventually allowed Cath to take Toby to Meriel's house after reports that the storm was abating and there was no damage reported in the area around her house. Viv was there, and Tom, and soon afterwards, Mike arrived, having heard of the emergency. He and Cath silently hugged each other and allowed the tears to fall unheeded.

Once drinks had been dispensed now the power was back on and Toby settled into a bed with some of the toys Meriel had bought for his visits, they sat down to discuss what had happened.

Cath said nothing to Vivienne about her neglect of her child. Instead, she told them about the loss of her children. 'Now it's time I stopped running and faced life without them,' she said to a sympathetic audience. 'I ran away without a thought for how Bryan was feeling, or how he needed me. I think we often believe we are the only ones feeling the pain of loss when a tragedy happens. Instead of comforting each other, we build a shell around ourselves, convincing ourselves that no one else is suffering, and no one understands.'

Vivienne and Tom went upstairs to check on Toby later and they were gone a long time.

'I think it would be a good idea for everyone to stay here for what's left of the night,' Meriel said.

'If you can cope with us all, I agree it would be best,' Mike said. 'The roads are still very dangerous.'

'I'll bring down the spare bedding and we can use the couches and chairs.' Meriel looked at Mike who went with her to help.

On the landing the door of Toby's room opened and Tom and Vivienne came out and softly closed the door.

'We have something to tell you,' Vivienne whispered. Meriel followed them back into the room and Mike hesitated before announcing he would go downstairs and wait.

'Toby is my child,' Tom began.

Surprise must have been clear on Meriel's face but she gave a half smile and waited for what came next.

'We were married you see,' Vivienne explained, 'But, well, things went on that I couldn't accept. And we parted. Now we've decided to give it a second try.'

'Aware of the – problem, you stand a better chance of success,' Meriel said, unable to comment further, afraid of saying the wrong thing.

'Ray and I were together for years,' Tom whispered, 'But we separated for six months as a trial. It didn't change the way we felt about each other. I married Vivienne because I loved her, I still do, very much, but it was partly to hide my homosexuality from my parents, who wouldn't understand,' he said.

'And, you can live with this?' Meriel asked Vivienne.

'I know you'll think I'm crazy, but I do love Tom and I'm prepared to accept his occasional lapses.' She touched Tom's cheek affectionately. 'And, he will accept mine.'

Meriel wished them luck and left them to sit beside their son and discuss their future. She thought Vivienne was brave and perhaps foolish, but her good wishes were genuine and she hoped she would remain friends with them both.

The calm after the storm was like a rebirth as Joanne stepped outside into the glittering, clean scenery. She and the boys had left the hotel early, and she stood now, looking around and marvelling at how calm and ordinary the day was, when her life had fallen apart. It was barely light and the flashing lights and shouting voices were harsh in the quiet of the morning. She called the boys and took them out to find some breakfast. She drove through the town and stopped outside the Gingham Cafe where Dai was just opening up.

'Can you do breakfast for three?' she asked. There was no need to explain about the lack of electricity. Everyone knew about the landslide and reports of the damage had reached every house via radio and television.

'I came last night, trying to find you, make sure you were safe,' Dai said as he took their order. 'But the police refused to let me through. I was told that your house was slightly damaged but you and the boys were unharmed.'

'We haven't seen the television news,' Justin complained, so Dai brought a small set in and set it up near their table. They watched with interest as the cameras panned the devastation.

'The semis, close to where the land slipped into the sea suffered most, and the theory is that this was because they had been built partly on solid rock and partly on infilled ground,' the reporter explained. 'There was movement on the impacted soil which dropped when the cliffs gave way. This has not been confirmed, and the real cause is not yet known.'

The boys were excited at the realization that they had lived through such a disaster unscathed, but Joanne showed little interest.

Guessing that something else was on her mind, Dai asked, 'What has happened, Joanne? Something about John?'

She stared at him hard then said, 'You knew, didn't you?'

'About John and—?' He hesitated, afraid of saying more than she knew.

'About John and my sister. How long, Dai? Tell me how long?'

'I think you should talk to John and Samantha.'

His use of her sister's name was all the confirmation she needed.

'I won't talk to John again except through a solicitor,' she said, pushing away the food he had cooked.

She drove home with her mind in turmoil. How could she explain this to Jeremy and Justin? They were so young. How could she make them understand?

Back at the house she wandered around checking half-heartedly for damage. Broken windows, a number of cracks in the walls and shelves askew. She idly ran her fingers through the dust. What did it matter? The house on which she had lavished such care was already part of a previous life.

She had whispered the few comments to Dai, while the boys

211

were engrossed in the television report so she was surprised when Jeremy asked, 'When will we meet our auntie and our stepsister, Mam?'

'What?'

'Auntie Samantha, when will we meet her?' Jeremy asked.

'Will we get extra birthday presents now?' Justin asked hopefully.

'What d'you know about Samantha?' she demanded.

'We heard Helen and Reggie talking about her one evening when we were playing monopoly with Henri,' Justin said.

'So everyone knew,' she said, half to herself.

'I expect so. Why didn't you tell us we had an auntie?'

'It's a bit complicated to explain.' she said, hurrying from the room, unable to cope with their questions. She had been wrong when she told Dai she wouldn't speak to John again. He would have to help her explain all this to their sons.

She knew he would be here soon. He would have to come. She braced herself to face him and tell him to leave. Perhaps her sister would come with him. Perhaps that would make it easier.

Opening John's notebook at the page showing Samantha's number, she sat to wait.

Cynthia and Christian, with Marcus, went early on the morning after the storm to collect their sons from Helen and Reggie. They had stayed at an hotel overnight and neither of them had slept.

'Let's not stay,' Christian said as he knocked on the door of the flat. 'Let's thank her and leave as soon as we can. There's so much to do today.'

Helen was red-faced and an argument had obviously taken place. Henri was crying, the boys looked upset. Reggie was hiding behind a newspaper.

Oliver blurted out, 'Mummy, Helen still says Henri's baby is our fault!'

'What are you talking about, Helen? How can my boys be responsible for Henri's pregnancy?'

'We were trying to persuade them to tell us who Henri's been with,' Helen said, unrepentant. 'They're all friends and they must know who she's been with.'

'You had no right to question them without us being here,' Christian said.

'If the boys tell me they haven't done anything, then I believe them,' Cynthia echoed. She glared at Helen and asked Rupert, 'Do you know anything about this?'

'I didn't do anything except kiss her,' he said outraged and tearful. 'And I know you can't get pregnant from a kiss.'

'Pity,' Marcus said jauntily, 'I'd like to be an uncle.'

'Shut up,' the twins chorused.

'Just tell us, Henri,' Helen pleaded.

Christian stood in front of Henri and said quietly, 'Well, young lady, I think it's time you answered your mother's question, don't you?'

The house was a mess but Joanne was unaware. When she heard the car, she didn't move. When John opened the door and walked in she didn't look up.

'Joanne, I'm sorry,' he said.

'I'm not. I've been unhappy for years, now I can tell you to go.'

'We have to talk about this.'

Justin poked his head around the door and said, 'If this is about us driving the car we only did it once, didn't we, Jeremy?' Too late, Jeremy slapped a hand over his brother's mouth.

John went in to talk to the boys and Joanne didn't try to comprehend the low murmuring. She had no idea how long they talked but eventually he came back to her and said, 'I'm taking the boys to meet Samantha and our daughters.'

The plural made her turn and face him. 'Daughters?'

'Three. One aged eleven, one seven and one only three.'

She didn't reply, turning her head away from him again, she stared at the wall. Now she knew everything. Her life was in tatters but she knew it all, nothing else could happen.

Then Helen phoned and haltingly explained that they now knew the father of Henri's child. It was Jeremy.

Slamming down the phone she turned to John and said, 'Samantha will have to wait!'

Calling for the boys to go with her, she hurried to the car, explaining as she ran, and demanding that John went with her to discuss this latest in a line of disasters.

Henri answered the door.

'They know,' she said succinctly to a white-faced Jeremy.

In Meriel's house the occupants woke slowly. Breakfast was cereal and sliced bread and they had just finished when there was a knock at the damaged back door. It was Evan.

'Are you all right, Meriel?' he asked.

'We all are,' she said. 'Go back to Sophie.'

'I don't think I can bear to talk to her after what she did last night, running away and leaving Toby like that.'

Toby waved a milky spoon on hearing his name. Evan went to step past Meriel to see him, but Meriel said pointedly, 'Goodbye, Evan. Thank you for your concern.'

Mike stepped forward and placed a proprietory arm across Meriel's shoulder and she took his hand in hers. 'Cathy is going to phone Bryan,' he said. 'I offered to walk down to the telephone box with her,' he said. 'Want to come?'

'I want to go to see if Cynthia and the others are all right.'

'Telephone box first, then to see Joanne and Cynthia. All right?' He kissed her lightly on the cheek.

'I can go with you to see Cynthia,' Evan said. 'Their houses, Cynthia's and Joanne's, aren't the worst hit. The semis were more or less demolished.'

'Thank you, Evan, but we'll manage.' Firmly, she ushered him out of the house and reached for her coat.

Vivienne and Tom gathered their things and took Toby home. Cath looked shaky at the prospect of talking to her husband, but was reassured by having Mike and Meriel with her.

'I'll come back here after talking to Bryan and search in the fridge for something for lunch. It isn't working but it is full,' she said.

'So, salad it is,' Mike teased.

Mike and Meriel stayed outside the phone box while a tearful Cath made her call. Instead of the anger and recriminations she had expected, Bryan spoke of his sadness that they had both had to grieve alone. Then the crying that should have been allowed to escape long before was released.

They arranged to meet at the chalet, to talk and find out whether their marriage that had been so cruelly destroyed, could be mended.

Meriel and Mike found Cynthia and Christian at home, their

house having suffered only superficial damage. The boys were in the lounge, complaining about the lack of television, Cynthia was suggesting books, and various games, to a chorus of groans. Christian was checking every room, while outside, men and women were still busy sifting evidence, making notes and taking photographs as they tried to piece together the sequence of the events of the violent night.

Joanne and John were there and Henri's pregnancy was discussed.

'The world has been tipped on its head,' Cynthia said. 'The months of anxiety when there was the suspicion of subsidence, and the storm destroying two houses, and now Henri's problem.'

'It's our problem too,' Joanne said. 'Jeremy and I will have to help her through this.'

In Churchill's Garden a few days later, Cynthia appeared and began talking about her latest shopping spree as though nothing had happened. Cath talked openly about the death of her children and the meeting with her husband, which was painful, but left her with hope.

Meriel shyly insisted that she and Mike were just good friends.

Vivienne, who had Toby with her and was feeding him sweets at a rate of knots, told them of her return to the husband she had left two years before. She did not mention the reasons for the break-up and knew that Meriel would never reveal her secret.

'Now, Joanne,' Helen said. 'What about you sharing your news with us, eh?'

Joanne was beautifully dressed in a suit of pale blue with a frilly white blouse and long dangling earrings that matched a brooch on her lapel. Her make-up was flawless, her hair immaculate. She looked completely at ease.

'Oh why don't *you* tell them, Helen, you'll tell it *much* better than I.'

Helen looked subdued as she muttered, 'No need to talk about it if you don't want to, we'll understand, Joanne.'

'I don't see why I should pretend it's a secret, you've known for a long time, haven't you, Helen?'

'I can't help picking up bits and pieces, odd items of news. People talk to each other in the shop without being aware that

I'm there sometimes, Just treat me like one of the fittings they do,' she said attempting a laugh.

'All right what would you like first? The bits and pieces and odd items about John having a second family, with my sister Samantha? Three children they have, all daughters. Now, would that make me their aunt or their half-stepmother? Or pre-stepmother? Is there such a thing? Very confusing, that one.'

Cynthia was shocked. 'Joanne, I'd no idea—'

'—Or the bits and pieces about my son, Jeremy, who's about to be a father, at fifteen?' She stood up and announced that she was going for more coffee. 'To allow you to get the first exchange of opinions over,' she said with a forced smile.

Meriel and Mike had discussed her pregnancy and any doubts she'd had were firmly in the past. His delight and happiness showed in the silly smile that, he told her, just wouldn't fade away, and in the flowers he brought her and the proposal that came with the flowers. She hadn't told her friends in Churchill's Garden. Being 'just friends' was enough for the moment.

She wanted to savour this wonderful new life on which she was embarking. Time to tell others when they had wallowed in their happiness a while longer. Besides, there had been enough gossip for one day, with Joanne's news and Cath's revelations. No, she would save her wonderful news for a morning when it would be given the importance it deserved.

It was a day when happiness was all around. She was in such a constant air of excitement that she was looking for excuses to laugh. She found one when she suddenly realized that Joanne, with her emphasis on youth and being beautiful, would soon be a grandmother. How would she cope?

Gradually life in the houses near the cliff returned to normal. Repairs were assessed and the demolition of the pair of semis took place.

Sophie went to stay with her friend in Abertrochi and Evan found accommodation in a small hotel. Evan called several times to talk to Meriel but she never allowed him through the door. Now he needed her, she had the strength to remember the times she had needed him and help had not been forthcoming. In something near despair he went to find Sophie.

* * *

Joanne's house needed very little work, and most of that was cosmetic. She wrote to John via his office and told him she was putting the house on the market as soon as the decorating was finished. Dai came frequently to help her sort out insurance claims and deal with the workmen, but eventually, she thanked him, and told him she no longer needed him. This was a time in her life when she needed to be on her own, to make her own decisions. She went to the Gingham Cafe and they shared a pot of tea and some scones, then he said, 'You know how I feel about you. I love and respect you. I admire you as a mother and as a talented and beautiful woman. Share my life, Joanne. You and I could have a wonderful future together. Equal partners, building a business together. You, me and your sons. What do you say?'

'I have to say sorry, my dear. I'm fond of you, but I need to go on alone, for a while at least.'

'But Joanne, I thought you felt the same as me?'

'Sorry, Dai, I really am. I value your friendship, and your love and I want that to go on and on. Knowing you has given me the strength to deal with all this. But now I want to see who I really am, find out my strengths and weaknesses by facing this without your support.'

She got into her car and drove home feeling the lightness of having discarded a burden. She was free to be her own woman. Her sons, they were all she needed to fill her life, her sons and a grandchild to dote on, and a job. She put all thoughts of starting her own business on to the back burner. She didn't feel strong enough to face that. No, serving in a clothes shop and being nice to people, helping them to choose clothes for a special occasion, that was what she would do. She hummed cheerfully as she approached her drive. Life had thrown her around cruelly but now she felt strong and knew her future looked good.

Cynthia said very little about the landslip once she had made certain everyone knew the fault was not with Christian. She pushed the dreadful incident aside and began to remind her friends how fortunate she was. How happy in her marriage and how much she appreciated her wonderful childhood, on which her happiness was based. Then her parents turned up.

Marcus was sitting at the kitchen table reading a magazine

one morning. It was twelve thirty. His brothers had gone into town with their mother to buy shoes and trousers and sweaters, he had decided to stay home and, in the absence of Millie, was in charge.

He looked at the freezer to decide what they would have for lunch and, having chosen fish fingers, took them out and placed them on the grill tray. A voice calling from the doorway startled him and he almost threw the fish fingers up in the air. The woman smiling at him was a witch! She was dressed in black, had very untidy hair and her teeth didn't look too clean. He looked at her nervously, backing away, still holding the grill pan. Then he saw there was a man behind her. A fat man, bald, and with eyes that popped out as he smiled and raised his eyebrows as a greeting.

'You Marcus, then?' the man asked. His voice was gravelly and low.

'Yes, but who are you?'

'Where are Rupert and Oliver, then?' the woman asked.

'Coming now this minute,' he said, 'With Mum and Dad, right behind you they'll be.' He still held the grill pan as a sort of weapon. 'Will you go please,' he said. 'Mummy doesn't like visitors she isn't expecting.'

'Oh, she'll like us, Marcus. We're your granny and grampy. Isn't this nice?' They came in and sat at the table, the woman looking around her and the man glaring at a troubled Marcus.

'Better put them fish things under the grill or you'll drop them,' the man growled.

Marcus put them on the table. 'I don't have a grandmother or grandfather,' he told them. 'Mummy would have told me.'

A car was heard stopping outside the kitchen door and Marcus let out a huge sigh of relief and ran through the door, 'Mum, Dad, there's a man and woman in there and I think she's a witch and she says she's my grandmother!'

Christian walked into the kitchen with Cynthia close behind him.

'Hello,' the woman smiled. 'At last we've found you. Saw the piece about the landslide in the paper and recognized your picture. Isn't this nice?'

'Go to your rooms, boys,' Christian said. The boys obeyed without question.

Christian turned to the smiling couple. In a low voice he

said, 'Go away and don't come back. There's nothing for you here.'

'Living like a king and queen you two are and there's us with grandsons we didn't even know about. Lovely it is to see them.'

'I'll count to ten then I'm calling the police.'

He opened the door and stood there, while Cynthia watched the two people she hated most in the world make up their mind. They stood up as Christian counted threateningly, then ambled to the door. Christian followed them out. She was trembling when he returned, holding his mobile phone, closing and locking the door behind him.

He hugged Cynthia. 'I hate doing it but we have to lie to them.' He called the boys back down.

'I've told the police,' he said. 'They knew all about them. Ill they are but completely harmless. They go around inviting themselves into houses hoping for a free meal.'

'Sorry if they frightened you,' Cynthia said.

'I think they wanted some fish fingers,' Marcus said. The twins both put an arm around their younger brother. 'Don't worry, they won't be back,' they told him. Both Cynthia and Christian crossed their fingers.

Churchill's Garden was full. The sales were keeping the shops busy and the streets of Abertrochi were crowded with shoppers hoping for a bargain.

'Of course John is devastated,' Joanne was saying as she walked in. 'He really didn't want to leave me and the boys. Samantha was the mistress and I the important wife. But I told him no matter how he pleaded, I would never take him back.'

Cynthia and Christian were planning a big celebration after being told the contract was being reinstated. She couldn't wait to tell her friends about the London weekend darling Christian had arranged.

'I'm glad I went back to Tom.' Vivienne said. 'I know we won't live a life as inseparable partners. We have a lot in common but I love to dance and Tom understands that and won't stop me. We'll both try to accept our differences for Toby's sake. He needs a proper family. I've settled down now to spend every moment I can with him and he's much happier.'

She had earlier asked the girl behind the counter to look after Toby that evening while she and her friends went to a rave, unaware she had been overheard by Cath and Meriel. 'I never leave him with strangers now.'

Cath and Meriel exchanged glances. How easily they all exaggerated their situation, making out everything was perfect. Everything was wonderful for Cynthia, Joanne and Vivienne. No one had any worries.

Cynthia was boasting about how well she looked after Christian and how wonderfully happy they were, when two figures walked into the cafe and looked around, obviously searching for someone. She bent over and delved into her capacious leather bag and when she straightened up her parents were standing at the table.

'Surprise, surprise,' her mother said.

At once, Cynthia stood up and led them outside. On her mobile she dialled Christian's number. She handed the phone to her father and watched while his face widened into a smile. Going back into the cafe she sighed dramatically.

'A family desperately in need,' she explained. 'Darling Christian and his lame ducks. He's promised to help them get a decent place to live, away from the squalor they've suffered recently.'

She looked out through the gift shop to the pavement outside where Christian's car had just pulled up. She saw the couple argue, then get into the car. He would sort it out. Probably pay them to stay away. Christian always put things right.

Everything was returning to normal. Ken was no longer a partner but she thought with pleasure of Ken's mother who was once more a part of their lives. Mrs Morris would be a surrogate grandmother for the boys and their secret would be safe with her.

'I had such a wonderful childhood with my Aunt Marigold, and Christian didn't want for a thing with his darling grandmother.' She repeated the oft told story. 'We are thankful for our good fortune and give something back when we can. Now, shall we have more coffee? And some cream cakes on me.'

She smiled confidently, but when she left her friends, she stood outside Churchill's Garden, and looked fearfully up and down the street in a way that would become a habit.

PILLGWENLLY 22·6·06